FIRE MUST BURN

FIRE MUST BURN

Allison Montclair

SEVERN
HOUSE

First world edition published in Great Britain and the USA in 2026
by Severn House, an imprint of Canongate Books Ltd,
14 High Street, Edinburgh EH1 1TE.

severnhouse.com

Cover and jacket design by Piers Tilbury

British Library Cataloguing-in-Publication Data
A CIP catalogue record for this title is available from the British Library.

ISBN-13: 978-1-4483-1593-2 (cased)
ISBN-13: 978-1-4483-1887-2 (paper)
ISBN-13: 978-1-4483-1594-9 (e-book)

This is a work of fiction. Names, characters, places and incidents are either
the product of the author's imagination or are used fictitiously. Except where
actual historical events and characters are being described for the storyline of
this novel, all situations in this publication are fictitious and any resemblance
to actual persons, living or dead, business establishments, events or locales is
purely coincidental.

All Severn House titles are printed on acid-free paper.

MIX
Paper | Supporting
responsible forestry
FSC
www.fsc.org   FSC® C013056

Typeset by Palimpsest Book Production Ltd., Falkirk, Stirlingshire, Scotland.
Printed and bound in Great Britain by TJ Books, Padstow, Cornwall.

The manufacturer's authorised representative in the EU for product safety is
Authorised Rep Compliance Ltd, 71 Lower Baggot Street, Dublin D02 P593
Ireland (arccompliance.com)

Praise for the Sparks and Bainbridge Mysteries

'Montclair's light, comic touch and gift for well-placed clues are on full display'
Publishers Weekly on *An Excellent Thing in a Woman*

'A page-turning mystery full of local color and angst-filled romances'
Kirkus Reviews on *Murder at the White Palace*

'The banter between Iris and Gwen remains brisk and hilarious, and Montclair does a particularly good job throwing readers off the culprit's scent. Series fans will be over the moon'
Publishers Weekly on *Murder at the White Palace*

'Along with providing a solid cast of characters, Montclair does a swell job of bringing 1946 London to life'
Booklist on *The Unkept Woman*

'Montclair portrays 1940s speech and culture well, with many allusions to postwar concerns. This will appeal to mystery readers who enjoy humor, historical fiction, and well-written crime-solving teams'
Library Journal on *The Unkept Woman*

About the author

Allison Montclair is the author of the Sparks and Bainbridge Mysteries, beginning with *The Right Sort Of Man*, the American Library Association Reading List Council's Best Mystery of 2019. Under her real name, she has written more mystery novels and a damn good werewolf book, as well as short stories in many genres in magazines and anthologies. She is also an award-winning librettist and lyricist with several musicals to her credit that have been performed or workshopped across the USA. She currently lives in New York City where she also practiced as a criminal defense attorney.

To the cousins: Bruce, David, Bill, Ellen and Kate.
One cannot choose one's family,
but if I could have, I still would have chosen you.

'So little pains do the vulgar take in the investigation of truth, accepting readily the first story that comes to hand.'

Thucydides, *The History of the Peloponnesian War*, I. 20, trans. by Richard Crawley

PROLOGUE

T he banks of the River Cam were a bustle of activity on the first day of the Lent Bumps. From First Post Corner down to Baits Bite Lock, eight-man boats at 150-foot intervals were secured to the bank by the towpath while their crews stretched and flexed in the chill of the late winter air.

Male crews, of course.

As the start time approached, they shed their coats and pounded on their chests and thighs to encourage both circulation and the admiration of the few female students and local girls who came out to cheer them on. Not a few flasks were passed around, ostensibly to provide warmth, energy and nips of courage.

On both sides of the river, marshals and umpires prowled the banks, glancing at their watches or calling out instructions.

With all of the hubbub by the water, no one paid any attention to a dark green eight-wheeled Leyland Octopus flatbed lorry as it rumbled up to a spot some fifty feet from Baits Bite Lock where the last of the ranked crews, the second boat from Pembroke, were now settling behind their oars, awaiting the boom of the tiny cannon that signalled the countdown to the start. As the lorry stopped, its engine idling, its cab blocked the view from the riverside of its cargo, another narrow, eight-oared boat that projected precariously beyond the rear of the bed. A head poked out from behind the cab. A woman's head, topped with unruly, brunette hair. She scanned the scene in front of her, then turned to three other women who had been clinging for dear life to the ropes securing the boat to the lorry's tray.

The brunette's name was Iris Sparks. She was seventeen years old, and about to cause an uproar.

'All clear,' she said, and the four of them scrambled to remove the ropes from the boat.

Several more women separated themselves from the crowd on the towpath and sauntered back towards the Leyland, two of them wheeling bicycles. The four on the flatbed carefully slid the boat from the tray to the waiting arms of the women below. They placed it on the ground behind the lorry so it would stay hidden, should anyone bother to look their way. Then Sparks handed down oars and two long poles before hopping down.

'What's the situation, Sauce?' she asked one of the cyclists.

'Tildy is at the next launch point,' reported Sauce, glancing at her watch. 'The four-minute cannon should be in about—'

A loud boom sounded in the distance up the river.

'Yes, well, that was it, wasn't it?' said Sauce with a laugh. 'When Pembroke is coming to that point, she'll wave her hand-kerchief, and the girls stationed down the path will relay it to you. Best of luck, ladies!'

She and the other cyclist mounted their bikes and pedalled off, turning down the towpath to await the beginning of the race.

Sparks and eight of the women shed their coats and tossed them into the cab of the lorry. The eight women grabbed oars, four with their left hands, four with their right, while two more picked up the poles.

'I'll wait for you at Ditton Corner if you make it that far,' called the driver.

'We'll make it,' said Sparks.

'Good luck to you,' he called.

'Right,' said Sparks to the others. 'Positions.'

They stood four to each side of the boat and placed their oars inside. Sparks stood at the cox, while the two women carrying the poles brought up the rear. Jessica, behind her on the bow side, shivered in the cold.

'I wish we had waited for the May Bumps,' she said.

'We wouldn't have been able to keep it secret until then,' replied Sparks. 'Not with this many people involved.'

The cannon boomed again. The one-minute warning.

'To shoulders, ladies,' said Sparks. 'Heave-ho!'

They grabbed the sides of the boat and lifted. Sparks looked out at the Pembroke boat, which was being shoved away from the banks by their polemen, the coxswain holding high the bung at the end of the chain connected to the bank at the launch station. She listened for the countdown.

'Thirty seconds, ladies,' she reported. 'We move at twenty. Five, four, three, two, quick march!'

They started towards the river at a jog. The starter's cannon boomed as they were halfway there, and the Pembroke crew pulled their oars, sending their boat upstream, gathering speed with each subsequent stroke. Their classmates and supporters moved along the towpath in pursuit, clearing a space for the ladies.

They reached the bank and lowered the boat into the water. Sparks grabbed the bung and clambered into the cox seat.

'Bow side, fix blades,' she called, and four oars went into the riggers.

'Bow side holding,' called Jessica.

'River side, fix blades. River side in. Bow side in.'

The rest of the eight women got into the boat, bracing their feet and grabbing the oars.

'Number off from bow!' called Sparks.

'Bow!' 'Seven!' 'Six!' 'Five!' 'Four!' 'Three!' 'Two!' 'Stroke!'

'Push off,' Sparks said, holding the bung over her head, and the two women with the poles placed them against each end of the boat and shoved it away from the bank.

The marshal on the opposite bank, who had been watching the Pembroke crew recede into the distance, finally turned back and saw them.

'Here, what do you think you're doing?' he shouted.

'Racing the bumps!' Sparks shouted back, keeping her eyes on the distant banks. 'Square on the ready!'

Eight oars went up, blades perpendicular to the water.

'But you're women!' shouted the marshal.

'We know!' they all shouted.

A handkerchief fluttered in the distance.

'Row!' shouted Sparks, dropping the bung.

Eight blades dipped into the water. The women pulled, and they were off, Sparks calling the strokes. They picked up speed, passing the stragglers on the towpath, many of whom stared in astonishment to see an all-woman crew, which elicited scattered cheers from the women and some shouts of derision from the men.

'Settle on three,' she called. 'Two, one, settle!'

They fell into their regular stroke now that they were at speed.

The pedestrians won't be a problem, thought Sparks as she kept calling out strokes, her hand on the tiller keeping the boat the proper distance from the bank as it curved slightly to the left.

They reached the next launch post where Tildy sat on her bike, looking at her watch.

'Sixty-eight seconds!' she shouted as they passed her, then she pedalled away, weaving between the clumps of people walking.

The water was smoother here, and Sparks called out a power twenty. The crowd on the towpath was getting thicker as they passed more of the launch points. She spotted Sauce at their next checkpoint, trying to fend off the attentions of a Caius second-year as she watched their boat approach.

'Fifty-nine!' she shouted.

'We're gaining on them, ladies,' called Sparks. 'Keep it up!'

Sauce jumped on her bike and sped by, blowing a kiss back to her aspiring suitor.

Some of the men seemed to be getting the idea that Sparks and her confederates were serious about competing. The shouts from the bank became more and more hostile, and were joined by whistles and gestures from the marshals to stop and pull in to the shore.

Which they ignored, of course.

Some of the Pembroke men began sprinting along the towpath, trying to catch up to their crew, but the boat was much faster. Then she saw one man climb on a bike and pedal off.

'The cat's out of the bag, ladies!' she called. 'Power twenty in two, one, now! Six, finish timing!'

They pulled harder, the sweat pouring off of them, soaking through their jumpers.

Tildy was at the next checkpoint, waving excitedly.

'Thirty-five seconds!' she yelled. 'They're slacking off! You can catch them.'

'Regular stroke in two, one, row!' cried Sparks, steering them through the corner. 'Here comes the Gut! And Pembroke's in sight!'

The Gut was a narrow stretch, and they could feel the current change as they hit it, crossing to the non-towpath side to take the inside corner. But at the other end was the Pembroke boat, whose oarsmen had apparently given up on catching the next crew in line and were easing up their pace, having no idea they were being targeted. The crew were more or less blocked by their coxswain from seeing the ladies catching up to them, and the coxswain had his eyes upstream.

Then the Pembroke cyclist finally caught up to them, shouting and waving his arms downstream. The coxswain turned to look behind him, and even from that distance Sparks could see the disbelief registering on his face. He turned back to urge his crew back to speed, but one by one each of the oarsmen leaned out to catch a glimpse of the oncoming wraiths, which caused the Pembroke boat to rock slightly and lose more speed.

'They've spotted us, ladies!' shouted Sparks. 'Power thirty in two, one, row! Give me everything you've got! Newnham! Newnham!'

The chant was picked up by the women along the banks, led by Tildy and Sauce as they pedalled alongside. The Newnham crew whipped around Grassy Corner, gaining inexorably on the Pembroke crew, who had fallen out of rhythm and were frantically trying to regain it as their coxswain shouted himself hoarse. He glanced behind him, his eyes meeting Sparks's, and she grinned as the prow of the Newnham boat closed in.

'Ramming speed on two!' she shouted. 'Two! One! Row! Row! Row!'

They were in the Plough Reach, a short, straight stretch, and just before the river turned to the right at Ditton Corner, the gutta-percha knob on the bow of the Newnham boat bumped the stern of the Pembroke boat.

Both crews kept rowing, the women shouting in triumph.

'Well?' called Sparks to the Pembroke coxswain.

'They're not even in the race,' protested the man sitting five in the other boat.

'Where did you start?' asked the coxswain.

She finally had a chance to get a good look at him. He was a fair-haired man, not much taller than her, with light blue eyes which at the moment were scrutinising her intently.

'At Baits Bite,' said Sparks. 'After you did.'

'How did you do the interval?'

'We stationed a woman at the next starting post. She signalled us when you passed it. If anything, we gave you more of a head start because you were already at speed.'

The coxswain looked at her as the two boats pulled in tandem, then he nodded, satisfied, and raised his hand to acknowledge the bump.

'Weigh enough, lads,' he said.

'Tony, you can't be serious,' said the man sitting at the stroke.

'They raced fair,' he said. 'The way I see it is we can be sporting about it or unsporting. Weigh enough, lads.'

'We already were starting last,' moaned one of the crew as they lifted their blades. 'Now we get bumped by girls. We'll never live this down.'

'Check it down, ladies,' called Sparks, and her crew dipped their oars to slow their boat's momentum.

The Pembroke boat drifted beyond them, then both boats eased towards the bank. As Sparks stepped onto the bank to secure the boat, she looked upriver to see the Pembroke coxswain looking back at her. He smiled and gave her a quick thumbs up.

Now, that is a fine-looking man, she thought.

'Well done, ladies!' she called. 'One foot up and out, then we stow this beauty and it's on to the Pike and Eel to celebrate!'

And then they were all jumping up and down on the towpath screaming, 'Newnham! Newnham! Newnham!' as a collective outrage of marshals and umpires descended upon them.

ONE

London, 1947

'No more pineapples, can you believe it?' grumbled Iris as they walked up Edgware Road. 'I had just got used to having them back, and now they're gone again. I love pineapples. How did they become a pawn of international trade negotiations?'

'Something about the Portuguese wanting dollars for them,' replied Gwen. 'And England has a limited supply.'

'The pound isn't good enough for the Portuguese? The nerve of those people! First they sit out the war, then this. If I didn't like pineapples so much, I would boycott them on principle.'

'It's too bad those mystery planters on top of your boat didn't hold any pineapple trees,' said Gwen.

'True, but the tomatoes have been spectacular, at least. Unfortunately, the birds have discovered them, and I don't have any netting to keep them away. If you hadn't sent your son to the country for the summer, I would hire him as a human scarecrow.'

'A job jumping up and down, waving his arms and screaming all day would have been perfect for Ronnie,' said Gwen.

The two women were walking back to Maida Vale from their offices in Mayfair where they ran The Right Sort Marriage Bureau. It was a late Wednesday afternoon in early July, and the air was cool and damp, though it wasn't raining at the moment. Nevertheless, the ladies had their umbrellas with them. Gwen's was a recent purchase from a speciality shop recommended to her by her martial arts tutor, and she was still self-conscious about carrying it, with the extra weight in the handle more of a distraction than a reassurance.

'It sounds so strange to have a Minister of Food,' continued Iris. 'Something so basic shouldn't be controlled by politicians.

Next thing you know they'll create a Ministry of Air and start rationing oxygen. I don't like Strachey in the job. All he knows about food is eating it. Hell, if that's a qualification they should make me Undersecretary of Wine.'

'I promise to vote for you when you stand for election,' said Gwen.

'Strachey's sister was Principal at Newnham when I was there. I can't tell you how many times she nearly caught me on the Clough Hall roof. I dislike the entire family.'

'At least he's relaxed some of the restrictions on wedding cakes. That will be good for business. I thought the one at the Haights' reception was quite yummy.'

'That was a nice wedding,' said Iris. 'And a quick engagement. Well done, us!'

There had been a plethora of weddings in June, and each resulted in the prompt payment of the contractual bounty the couples owed for being matched so well. As a result, the firm was financially flush after a lean stretch over the winter. They had taken advantage of their new stability to institute reduced summer hours, even planning for holidays in August, their first since they began the enterprise the previous year.

'What's the latest on your landlord?' asked Gwen. 'Or should I call him a waterlord?'

'His parents are still ailing, so he continues to reside in Yorkshire for the near future,' said Iris. 'I wish them a full recovery, but not a speedy one. I am enjoying the narrowboat life.'

'Are you looking for any place for after he returns?' asked Gwen. 'Perhaps something fixed to the earth's surface?'

'Not until it's absolutely necessary. May I tell you a secret?'

'Of course.'

'I've been taking piloting lessons with Casper, my neighbour.'

'Piloting? You mean narrowboat piloting? Don't you need some form of licence to do that?'

'Apparently not,' said Iris. 'Not that the lack of a licence ever stopped me from driving anything, but that's a whole collection of thrilling tales.'

'Which I don't want to hear. But are you actually planning to take your boat out into the wild?'

'I think it would be great fun. See England at my own pace, not tied to railway schedules. Since the war ended, the narrow-boat traffic on the canals has dropped considerably, so I might be able to manage it without bumping into anything important. And I'd be taking my whole digs with me, so apart from fuel and the overnight mooring fees, it would be quite economical.'

'But you'd be alone the entire time.'

'I've been alone for a while now,' said Iris sombrely. 'It's been six months since Archie died. I'm not ready yet to look for the next disastrous relationship with a man, and despite *The Friendly Young Ladies* aspects of the setting, I'd rather not bring any female companions aboard, either.'

She sighed.

'What?' asked Gwen.

'I'm turning thirty soon.'

'I know. We should celebrate.'

'Celebrate what? The fulfilment of my mother's predictions? That I would be alone at thirty if I didn't change my wicked ways?'

'When did she say that?'

'When she caught me sneaking a boy into the house while I thought she was out handing out pamphlets.'

'How old were you?'

'Fifteen. She made me read the entire pamphlet aloud to him, which was mortifying for both of us. We're being followed, by the way.'

'Are we?' exclaimed Gwen.

'Not so loud,' Iris cautioned her.

'Sorry,' said Gwen, dropping her voice. 'Followed by whom? And for how long?'

'A man wearing a dark blue cap, dressed like a dock worker. I noticed him smoking on the corner when we left the office. I thought he was a long way from the nearest dock.'

'You didn't say anything then.'

'I wanted to see what he was going to do next,' said Iris.

'He tailed us on Oxford Street, then flagged down a car and vanished. But he's reappeared since we've hit Edgware. I haven't spotted the car, but I'll bet it's somewhere close by.'

'What should we do?'

'For a start, let's look at the ladies' shoes in the window at Forley's.'

They paused in front of the shop, Iris surreptitiously producing her compact from her purse and angling the mirror to see down the pavement to her right.

'He's still coming towards us,' she muttered. 'He's alone, but that doesn't mean there aren't others about. Keep looking at the shoes. If necessary, I'll make the first move.'

Gwen said nothing, but gripped her umbrella tightly. It was all she could do not to turn and stare at the oncoming follower. She forced herself to focus on the slingbacks and kitten heels on display. A man's footsteps approached, then stopped next to them.

'Excuse me, ladies, I'm looking for a pub,' he said.

They turned to face him. He had removed his cap, revealing a shock of brown hair sticking out in different directions.

'There are plenty about,' said Iris.

'I mean, a particular pub,' he said. 'The Portland Arms. I'm supposed to meet me mate there.'

'I know the place,' said Gwen. 'It's about a twenty-minute walk from here. Take a right on Hall, then keep going until you reach St John's Wood High Street, and then another right. It's on the corner across from the gardens.'

'Thanks, miss,' he said. 'Would the two of you fancy joining us for a pint? Timmy's a good lad. I can vouch for him.'

'Sorry, we have a prior engagement,' said Iris smoothly.

'Well, can't blame a fellow for asking,' he said with a grin. 'This is a nice part of town. I've only been here once before. Friendly little place called the Heroes of Alma. They do a decent shandy there, if you're ever interested.'

'We'll have to check it out sometime,' said Iris. 'Thanks for the recommendation. Enjoy your evening.'

'Ta,' he said, replacing his cap and moving on.

'What just happened?' asked Gwen as they watched him disappear around a corner.

'Contact has been made,' said Iris. 'Shall we go?'

'Go? Go where?'

'To the Heroes of Alma, of course.'

She resumed walking up Edgware. Gwen, confused, caught up to her.

'I was given "shandy" as a code word,' explained Iris as they turned onto Elgin.

'When?'

'A few days after you were forced to sign the Official Secrets Act after our last unexpected adventure.'

'I did that to protect you.'

'I know you did,' said Iris, grasping her partner's hand for a moment. 'I'm grateful. But it also put us in a precarious position. I have a feeling that the other shoe is about to drop directly on our heads.'

'Oh, dear,' said Gwen. 'I had been hoping they had forgot about us. It's been three months.'

'It could have been three years or three decades. We're still beholden to them, and they never forget.'

The Heroes of Alma was tucked away at the end of Alma Square in a little nub end of the street, two buildings on each side before it butted up against a wall separating it from a house on the other side. The door was in the centre, flanked by windows with strips of narrow red and white striped awning. Some small round tables were set up outside with wooden folding chairs surrounding them. Three men were drinking at one, discoursing on the problems of the world and offering their own competing solutions. Another man sat alone at the other table, reading the *Telegraph*. The first three men raised their glasses in salute as the women passed by them to the door. The *Telegraph* reader barely glanced at them.

He's the bodyguard, thought Iris, wondering if he had a weapon at the ready behind the newspaper.

The interior of the pub was not much bigger than a regular front parlour, with four square oak tables and a small bar at one side. A plump, middle-aged woman sat on a stool behind the bar, nodding at the two as they entered. The only other customer was an older, balding gentleman seated at one of the tables, a partly smoked Dunhill in his left hand, a small glass of whisky in front of him, a grey trilby resting on the centre of the table.

'It's that man again,' said Sparks when she saw him. 'The Minister of Aggravation and Mysteries at the Office of Twerps.'

'Miss Sparks, Mrs Bainbridge,' acknowledged the Brigadier. 'Good to see you both. Hetty, we'll be in back. What will you be drinking, ladies?'

'Do you actually have shandy here?' asked Sparks.

'We do,' said Hetty.

'I'll have one.'

'The same, please,' said Mrs Bainbridge.

The Brigadier stubbed out his cigarette in the ashtray, stood, gathered his drink and his hat, then led them through a door in the rear and down a narrow hall to the back where there was a kitchen with a small table and some chairs. He motioned for them to sit. Hetty appeared a moment later with two pint glasses of shandy which she placed in front of the ladies, then vanished, closing the door behind her. The Brigadier waited for a moment, then opened the door a crack to make certain she had gone back to her post behind the bar.

'Good,' he said, closing the door and locking it. 'I won't be keeping you long.'

'Nice of you to pick a spot in our neighbourhood,' said Sparks.

'I like this pub,' said the Brigadier. 'It's quiet, out of the way, and you can see who is coming with plenty of warning.'

'And you have the use of the kitchen,' observed Sparks. 'Well, to absent friends.'

They held up their respective drinks for a moment, then drank.

'Refreshing,' commented Sparks. 'Now tell us why we're here.'

'I need something done by someone outside of my department,' said the Brigadier.

'Why aren't you using someone in your department?' asked Sparks.

'Because I am increasingly concerned about infiltration by

communist sympathisers and double agents,' he said. 'The number of people in whom I have faith drops by the day.'

'You have faith in me? That's news,' said Sparks.

'I have faith in you, Sparks, because you quit the office rather than join in a project which in retrospect would have been a massive error had it been put into action,' said the Brigadier. 'My apologies for not elaborating, Mrs Bainbridge, but Sparks knows what I'm talking about.'

'I'd rather not know any more than I already do,' said Mrs Bainbridge.

'And I have faith in you, Sparks, because of your willingness to throw yourself into situations that have occasionally run up against our own policies, and each time you have proved yourself in the right,' continued the Brigadier. 'Which is why I have protected you as much as I could.'

'But you also found it useful to maintain my reputation as a renegade, haven't you?' asked Sparks.

'I have,' said the Brigadier. 'That, along with your leftist background from your university days, and your contacts with a Soviet Intelligence operative last year, means that anyone looking into you might assume you had been turned, or are at least capable of turning.'

'Why would a double agent be running a marriage bureau?' asked Sparks.

'It's as good a front as anything. It allows you to meet people from all walks of life, including any level of His Majesty's government.'

'What specifically are you asking me to do?'

'It would involve both of you, in fact,' said the Brigadier. 'And your marriage bureau. There is a man we're concerned about who has been with our Far East operations based in Shanghai. He's transferred back home to work under the Foreign Secretary. Bevin likes him, so he looks to be on the rise, and will have access to a number of ongoing operations and their personnel. Most importantly, he's single.'

'Ah,' said Sparks. 'I think I see where this is going.'

'The Secretary prefers career civil servants to be stable and married,' said the Brigadier. 'I've personally never seen any causal connection between matrimony and stability, but there you are. There are two parts to this plan. I want you to get this man to sign up for your professional services. Then I want you to set him up with someone who can delve into his affairs.'

'A honeytrap?'

'Not quite that involved. More of a sounding out in a way that will be less likely to set off his alarms. Once we're satisfied, she'll break it off, and, depending on which side he falls on, we'll move in as appropriate.'

'I have a question,' said Mrs Bainbridge. 'What if he proves to be loyal to the Crown? What does The Right Sort do with him then?'

'If he's loyal, go ahead and find him a proper bride,' said the Brigadier with a shrug.

'How are we supposed to recruit him?' asked Sparks.

'That's the main reason I chose you,' said the Brigadier. 'You already know him.'

'Who?'

'Anthony Danforth,' said the Brigadier, watching her closely.

'Tony,' she said, closing her eyes for a second. 'Tony Danforth. I knew him at Cambridge.'

'We know,' said the Brigadier. 'When is the last time you saw or heard from him?'

'When he came back from Spain,' she said. 'Late '38 maybe? We had dinner. He had plans to go to Singapore then. We exchanged a few letters, but we lost touch after that.'

'I have to ask you this, Sparks, and it is absolutely essential that you be truthful with me,' said the Brigadier. 'Were you lovers?'

'Lovers?' she repeated. 'No. Friends. Good friends for a while. But it never reached that level.'

Gwen willed herself to keep her expression blank as she watched her partner.

'What I find interesting, knowing you as I do,' said the Brigadier, 'is that you haven't leapt to his defence or attempted to dissuade me from this course of action.'

'I'm not a wide-eyed student any more,' said Sparks. 'I fully respect the dangers of the world we live in. I know who Tony

was then. I don't know who he is now, but I think I know what
he was capable of becoming. And I think I know you well
enough by now to know that you wouldn't be asking me for
help unless the situation was serious.'

'It is,' said the Brigadier.

'I also noticed that you have cloaked all of this in a semblance
of choice, rather than pointing out the obvious.'

'Which is?'

'That you have us both under your thumb. If I said no right
now, would you honour it?'

'I would,' said the Brigadier.

'What do you think?' Sparks asked her partner.

'I follow your lead in this,' said Mrs Bainbridge.

'But what do you think?' persisted Sparks.

'I think that the Soviets are as great a threat now as the
Nazis were,' said Mrs Bainbridge. 'If there is any small way I
can help with the fight, I offer it.'

'This isn't small,' said Sparks.

'As I said, I follow your lead.'

'Right,' said Sparks. 'I'm in. We're in. Who's playing the
not-so-sweet honey?'

'Someone new to my team,' said the Brigadier. 'So new that
I've kept her separate from the rest. She'll be showing up at
your office to sign up within the next few days. After that,
you'll receive instructions on where to find Mr Danforth.'

'And that has to be just me,' Sparks said to Mrs Bainbridge.

'Of course,' replied her partner. 'It wouldn't make sense for
both of us to run into him.'

'Anything else I need to know?' asked Sparks.

'Not at the moment,' he said, standing and reaching for his
hat.

'Are you well, sir?' asked Sparks.

'Excuse me?'

'Since I last saw you, you seem thinner. And more tired.'

'This work takes its toll,' he said. 'No need to concern
yourself with my well-being.'

'We need you to stay alive, sir,' said Sparks. 'You're the one
keeping me out of jail, remember?'

They re-entered the pub and deposited their empty glasses on the bar, the Brigadier leaving a healthy tip as he paid.

'I was never here,' he said to Hetty.

'You're always never here,' said Hetty. 'See you the next time you're never here.'

'You go ahead, ladies,' he said. 'It was a pleasure to see you as always.'

'And you, sir,' returned Sparks.

'Goodbye,' said Mrs Bainbridge.

They left, nodding to the patrons at the outside tables as they passed.

'"A pleasure to see you as always",' muttered Iris. 'I can't think of a single time it's been a pleasure. We do meet 'em, don't we?'

'We certainly do,' agreed Gwen.

'Was he telling us the truth in there?'

'As far as I can tell,' said Gwen. 'He's difficult to read. As are you when you're talking to him, by the way. Your defences rise to a higher level.'

'You were reading me?'

'If I'm following your lead, I need to know where you're going,' said Gwen. 'Especially if it's anywhere dangerous.'

'This shouldn't be dangerous,' said Iris. 'We're merely setting up the connection, then stepping back and letting it play out without us.'

They walked back to Edgware.

'Was I telling the truth in there?' asked Iris.

'You should know better than I.'

'I lie to myself as much as I do to anyone,' said Iris. 'Don't hold out on me, Madam Cassandra, tell me my fortune.'

'I once wanted to be a fortune teller, but there was no future in it.'

'I'm being serious, Gwen.'

'You were telling the truth – for the most part.'

'Ah,' said Iris. 'Where did I go astray?'

'When he asked if you were ever lovers.'

'You thought I was lying.'

'I thought you were being . . . ambiguous.'

'It was that word. Lovers. I don't think we were. Not really.'

'But?'

'But I think I answered a different question than the one he was asking.'

'So do I,' said Gwen. 'Do you want to tell me about it?'

'No,' said Iris. 'It doesn't change anything. And here is where I turn off. Are you seeing Sally later?'

'He's working late tonight.'

'Pity. I thought you'd be taking more advantage of Ronnie being away this summer.'

'I have been. During our lunch hour. It's a quick walk to his flat.'

'So that's where you've been going. I should have guessed.'

'I thought you had.'

'You always return looking as immaculate as ever. Let me think. You missed lunch with me yesterday, and three times last week. My goodness! You must be starving!'

'Hungry, but happy,' said Gwen.

'See you in the morning,' said Iris. 'The world must be peopled!'

'The world must be peopled,' returned Gwen. 'Goodnight, Iris.'

'Goodnight, Gwen.'

Iris walked down to the Regent's Canal where the *Cecilia*, her current abode, waited. She waved to her neighbour, Casper, who was as usual seated in a worn easy chair he had somehow manoeuvred onto the roof of his boat. He was smoking a pipe and watching the changing colours of the sky as the sun descended.

She felt enough of a glow from the shandy to forego adding more alcohol to her meagre evening meal, then sat out on the fore well, an unopened book on her lap. *It's That Man Again* wasn't on tonight, and there was nothing else on the radio that she wanted to listen to, so she contented herself with watching a family of ducks paddling about.

Some song was running through her head. What was it? She hummed a few bars, then placed it. 'The Internationale'. Of course, that would be the one to resurface even after she had suppressed it so many years ago.

She went back inside and changed into her pyjamas, then lay on top of the covers. The wind kicked up outside, and the *Cecilia* swayed back and forth, bumping gently against the dock.

Well, Tony, you're back in my life, she thought. And I'm on a boat.

How appropriate.

'The Internationale' continued to play in her head. What were those lines in the last verse? Something about crows and vultures. Mais si les corbeaux, les vautours disparaissent . . . But if the crows and vultures disappear, the sun will shine forever.

The crows and vultures have returned, thought Iris. Which one is Tony?

And which one am I?

TWO

The line of constables guarding the University Arms Hotel stretched from the entrance on Regent Street around to the side facing Parker's Piece, the large square park where the protesters were gathered. The gates to the hotel were closed and locked, a rare concession to the hostility of the crowd outside towards the dinner party within. The constables, many of whom had been pulled into a second shift to accommodate the needs of the event, knew that they were insufficient in numbers to withstand the protesters should the latter decide to mount an attack. They also knew it was highly unlikely that there would be an attack, given that the protesters were students from the University Socialist Society, more predisposed to making noise than to taking action. Still, in the back of the mind of each officer was the possibility that things could go wrong due to a combination of youthful exuberance, alcohol and political rage, and that even though the police station was only minutes away on the other side of the park, there might not be enough time for reinforcements to arrive.

So despite believing that the sound and fury would amount to less than nothing, each constable gripped his truncheon tightly, looking out at the sea of academic gowns and blazing torches with grim anticipation.

Inside the hotel, the University Fascist Society had taken it upon themselves to invite Sir Oswald Mosley, founder and leader of the British Union of Fascists, to dine, orate and be cheered, presumably because Hitler and Mussolini were otherwise engaged.

'Really?' said Sally when Sparks had told him about it. 'Will the dress code be black tie or black shirt?'

'Won't you come?' she pleaded with him. 'You have such a good voice for roaring at buildings.'

'I just got the F key repaired on my typewriter,' he said. 'I have a free evening to work on my play. There's a nice part for you in it, you should know.'

'You believe that writing a play is more important than changing the world, Mr Danielli?'

'The fascists and the socialists are both badly written theatre, so anything I can do to improve the art is more important,' he said. 'I don't think the world will change because of what happens in Cambridge tonight, and I don't think I'd be tipping the balance either way. Besides, you shouldn't be allowed anywhere with a torch. You're too short. You'll be singeing men's beards off.'

'If the fascists take over, there will be no decent theatre,' said Sparks.

'That will be enough cause for me to put down my typewriter and pick up a machine gun,' promised Sally. 'But tonight, I need to go over the manuscript of the second act and put all the Fs into it. It should improve the clarity of the writing immensely, although it might arouse the attentions of the censors in some cases. Have a good roar without me, Sparks. But don't start the next world war until I'm done with the third act.'

'Where's the fun in that?' said Sparks. 'But I promise I'll carry a torch only for you, darling.'

'Would that were true,' he said with a laugh.

She punched him in the arm affectionately and walked away, belting, 'I've Got to Sing a Torch Song' to the bewilderment of passers-by.

Which is how she found herself in the midst of two hundred or so like-minded colleagues, screaming, 'We want Mosley, dead or alive!' and singing 'The Internationale' at the tops of their lungs. All the verses. In the original French, of course, because they were Cambridge students and liked to show off. Much of the preparations for the protest had in fact been devoted to learning the song, which was as much of an intro-duction to socialism as many of them had had up to that point in their lives, chalking up the evening's gathering to enjoying a moment of rebellion that had as much to do with being independent and away from their parents as anything else.

Sparks, however, was genuinely committed to the cause, having been raised through her teens by her very progressive mother after her parents' divorce. She held her torch high (she had to – Sally was right about the dangers of combining fire with her lack of height), and after an hour of heartfelt speeches mixed with some bad revolutionary poetry by John Cornford and Maurice Cornforth, followed by a discourse on Marxian economic theory by Maurice Dobb, a don at Trinity College, her arm was in agony.

How does that statue in New York manage it so easily? she wondered.

Thankfully, the decision was made to march through the town to Peas Hill, giving her the opportunity to loosen up her joints and bring the torch down to a less painful level, taking care not to ignite her hat. The crowd proceeded up St Andrew's Street, passing by Emmanuel College, somewhere inside of which she knew Sally was working away on his play.

'Uck o, Danielli!' she shouted in his general direction, drawing puzzled looks from her nearby fellows.

The marchers turned left on Downing Street, then right onto Corn Exchange, which was narrower, causing a temporary bottleneck until they managed to sort themselves into an array with five abreast. Two more turns brought them to the market-place in front of the Guildhall. The stalls were closed for the evening but the area still smelled strongly of fish despite the competing fumes from the torches.

More speeches followed, each speaker denouncing fascism as ardently as they could, but by this time repetition and declining oratorical ability had taken their toll on Sparks, whose mind had wandered to considering the problem of how to dispose of a lit torch without causing a major conflagration. She saw a number of students tossing theirs into a metal rubbish bin, and decided to add hers to what she hoped would be a safe resting place for it. As she did, shrill whistles suddenly sounded from all sides.

'The bulldogs!' someone yelled. 'Run for it!'

Then there was pandemonium as the Proctor's own law enforcement poured into the marketplace, grabbing anyone they could. Around her, students panicked and dashed off in all directions. She sidestepped a man running directly at her while looking back over his shoulder, but was almost knocked off her feet by another crashing into her from behind.

She wasn't built for being in the middle of a scrum. She broke for the narrow alley to the right of the Church of St Edward the King, then stopped as she reached the left turn past the antiquarian bookshop. There was a pair of bulldogs at the other end where the alley emerged onto St Edward's Passage. She couldn't go back. She was trapped.

Then a voice called, 'In here! Quickly!'

She turned and saw a young man in the open doorway of the bookshop, beckoning to her. He was wearing a black academic gown. There was something familiar about his face, but she wasted no time trying to identify him, choosing instead to scoot inside as he held the door.

'Mind the step,' he cautioned her.

'Thanks,' she said.

He closed the door behind her and locked it. The blinds in the store windows had been drawn so it was almost completely dark.

'Keep your voice down,' he whispered, peeking around the side of one blind. 'The owner and his family sleep upstairs.'

'How is it that you have a key?' she asked.

'I work here a few hours a week,' he said. 'Luckily for you. That wasn't the best escape route.'

'I suppose not,' she said. 'How long do you think we should wait it out?'

'I'd give it half an hour,' he said. 'Until the bulldogs have caught enough to sate their appetites. You're Iris Sparks, aren't you?'

'I am,' she said in surprise. 'And you have me at a disadvantage. I'm afraid I didn't get a good look at you.'

'Picture me sitting cox in a boat, my expression one of abject humiliation,' he said.

'Ah!' she exclaimed. 'From the Pembroke crew. You're Anthony Danforth.'

'Tony, please,' he said. 'Any woman who has beaten me so soundly has earned the right to call me by my familiar name. And I'm flattered that you know it.'

'I may have made a few enquiries after last week,' she confessed, smiling in the dark.

'As did I. I read your article in the *Thersites* on controlling population growth. I thought it was very well-reasoned.'

'You read the Newnham magazine? Not many men around here would admit to that.'

'I read all the college publications,' he said. 'I like to know who all the interesting people are.'

'And I interest you,' she said.

'You do.'

'Well, in that case . . .' she said.

She pressed up against him in the dark and kissed him.

'That was unexpected,' he said when they came up for air. 'Was it the narrow escape or the smell of old dusty tomes that brought that about?'

'I cannot deny the erotic stimulus of rare books,' she murmured. 'But this is more of a social experiment of mine.'

'Explain, please.'

'My theory is that romance as it is currently practiced is an unnecessary and inefficient investment of time, money and emotion. All of those rigid courtship rituals observed to the letter, leading up to that supreme moment – the first kiss. But what if it's a complete bust? I have only three years here, so why waste time on the duds? A kiss is something worth having independent of all that other folderol. My reactions to it are more physiological than anything else, but I trust those more than I trust either my emotions or my ability to assess a man, especially when he's still wet behind the ears. So if I find someone attractive, I say let's go for the goal straight away, uncluttered by doubts or expectations, and then see if he's worth the follow-up.'

'I see,' he said, bemused. 'May I ask, and this is purely for the sake of my fragile male ego, how was I?'

'Not bad at all. Of course, I only have the one data point.'

'Insufficient for analysis,' he said, gathering her in his arms. 'And if we remove the element of surprise from my side of the equation . . .'

They kissed again, this time with more active participation on his part.

'Now, that was first-rate,' she said when they finally parted.

'Good to know,' he said.

He listened outside for a moment.

'The commotion seems to have died down,' he said. 'I'll walk you back to Newnham. If we come across any straggling bulldogs, we're out on a date and quite shocked to learn that such pinko goings-on have been going on.'

'A plausible cover story,' she said. 'Thank you.'

He unlocked the door, listened again, then stepped outside, motioning for her to join him once he saw that the area was deserted. He closed the door behind her, locking it quietly, then offered her his arm. She took it.

The alley was illuminated only by the lights coming from the windows of the flats overlooking it. They walked quietly to St Edward's Passage and turned to the right. The only signs of the evening's mayhem were the odd discarded placard or burned-out torch.

'What did you think of the rally?' he asked as they strolled towards the Cam.

'It was a decent turnout for a Thursday,' she replied. 'I found that encouraging.'

'And the speeches?'

'I thought Cornforth was particularly good. Forceful, succinct, no self-glorification, unlike Cornford. As for Dobb, I would be very much interested in attending one of his classes, but I felt like I was attending one of his classes.'

'It wasn't the most rhetorically inspiring speech,' Danforth said with a laugh. 'But you should definitely sign up for him next term if you have any interest in economic history. I recommend that we take the Mathematical Bridge. It's less likely to be bulldogged at the moment.'

'I will be guided by you, Mr Danforth.'

'Please call me Tony, Iris.'

'I will,' she said. 'But call me Sparks. Everyone does.'

'Sparks, it shall be.'

They passed over the bridge, a construction of wooden beams and trusses that took them over the narrowed Cam. To their left were staff cottages, so they went straight through the Fellows' Garden and skirted the tennis courts on the other side. From there they cut across to Sidgwick Avenue, which brought them a few minutes later to the bronze gates of Newnham College.

Which were closed and locked.

'It's after ten,' muttered Sparks. 'Blast.'

'Will you get in trouble?' asked Tony.

'Only if I get caught,' said Sparks. 'Come with me.'

She led him along the walls to a section of wrought-iron fence, beyond which was Clough Hall, its white trim gleaming in the half-moonlight, lights still on in most of the rooms.

'Give us a leg up, would you?' she asked.

'I'm in an experimental phase myself, you should know,' he said as he interlocked his fingers and held his hands by the fence.

'Interesting,' she said as she placed her right foot on the step he had made for her.

'Worthy of a follow-up?' he asked as he boosted her up. 'I realise I'm going about this backwards under your scheme, but could I take you to lunch Saturday? Maybe to the cinema after, although I'm hoping that the quality of the conversation will make that unnecessary.'

She hauled herself over the top, dangled by one hand for a moment, then dropped softly to the grass on the other side. She turned to face him through the bars.

'Do not discount the cinema,' said Sparks. 'It is an essential part of character. I will be judging you on which film you choose.'

'Extra pressure, good,' he said. 'I shall meet you here – well, not here, exactly, but in proper form at the front gate at eleven thirty.'

'Agreed,' she said.

She stuck two fingers through the fence, and he held them for a moment.

'Goodnight, Sparks,' he said.

'Goodnight, Tony. Thanks for the sanctuary.'

He watched as she ran silently towards Clough Hall. She stood under one of the lit upper-storey windows and whistled softly. A moment later, the window opened and a rope snaked down from it. She swarmed up it like a pirate and disappeared. He grinned, then turned and walked back to Pembroke College.

* * *

Lunch was at the Whim Café, and they ended up not going to the cinema after all, the conversation continuing while they leaned across a small table on the upper level, wolfing down scrambled eggs with broiled tomatoes and toast, refilling their cups with more coffee when they felt there was any hint of being asked to make way for any waiting customers. Around them was activity and noise – the Footlights crowd arguing over programming, aspiring authors ostentatiously scribbling in notebooks, hoping to be interrupted by other aspiring authors asking what they were writing, and the outnumbered women seated with anywhere from three to five men each, all desperate, all hopeful, all ultimately frustrated.

Sparks and Danforth interrogated each other thoroughly over a wide-ranging selection of topics. He was a second-year, so she had many questions as to his experience with courses she was thinking about taking, while he wanted to know more about her adventures since arriving.

'How did it turn out with your crashing the Bumps?' he asked.

'We were fined and banned from taking our boat out between the Jesus and Baits Bite Locks for the remainder of the Lent and Easter terms,' she said. 'We expected that. There was never any danger of rustication for disrupting the Bumps. We made our point.'

'And this social experiment of yours, have there been many other, erm, data points?' he asked.

'Do you mean have I kissed anyone besides you?' she returned, smiling.

'Yes.'

'If I am going to maintain scientific objectivity, I must adhere to the complete confidentiality of my test subjects,' she said loftily.

'But this, right now with me, is a follow-up.'

'Obviously.'

'I confess to being uncertain how to proceed from this point,' he said. 'Do we travel back to the past to our first meeting, then part?'

'I am bound by time's arrow like everyone else,' she said.

'How do you feel about marriage?'

'Why, sir!' she exclaimed, wide-eyed. 'This is so sudden! We still barely know each other.'

'I mean, about the institution. Given your approach to romance.'

'I think it's an antiquated system designed to bring about the political and economic subjugation of women,' she replied.

'That seems harsh,' he said, taken aback.

'Do you believe that women can do anything that men can?' she asked.

'No,' he replied.

Her face fell.

'I believe that they can do more,' he said. 'And someday, the world may allow them to.'

'Hmph,' she said. 'I think you're only saying that because you're hoping that we end up in bed together.'

'What if I said that wasn't true?' he asked. 'The bed part, I mean. Would you then relegate me to the bottomless pit with the other duds?'

'Not at all. Most of the boys – excuse me, men – who have sought my attentions here have been single-mindedly focussed on getting me on a horizontal plane rather than an intellectual one. You, on the other hand, seem to enjoy the conversation. I like that.'

'Same here,' he said. 'Tell me, and this is once again to delve further into your approach, how does—' He dropped his voice for the next word, mouthing it more than giving it voice. '—sex come into it? Is it a logical development of a successful kiss?'

She glanced around the nearby tables. No one had reacted.

'I don't know how much of a part logic plays in it,' she said. 'The kiss is a condition precedent, of course, but it doesn't always automatically follow that it sets that particular course of events in action. Sex—' She dropped her voice in an exaggerated imitation of his. '—carries with it its own set of complications, emotional, practical and otherwise.'

'So you are saving yourself for the right man, whether or not matrimony is involved.'

'Oh, that particular ship sailed a while ago,' she said with a grin. 'And other ships have— well, the metaphor is going to become grossly unsubtle. Again, I don't attach romance to the actual act, and as a result, I have had more fun and less angst in my brief life.'

'Has the first kiss project helped with the winnowing?'

'Immensely.'

'But I'm not a man you would consider a good candidate.'

'Who says you're not?'

'Everyone I've asked so far,' he said ruefully.

'So you're saving yourself for the right woman,' she said mischievously.

'More like I've been throwing myself at the wrong ones,' he said. 'Let's go for a walk.'

'Where to?'

'Just about,' he said.

He paid the bill, and they left the Whim, eventually finding themselves strolling along the path of their flight two nights before. In the light of day, the Fellows' Garden was filled with bare trees and gnarled bushes huddling in the cold, damp winter, awaiting the slightly less cold, damp spring.

'Distinct lack of cover here,' observed Sparks. 'If seducing me is your intent.'

'It isn't,' he said. 'I wonder if they'll preserve this garden when they put up the new building.'

'I hadn't heard about that.'

'All of the servants' and porters' buildings are going to be razed for a new residential building for Queens' College,' he said. 'Once again, the working class being trampled upon for the sake of the privileged.'

'Are you privileged?' asked Sparks.

'I'm afraid so,' he said. 'You?'

'Working class of the less trampled variety. Mum was a schoolteacher, Dad a businessman.'

'What sort of businessman?'

'I believed "failed" is the proper description. "Drunk" would also be an appropriate adjective.'

'Sorry to pry.'

'No, no secrets here,' she said.

'Yes, you've told me much that others would generally keep

hidden,' he said. 'Tell me, are you able to keep secrets when called upon?'

'I am,' she said, looking at him curiously.

'How serious are you about the socialist agenda?'

'Quite serious. Why?'

'A lot of folks dabble, but stop before going to the next level,' he said. 'Are you one of those?'

'I don't dabble. I plunge in headlong.'

'Are you free Wednesday evening?'

'As far as I know. Why?'

'Maurice Dobb is having a small get-together at his house. You should come.'

'What's the occasion? More economics?'

He smiled.

'The next level,' he said.

London, 1947

'And that's how I almost became a communist,' said Iris.

She had decided in the morning to tell Gwen more about Tony during their walk to work, and her partner listened without interruption the entire time.

'The get-together with this Dobb person was a recruitment?' she asked at the end.

'A recruitment disguised as a party,' said Iris. 'A Party party. A mix of dons and students. There were relatively few freshers, even fewer women, so I was flattered to be invited, and the subject of much attention, of course.'

'Of course.'

'Tony stayed by my side the entire time,' Iris continued. 'My gallant protector and sponsor.'

'This was a secret society of some sort?'

'Oh, not that party. I mean, there were plenty of secret societies about, and I daresay half the guests that night were members of the Apostles as well, but Cambridge back then – they said that one out of every five students was with the socialists, and one of every five socialists joined the communists, so there was nothing unusual about any of it.'

'But you weren't seduced. Politically, I mean.'

'No. There had been an incident the year before that bothered me. A Russian physicist on the faculty had gone back for a visit to his family, and the Soviets wouldn't let him leave. I couldn't see affiliating myself with anything associated with them after that. So I chose after a few more exploratory meetings not to join the CP.'

'How did Tony take that?'

'He was disappointed, but we remained friends.'

'Only friends, though? It never went any further?'

A quick flash of memory . . .

She sat at the head of the bed, her back against the headboard, her legs drawn to her chest, her arms wrapped around them.

'Is something wrong?' she asked softly.

'I'm sorry,' he said disconsolately. 'I don't seem to be able to manage it.'

'We didn't get that far,' said Iris. 'I thought we would, but we didn't.'

'Do you wish you had?' asked Gwen.

'Not now,' she said. 'Given how things went later, it's a good thing that it didn't.'

'What happened later?'

Once again, she sat across from him in the Whim. Their last time together there, the end of 1936. She wouldn't meet his eyes.

'Come with me,' he urged her.

'You must be mad,' she said.

'Why not?' he asked. 'It isn't about joining the Party, it's about fighting against fascism. That's something you and I both agree on. A bunch of us are going – Cornford, Julian Bell, Dave Guest, Bruce Cater, others. The crème de la crème, or maybe I should say la crema de la crema.'

'Your accent is terrible.'

'And you speak Spanish better than any of us. That's another reason you should come.'

'To be what?' she snapped, finally looking at him. 'Your interpreter? Your camp follower?'

'I didn't mean it like that. But with your abilities . . .'

'My abilities,' she said. 'I'm reading History and Modern

Languages, I've never fired a gun in my life, and I don't want to shoot at anyone. Or be shot at.'

'Not all of us will be on the front lines,' he said. 'The International Brigade is going to be largely in support operations. You could drive an ambulance, or make bandages, or sandwiches, or something.'

'Easy for you to say,' she said. 'You've got your privilege to fall back upon if you don't finish school. I haven't.'

'You can finish when you get back,' he said. 'It shouldn't be long.'

'You have no idea how long it will be,' she said.

'Maybe not,' he said. 'But Spain is where the fight is going to be.'

'No, it isn't,' she said. 'Which is why I'm spending the Lent Term in Berlin.'

'You are? To do what?'

'To get to know the real enemy,' she said. 'Spain is just the prologue, Tony. The real war is coming from Germany.'

'Not if we nip fascism in the bud, and we will if enough of us join. Come with us. With me.'

'I'm sorry, Tony,' she said, reaching across the table and taking him by the hand for a moment. 'Good luck, and goodbye.'

'And that was that,' said Iris.

'He survived, though,' said Gwen.

'He did. The others – Cornford, Bell, Guest, Cater – all of them were killed there, along with many others. Cornford left behind a mistress, a baby son, and some heroic poetry.'

'You sound bitter about it.'

'It was a fools' war,' she said. 'The International Brigade never stood a chance. And they were just as prone to infighting and backstabbing in their own ranks as anyone, as it turned out.'

'You said you saw Tony when he returned. What was he like then?'

'We had dinner. He wouldn't talk about what happened there. He barely spoke at all. He told me he was going to Singapore to teach. Then, when we were parting, he said, "You were right, Sparks. About everything." And that was the last time I saw him.'

'What do you think he's like now?' wondered Gwen as they arrived at the building holding their offices.

'I can't imagine,' said Iris. 'Take all that he had already gone through, then add seven years in the Far East, fighting the Japanese. Maybe he can talk about things now. But first, we have to meet his pre-selected match.'

Mrs Billington, their sole employee, was already at her desk when they arrived.

'Good morning, ladies,' she said. 'You have three interviews scheduled before lunch. All women. We need to bring in some new male blood – we're running low.'

'You're making this sound unnecessarily vampiric,' said Gwen.

They went into their shared office and unpinned their hats.

'Did you really feel that way about marriage back then?' Gwen asked as they sat behind their desks.

'I was young, full of myself and suffering from delusions of grandeur,' said Iris. 'I had all sorts of big ideas. That's what university is for.'

'And now?'

'Not so young and constantly confronted by the smallness of reality,' said Iris. 'And now marriage is our business, so let's get to work, partner.'

The nine-thirty appointment was Miss Calpurnia Ford, a twenty-five-year-old switchboard operator from Balham.

'I was engaged,' she informed them after they took her preliminaries. 'But he was so changed when he came back from the war. He knew it, I knew it. He said he was still willing to go through with it because he had made a promise, but I didn't want to be a woman someone had to go through with it with to get married. So I released him, and I think he was relieved. I know I was. But I had waited for him all that time without, you know, going out and meeting anyone, and we ran in the same circles and knew all the same people, and I couldn't face any of them any more, so here I am.'

'And here we are,' said Sparks. 'Let's talk about what sort of man you're looking for.'

When she had left, Iris glanced over at Gwen, who shook her head.

The ten-thirty was Virginia Barton, a studious-looking librarian in her early thirties from Bayswater.

'I don't like people much,' she said. 'That's the problem. I don't like crowds, and I don't like parties, so meeting men is a chore.'

'Is that why you came to us?' asked Mrs Bainbridge.

'Yes,' said Miss Barton. 'Because I also don't want to be alone for the rest of my life. It's so dispiriting. I'm not looking for anything romantically earth-shattering, nor do I want children. Just someone to sit with at the end of the day, with quiet conversations and books or listening to music by the fireplace. Someone I can grow old with. Is that asking a lot?'

'We don't promise results or guarantee happiness,' said Mrs Bainbridge. 'But we also don't expect people to settle for less than they desire. Ask for all that you want with us, Miss Barton, and we'll do the best we can.'

When she had left, Gwen leaned back in her chair.

'She's going to be a real challenge,' she said. 'But she's not our special emissary from the Brigadier.'

'Agreed on both points,' said Iris. 'I wonder if she's even coming today.'

The eleven-thirty was lively, a petite twenty-three-year-old with a mass of blonde curls.

'All right, my name's Evelyn Lowle, but you got that on the form, I suppose,' she said. 'I'm from Manchester, but you got that from hearing me talk.'

'We do,' said Sparks. 'What brings you here?'

'Sitting across from you? Or meaning London?'

'Why don't you start with London?' suggested Mrs Bainbridge.

'I followed a boy here, silly little fool that I was,' she said. 'He was a year ahead of me at university, and we were madly in love. He gets done, comes to London to seek his fortune, then I come here a year later seeking him, only when I see him, there's nowt there any more, you know? And I find out he's moved on to a proper London girl, and I'd cut all my ties back home, so I was stranded here. So I was having a proper strop for a good while, but then I said to myself, "Evie, quit skriking and give your head a wobble. He's not the only fish." The problem is, I don't know anyone in London. So I came here.'

'I see,' said Mrs Bainbridge. 'What was your life like in Manchester before you went to university?'

'Working class all the way,' said Miss Lowle. 'Dad's a book-keeper, Mum teaches piano. She fancied I'd go to Royal Manchester or one of the other conservatoires one day, but hearing nowt but piano students non-stop in the front parlour made me lose interest in it pretty early.'

'I'm remembering all of my early piano lessons now,' said Mrs Bainbridge with a laugh. 'Which piece was the straw that broke the camel's back for you?'

'Oh, I don't even remember any more,' said Miss Lowle. 'I've blocked that part of my life.'

'What sort of man are you looking for?' asked Sparks.

'Don't know, rightly,' she said. 'I guess I'm looking for someone who is looking for me, so I'm open to possibilities. What do you think?'

'I think that you're laying on the accent a little thick,' said Sparks. 'You don't have to throw in every bit of Mancunian slang you know in the first two minutes.'

'Also, the piano teacher mum is a nice touch,' added Mrs Bainbridge. 'But you'd better be ready to name a few pieces in case the question comes up.'

Miss Lowle looked back and forth at the two of them in astonishment. Then the look was replaced by a sly smile.

'Wow. He told me you would be the tougher one to fool,' she said to Mrs Bainbridge. 'But I couldn't get by either of you, could I?'

'Who told you?' asked Sparks.

'The Brigadier, of course.'

'I have no idea what you're talking about,' said Sparks.

Lowle looked confused for a moment, then her face fell.

'Gosh, I'm doing it all wrong,' she said. 'I'm supposed to give you the password. Shandy.'

'Much better,' said Sparks. 'Let's talk.'

THREE

'What's your name?' asked Sparks.

'It's Evelyn Lowle as far as the two of you are concerned,' she replied. 'And the address on the application is where they've put me for this assignment. I don't have my own telephone there, so you'll have to use the landlady's number to reach me. A girl just out of university coming to London for an entry-level desk job can't afford her own telephone.'

Her accent is much less pronounced now, noticed Mrs Bainbridge.

'What is your ostensible desk job?' she asked.

'Oh, it's real enough,' Lowle said with a bitter laugh. 'I'm supposed to be some kind of a resources analyst, but I'm really just a glorified clerk for the Ministry of Food, if you can believe that. And I actually have to do the work! It's exactly the sort of thing I was hoping to avoid when I signed up to be an operative. I sit behind a stack of reports, pounding away at my typewriter, all the while thinking, "Is this how Mata Hari got started?"'

'She was an exotic dancer and a courtesan,' said Sparks. 'How's your exotic dancing?'

'Not my forte, sorry to say,' said Lowle. 'How's yours?'

'Passable when I was at Cambridge,' said Sparks. 'But the lads there were just happy to see any woman wiggling about on a pub table.'

'Ah, he told me you'd bring up Cambridge early in the conversation,' said Lowle.

'It's relevant to your assignment,' said Sparks, bristling.

'Not particularly,' said Lowle. 'But go ahead and brag about it all you like. At least I got a real degree from Manchester, not the BA tit. they saddle the Cambridge girls with.'

'You're really from Manchester?' Mrs Bainbridge asked quickly, forestalling any retort from her partner.

'I am,' said Lowle. 'And I really went to Victoria University of Manchester, so I can rattle away about that if called upon. They're adding records there showing me under this name. All part of my new cover. Oh, speaking of which . . .'

She opened her bag and pulled out five pounds.

'I've now signed up for your service,' she said, putting it on Sparks's desk. 'Is there a contract for me to sign?'

'Is that necessary, given you're not really a client?' asked Mrs Bainbridge.

'No, she's right,' said Sparks, handing over the paperwork. 'In case someone is suspicious enough to break in here and look her up in our files.'

'Let me skim this for a moment,' said Lowle. 'Yes. That's fine. I like the paragraph where you promise not to date the clients. Was it like that from the beginning, or was that in response to some incident?'

'From the beginning,' said Sparks tersely. 'Nor has there been any difficulty adhering to it. Do you need a pen?'

'Got one,' said Lowle, pulling one from her bag and signing the contracts. 'Here you are.'

Sparks and Mrs Bainbridge countersigned, then Sparks handed Lowle her copy which she folded neatly and tucked into her bag.

'Right,' she said. 'So who's my first date?'

'Excuse me?' said Mrs Bainbridge in surprise.

'My first date,' repeated Lowle. 'Who are you going to set me up with?'

'I'm not sure I understand what you mean,' said Mrs Bainbridge. 'The whole point of this exercise is to get you into a relationship with Anthony Danforth.'

'Yes, precisely,' said Lowle. 'But if Miss Sparks succeeds in luring him here, and his first date turns out to be someone who has also just signed up, then his hackles will be raised immediately. I need to come into it with a tale or two of the men before him and why they didn't work out. So who would you recommend?'

'I did not consent to this,' said Mrs Bainbridge.

'I was told that you agreed to the operation,' said Lowle.

'I did, but not to inflict it upon our unsuspecting clients. That's completely unfair to them.'

'That is so very kind of you,' said Lowle. 'Look, I promise that whoever it is, he will have an enjoyable time with me. And after our date, I will tell him that he is a wonderful man and will make an excellent husband for some lucky girl, but he's not quite right for me. He will leave with his sense of self-confidence intact, perhaps even enhanced.'

'No, I don't like this,' said Mrs Bainbridge. 'We'd be using an innocent—'

'What about Mr Lonsdale?' interrupted Sparks.

'What?' replied Mrs Bainbridge, turning in her chair to face her partner.

'Mr Lonsdale,' said Sparks. 'He hasn't made a connection with anyone yet, and it's been, what, six different dates with him?'

'Seven,' said Mrs Bainbridge.

'Right, Miss Hart said no to him last week,' recalled Sparks. 'So one more failed attempt shouldn't raise anyone's eyebrows in his case.'

'That's rather mean,' said Mrs Bainbridge.

'What's the matter with him?' asked Lowle.

'Well, that would be revealing the comments by our female clients afterwards,' said Sparks. 'I don't think that's any of your business, honestly. But he would meet your criteria for a one-date relationship.'

'What's he like?' asked Lowle, looking apprehensive for the first time in the conversation. 'Oldish? Youngish? Good-looking? Not so good-looking?'

'Let's see,' said Sparks. 'Thirty-four, five foot ten, thin black hair, receding somewhat. Average-looking overall, I'd say, with kind of a reedy voice.'

'Is it the voice that irritated my predecessors?' asked Lowle. 'You have to tell me something so he can see why you'd be setting him up with me, right?'

'Well, we're in a desperate situation with him and you're new blood, aren't you?' replied Sparks with an evil gleam in her eyes.

'Miss Sparks, please,' cautioned Mrs Bainbridge.

'Very well. The main problem he has with women is that he likes to fish,' continued Sparks.

'Fish? As in – fishing?'

'Exactly,' said Sparks. 'And when I say he likes it, it's more like he's completely obsessed.'

'He's from Dunbridge out in the Test Valley in Hampshire,' added Mrs Bainbridge. 'From what he told us, it's a one-pub village but the trout and graylings are abundant. He intends to return there once he's found a bride.'

'Trout and graylings,' repeated Lowle. 'Does he talk about anything else?'

'Apart from other species of fish and the various methods of catching them, not that we've heard,' said Sparks. 'Most of our ladies chose not to return for a second date, and the one who did refused to go back for a third.'

'What happened to her on the second date?' asked Lowle.

'He took her out on a boat,' said Mrs Bainbridge. 'There were worms and hooks involved. She didn't take to the experience, although I'm not certain if it was the bait or the seasickness that did it.'

'Hah!' said Lowle. 'Well, I think I could survive one evening of that. And then I'll move on to the real target.'

'What makes you think Mr Danforth will like you?' asked Sparks.

'I'm pretty, blonde and young,' she said matter-of-factly. 'Older men coming back from the war like girls like me.'

'He's not old,' protested Sparks. 'He's thirty-one.'

'Yeah, well, that's old for me, isn't it?' said Lowle with a sharp laugh.

Oh, now I truly dislike her, thought Mrs Bainbridge.

'You do realise that won't be enough for a man like him,' said Sparks.

'And that's where the two of you come in,' said Lowle. 'Once you get him here, you interview him, right?'

'We do,' said Mrs Bainbridge. 'We do that with all our clients.'

'Of course,' said Lowle. 'Only you'll be a little more thorough with him, won't you? Then you report back to me, and I will become that woman for our first date. Sound good?'

'Fine,' said Sparks. 'One suggestion, if you don't mind, from someone with prior experience in this sort of thing.'

'Sure.'

'Don't be a hundred per cent of what he's looking for. Too much of a good thing will raise hackles as well.'

'Good point,' said Lowle. 'Thanks.'

'And be careful,' added Mrs Bainbridge. 'You may want to be Mata Hari, but it didn't end well for her. I believe they still have her head in the Museum of Anatomy in Paris.'

She smiled sweetly, and Lowle blanched for a moment. Then she brightened.

'You're having me on now,' she said, getting to her feet. 'All right, got to get back to the desk job.'

'Tell the Minister to allow pineapples back again while you're there,' said Sparks.

'Will do,' said Lowle.

She left. Iris walked out to the landing and peered down the staircase to make certain that she had exited the building. Then she came back into the office, shut the door and sat down heavily in her chair.

'I'm sorry,' she said to Gwen. 'That was worse than I had thought it was going to be.'

'Was it like this for you?' asked Gwen.

'I had to do things during the war that went even further than this,' said Iris.

'You used the term "honeytrap" when we met with the Brigadier,' said Gwen. 'Does that mean what I think it does? A sexual seduction?'

'Yes,' said Iris.

'And you did that?'

'Yes.'

'Did it work?'

'For a while,' said Iris. 'It's also what cost me my engagement to Mike Kinsey.'

'Oh,' said Gwen. 'I'm so sorry, Iris.'

'The worst part is that to this day, I don't know if it contributed anything of real value to the war effort,' said Iris. 'Information was gathered, false information was leaked to the enemy. In the grand scheme of things, who knows? One destroyed relationship amid hundreds of thousands dead didn't mean much to anyone.'

'Except to you and Mike.'

'Except to us. And we might have broken it off anyway, given it's me we're talking about, so maybe there isn't any weight to that any more.'

'Well, our Miss Lowle doesn't seem to possess any real feelings, so this won't weigh much on her, either.'

'Not now,' said Iris. 'Down the line, it will or it won't. And if it doesn't, then she's clearly cut out for this work. What did you think of her?'

'She's interesting,' said Gwen. 'Once she dropped the outer layer of lies, she was still lying to us. I guess she has to.'

'She was very good at irritating me. "I'm pretty, blonde, and young!" Honestly, I suspect a bottle of peroxide was liberally applied.'

'Some of us blondes are actually blonde, you know,' said Gwen mildly.

'She was trying to top me in so many ways, did you notice?' commented Iris. 'The new girl competing with the veteran.'

'You were being just as competitive.'

'I was not!' said Iris hotly. Then she paused. 'Was I?'

'You do bring up Cambridge a lot,' Gwen pointed out.

'Do I?'

'I'm afraid so.'

'That must be irritating,' said Iris. 'I wasn't aware I was doing that.'

'It's something you have in common with every other Oxbridge person I've met,' said Gwen. 'Honestly, if I weren't so envious, I would chalk it up to them overcompensating for frail egos.'

'You're envious of them? Of me, I should say?'

'In my family, Brewster girls were raised to be accomplished up to a point, then married off,' said Gwen. 'My brother went to Oxford as did generations of Brewster men before him, but there was never any suggestion of me going to university, and I never knew enough then to question it. And now that I do, it's too late.'

'You could attend lectures, couldn't you? Take some adult courses?'

'With the other rich, bored dilettantes, you mean? No, thank you. I have a business to run, a child to raise, a home to manage, a corporate board to sit on and a lover to love. I couldn't possibly squeeze in a university education right now. And I'm ten years past the age where it could have given my brain a taste of the infinite, which saddens me because I know by now that my brain is a good one.'

'It certainly is.'

There was a knock on the door, then Mrs Billington came in.

'How did things go?' she asked.

'Three new clients,' said Iris, handing her the forms and the money.

'We should be able to repopulate England at this rate,' said Mrs Billington. 'Or London, at least. Any ideas as to matches for them?'

'As a matter of fact, we thought we'd give Mr Lonsdale first crack at the third woman, Miss Lowle,' said Iris.

'Really?' exclaimed Mrs Billington. 'So soon after the worm incident?'

'Miss Lowle seems unperturbed by the thought of impaling invertebrates,' said Iris. 'Send him her information right away, would you?'

'Very well, Miss Sparks,' said Mrs Billington. 'Eighth time's the charm, I guess. It will be in the afternoon post.'

She left.

'Stage One has commenced,' said Gwen.

'I wonder how long before Stage Two,' said Iris.

Two days later, they received a message from Miss Lowle: 'First date tonight. Wish me luck.'

'I'm wishing her something,' muttered Iris.

'We really need to find Mr Lonsdale someone more suitable after this,' said Gwen. 'I cannot tell you how guilty I'm feeling about him.'

The telephone rang in the next room. They heard Mrs Billington's voice through the wall, then she appeared at the doorway.

'That was Dr Shandy's office for Miss Sparks,' she said.

'They had to cancel your appointment, but said to call next week. Are you not feeling well, Miss Sparks?'

'Nothing to worry about, Saundra,' said Iris. 'Thank you.'

She waited until Mrs Billington left, then got up.

'I'll be back in twenty minutes,' she said.

The telephone box for the contact was on the corner of Davies and Brook Streets. She stepped into the box, dropped a coin into the slot, then dialled a number. She let it ring three times, then hung up and waited. A minute later, the telephone jangled in the box. She waited for the third ring, then answered.

'Do you know Maggs Brothers?' asked the Brigadier.

'The bookshop on Berkeley Square? I'd live there if I had the money.'

'The target put in a request for a particular book. The shop has received it, but won't call him about it until tomorrow afternoon, so he'll have to collect it after work.'

'I'll intercept him there,' said Sparks. 'I'll have to buy a book for myself while I'm there, sir, and I fully expect you to reimburse me for it.'

'Don't break the bank, Sparks,' he said. 'No Gutenberg Bibles, understood?'

'Please, sir, you know I'm an atheist. That would only serve me as an overpriced doorstop.'

'How did you like the new recruit?'

'We rubbed each other the wrong way.'

'That doesn't surprise me.'

'She's so green,' said Sparks. 'Why did you pick her?'

'Because she reminded me of you, Sparks. Let me know how things go.'

'Will do, sir.'

He hung up.

'Everything go all right?' asked Gwen when she returned.

'I have a time and a place for our accidental reunion,' said Iris as she sat down and opened their telephone directory. 'And I'm getting a book out of it, so there's some good coming from all of this.'

She picked up the phone and dialled.

'Hello, is this Maggs Brothers?' she asked. 'Do you have a

decent used copy of *British Water Beetles*? The author is Balfour-Browne. Yes, I'll wait.'

'Water beetles?' queried Gwen.

'Water beetles.'

'Those would be like aquatic cockroaches?'

'Faint praise, darling,' replied Iris. Then she turned back to the telephone. 'Hello? You have it? How much? And that's in what condition? Well, I'm a little cracked myself, or so I'm told, so I won't hold it against you. But the plates are pristine? Excellent. Could you hold that for me, and I will pick it up tomorrow after work? Miss Iris Sparks. Thank you.'

She hung up.

'I've been wanting that one for ages,' she said happily.

She was nervous the next day. She couldn't decide whether it was because she was going into the field for the first time since the war, or because it was Tony.

Her friend. Who she was going to betray.

Well, not betray, exactly, she thought, trying to reassure herself. If he was innocent, she was helping him clear himself before his career took off, and that was a good thing.

And if he wasn't innocent . . .

If he wasn't loyal to the Crown, then he didn't deserve her loyalty, either.

A convincing argument, surely. So why wasn't she convinced?

Gwen was a comforting presence as they worked, choosing not to bring up the subject. Iris knew that her partner would gladly hear her out on any part of it, but she decided that she needed to do this on her own. Even with their joint forays into the criminal underground and other odd venues on their occasional investigations, intelligence work was something in which she had experience and Gwen did not.

She didn't have much of an appetite for lunch, and Gwen didn't press her. Far from it, in fact, as she merely rose from her chair at the appointed hour, gave Iris a knowing look, and disappeared, returning an hour later looking flushed but quietly ecstatic, a few telltale blonde tresses having escaped from her chignon.

At quarter past four, Iris glanced at her wristwatch, then rose from her desk.

'Wish me luck,' she said.

'Ring me at home when you're done,' said Gwen. 'Or better yet, stop by the house for dinner. I don't want to wait until tomorrow to hear everything.'

'I can't promise dinner,' said Iris. 'Unexpected university reunions can become late and liquid in nature. Don't worry if I don't call.'

'Call anyway,' said Gwen. 'Reassure me that you're still alive.'

'It won't be anything that dramatic,' said Iris, pinning on her hat. 'See you.'

Gwen watched as she left, her expression changing from encouragement to concern. But there was no more that she could do.

She resumed her tasks of trying to match up their clientele, concentrating on their newest candidates, Miss Ford and Miss Barton. Then the telephone rang. A moment later, the intercom buzzed. She answered it.

'It's Mr Lonsdale,' said Mrs Billington, a concerned note in her voice. 'Are you free to speak to him?'

'Of course,' she said, her heart sinking. 'Put him through.' She picked up the handset.

'The Right Sort, Mrs Bainbridge speaking,' she said in what she hoped was an authoritative voice.

'Mrs Bainbridge, Kenneth Lonsdale here,' came his voice, sounding even reedier on the telephone than it did in person. 'I hope I'm not interrupting anything important.'

'You are not, Mr Lonsdale. How may we help you today?'

'It's about this last girl you set me up with.'

'Miss Lowle? Why, was there something wrong?'

'That's just the thing, Mrs Bainbridge,' he said. 'There wasn't. I thought the moment we met, Hullo, here is a possibility. And she turned out to be the first girl you've sent me who knew the difference between a wet fly and a dry one, or didn't immediately run for the door when I offered to show her my Black Spider and my White-Winged Coachman.'

'Which are what, exactly?'

'Flies, Mrs Bainbridge, flies,' he said impatiently. 'Two of the finest in my collection.'

'You brought fishing flies to show on a first date?'

'Any woman who is worth my attention should know who I am from the start. Wouldn't you agree?'

'I do, Mr Lonsdale. So things began well.'

'They began well and they continued well throughout the evening. It was by far the most enjoyable experience I've had since I signed up with your agency.'

'I am glad to hear it, Mr Lonsdale. What went wrong?'

'At the end of the evening, I asked if we could see each other again. She said no. It was expressed with decency, even kindness, but it was still no. Frankly, I am at a loss to understand why.'

'I'm so sorry, Mr Lonsdale,' she said. 'I will see if there is someone more outdoorsy among our ladies. Perhaps—'

'No, Mrs Bainbridge,' he said. 'The purpose of my calling you is to tell you that I am done with all this.'

'But Mr Lonsdale—'

'Mrs Bainbridge, I know who I am,' he said. 'I believe that being a man of my particular passions is off-putting to city girls, and I have seen that belief validated by one unpleasant encounter after another. I thought this last one might be different, yet the end was the same. In some respects, it was even more disheartening because I had hope in the beginning, and that hope grew throughout the evening. The fall at the end was from a greater height as a result, and more painful because of that.'

'Oh, Mr Lonsdale, I cannot tell you how sorry I am,' said Mrs Bainbridge. 'Please give us another chance. I will not rest until I have brought you happiness.'

'No, Mrs Bainbridge, I am done,' he said. 'I appreciate the efforts you and Miss Sparks have made on my behalf. I know that you can't succeed with everyone. I am sorry to have become one of your failures. I am going to wrap up things in London and go back to Hampshire. If I am to be alone, I would at least like to be alone where the trout are biting. Goodbye, Mrs Bainbridge.'

'Goodbye, Mr Lonsdale,' she said. 'Thank you for calling to tell us.'

She hung up, then dabbed at her eyes.

We've hurt someone, she thought. Damn it.

Berkeley Square was a short walk from The Right Sort, so Sparks arrived much too early for her quarry. She was running on nerves and an empty stomach by this point, so she walked through the London plane trees dotting the park, inhaling the scent of the new-mown grass to soothe her frazzle.

Then she spotted him. Tony, unmistakably Tony, walking down the pavement towards the shop. She looked down into her bag as if she were searching for something, keeping him in view out of the corner of her eye. He went inside Maggs Bros.

She pulled out her compact, checked her make-up, snapped it shut and put it back. Then she took a deep breath and sauntered from the park to the bookshop.

Two shallow steps took her to the door, next to which hung a plaque with the royal coat of arms over it and the proud, white-lettered proclamation: Maggs Bros. Ltd., 50 Berkeley Square Est. 1853. RARE BOOKS MANUSCRIPTS AUTOGRAPHS. She opened the door, tinkling a small silver bell overhead. A clerk nodded to her from behind a maple counter to her left. On long tables in front of her were stacked giant volumes with worn bindings from centuries past, while more on shelves covered every inch of wall space up to the ceiling. A rolling stepladder stood at the ready to the right. There was a staircase at the rear leading to the upper storeys, which no doubt were crammed with even more books.

Tony wasn't there, which meant he must have gone upstairs. She walked over to the clerk at the counter.

'May I help you, miss?' he asked.

'Miss Iris Sparks,' she said. 'I called about a book yesterday.'

'Of course,' he said, turning to a shelf directly behind him.

He pulled down a large brown book with embossed lettering and placed it before her. She flipped it open to find plates of Coleoptera in glorious array.

'Wonderful,' she said, meaning it. 'I will take it. But I'd like to do some browsing before I go.'

'Of course, Miss Sparks,' he said. 'I'll be here when you're ready.'

She took the book, then made a slight show of examining the volumes on the display tables, some of which were nearly half her size. Then she took the stairs up to the next floor.

Where would he be? she thought.

History, most likely.

The History section was two storeys up. She took a quick recon of the first floor just in case she was wrong but didn't find him.

On the next level, tall, freestanding bookcases divided the room. She wandered through the centuries and civilisations from antiquity through the modern era. Then she spotted him in the middle of one narrow aisle, a pair of reading glasses perched on his nose, with said nose deep in a volume from the nineteenth century. The fair hair was now touched with grey here and there, topped by what looked like a brand-new homburg, and the glasses were not a part of any memory she had of him, but it was the same face, as beautiful as it was nine years before, the trace of melancholy that had infused it when he had returned from Spain now deepened.

Time to attract his attention in some subtle fashion, she thought.

Then she thought, the hell with subtle.

She walked boldly down the aisle, making sure to throw her left hip solidly into him as she passed.

He turned to glare at her as she kept walking.

'Excuse me, madam,' he said irritably. 'Would you mind taking care where you're going?'

She stopped, still facing away from him.

'I bumped you fair and square, you Pembroke git,' she said. 'So weigh enough and pull to the banks.'

She turned, smiling, and his jaw dropped.

'Sparks,' he said. 'Oh, my God.'

She wasn't expecting the embrace. It happened so quickly that her arms were momentarily pinned to her sides, but she was able to free them enough to wrap them around him.

'Excuse me, but that behaviour is not permitted in this

establishment,' a clerk admonished them sternly from the end of the aisle.

They quickly released each other.

'Sorry,' called Tony. 'I was caught by surprise. Won't happen again, I promise.'

'See that it doesn't,' said the clerk.

'Well, here we are,' said Tony, turning back to her. 'Once again acting inappropriately in an antiquarian bookshop. My God, Sparks, you are a sight for sore eyes. How long has it been?'

'Nine years,' she said. 'We had dinner right before you left for Singapore.'

'Well, the polite thing would be to say you haven't aged a bit,' he said, stepping back to look at her critically. 'But the accurate thing to say is that you have aged gloriously.'

'And you've become quite distinguished looking,' she replied. 'Tell me, what's it like being over thirty?'

'Ah, the thrust straight into my heart!' he cried, his fist pounding his chest dramatically. 'You'll find out all too soon, if my arithmetic is correct.'

'When did you get back?' she asked.

'A few weeks ago.'

'And you didn't call me straight away? Naughty boy!'

'I thought about calling, but you're not in the London directory and I didn't know where you had got to,' he said. 'And life has been a whirlwind since I came home.'

'You need to tell me everything,' she said. 'Over drinks. Which should start as soon as possible.'

'Agreed,' he said. 'I've got a book waiting for me downstairs, and I'm going to add this one. What have you got there?'

She held it up, and he smiled affectionately.

'Beetles, of course,' he said. 'Some things never change. Is every British water beetle in there?'

'Hardly,' she said. 'They say he's doing three volumes. What have you got?'

He held up a copy of Thucydides' *History of the Peloponnesian War.*

'It's the Crawley translation,' he said. 'I prefer it to Jowett's, plus I can't afford the Jowett. Ashendene Press put out a limited edition of the Jowett that's obscenely beautiful and expensive, but the translation's still the thing, isn't it?'

'I can't believe you didn't already have a copy.'

'I did,' he said. 'Took it with me to Singapore, lost it in a typhoon.'

'A typhoon! Goodness! That had better be one of the stories.'

'Right, let's get out of here.'

They descended the stairs to the front counter where the clerk had another book waiting for him.

'*Guide to 14 Asiatic Languages*,' she read. 'How many do you speak now?'

'Fluent Malay and Mandarin, passable Cantonese and Japanese, and a smattering of Korean,' he said as the clerk rang up the sale.

'I'm impressed,' she said, handing over the Balfour-Browne beetle book. 'I'm still stuck in Europe. And you're planning to learn more?'

'My new post,' he said. 'Let's go find a pub and I'll tell you all about it.'

They ended up at the Clarence, a small establishment on Dover Street. Tony secured a table, placing his package on the floor beneath his seat.

'What are you drinking?' he asked.

'In your honour, make it a Singapore sling,' she said.

'Done, and I'll have the same. Feeling peckish?'

'A bit.'

'I've been craving Scotch eggs. They didn't have those in China. Shall I order a plate to buffer the alcohol?'

'Please.'

When the drinks came, he held up his glass.

'To old friends,' he said.

She smiled and clinked her glass against his, suppressing her internal disgust with herself.

He took a sip and swirled it around in his mouth quizzically, then swallowed.

'Not at all like the ones at the Raffles,' he pronounced. 'It was the first drink one had when one came to Singapore. This one is missing a few ingredients.'

'Welcome to rationing,' said Sparks. 'What's missing?'

'Lime,' he said. 'And I don't taste any pineapple.'

'Sorry, I'll pick a more conventional drink for the next one. So – typhoon.'

'Nasty creatures, all of them,' he said. 'You talk about rain in England. You have no idea. I spent a foolish amount shipping my books to Singapore, then lost half to the weather and the rest to the Japs.'

'Were you in Singapore when it fell?'

'No, thank God. I was travelling in China, and got stuck there after the Japs attacked Malaya. I managed to get to Chungking, reported to the embassy, and asked what I could do to help. They found out I spoke Mandarin, and I spent the rest of the war working out of there.'

'That must have been brutal,' she said quietly.

'I did what was necessary,' he said, with a shrug that was meant to be casual. 'I was lucky in hindsight. Had I remained in Singapore, I probably wouldn't be here drinking with you now.'

'What's it like being home after all this time?'

'Ah, home,' he said. 'The place I left thinking I'd never return. They weren't exactly forgiving about it.'

'What, besides leaving, needed forgiving?'

'Coming back and expecting to be welcomed as the prodigal. My family tends to skip those portions of the Good Book involving acceptance and forbearance.'

'Fatted calves are also rationed nowadays,' she said. 'Are you living there now?'

'Staying in a hotel at the moment, but I just signed a lease for a flat not too far from work.'

'Right, you mentioned a new position.'

'I'm with the Foreign Office now, working the Far East desk.'

'How wonderful! Obviously, you know the territory, and I imagine . . . well, you haven't said anything about what you've been doing since the war.'

He leaned back and looked at her appraisingly.

'Before I answer that, you should know that Cyrus Norton was stationed in China with me,' he said. 'You remember Cyrus, don't you?'

'Of course,' said Sparks. 'He was at Pembroke with you, too.'

'He was,' said Tony, watching her closely. 'He told me that the two of you trained together before he was sent over.'

'I have no recollection of that,' said Sparks. 'Trained for what, exactly? I did mostly secretarial work during the war. Did they send him out there to take shorthand? Can one even take shorthand with pictographs?'

'That's what I expected you to say,' he said, grinning. 'As for what I've been doing since the war – you know, this and that.'

'Illuminating.'

'When I got back here, I asked around the, err, firm,' he continued. 'I heard you left there under a cloud after having a screaming argument with your boss.'

'People say the most unlikely things,' said Sparks. 'I don't know what you've heard about me, Tony. All I can say is whatever you think I was doing, I'm not doing it any more. Haven't for a few years now.'

'Why?'

'I had some serious disagreements over where things were going,' said Sparks. 'Let's leave it at that, shall we? We've both said more than we should.'

'Very well,' he said. 'So what have you been doing since peace broke out?'

'You're going to laugh,' she said.

'I could use a good laugh,' he replied. 'Tell me.'

'I started up a licensed marriage bureau with a friend last year.'

He stared at her in disbelief, then tilted his head back and roared with laughter.

'Stop,' she commanded him.

'This is— no, I don't even have a word for it,' he gasped, still shaking. 'You monstrous hypocrite! You told me that marriage was devised for the economic and political subjugation of women!'

'My thinking has evolved since then,' she said. 'Now I believe it's for mutual subjugation.'

'And I see you've put that theory into practice,' he said,

reaching across the table and tapping the ring on her finger. 'Who's the lucky gent?'

The ring that Archie had given her.

Her smile faded.

'The lucky gent died not long after giving me this,' she said. 'About six months back. I wear it in his memory, and to fend off unwanted attention.'

He straightened almost convulsively in his seat.

'Oh, no, Sparks,' he said, his merriment gone. 'I'm so sorry. Please forgive me, I never would have mentioned it.'

'Nothing to forgive, Tony,' she said, reaching across and clasping his hand for a moment. 'You didn't know. And—' She held his hand up. 'I see you're ringless. No luck with the locals while you were there?'

'My adventures have not been conducive to lasting romance,' he said ruefully. 'A marriage bureau, eh? Have you actually produced any marriages?'

'Many,' she said. 'Business is thriving, in fact.'

'Maybe—' he began. Then he shook his head.

'Maybe what?' she prompted him.

'I was wondering if perhaps I should avail myself of your services.'

'Really?'

'I am back in England, and have a real job with prospects of advancement,' he said, sounding as if he was trying to convince himself. 'But this milieu is as much a social one as it is a political one, and it has been suggested that I would present myself more advantageously as a married man.'

'Don't you know anyone here?'

'Everyone I knew here, I knew nine years ago,' he said. 'More, in most cases. And after nine years, you stop recognising the people you once knew.'

'You recognised me,' she pointed out.

'You are the special case among all of them,' he said. 'You wouldn't want to marry me, would you, Sparks? It could be awfully fun.'

'Sorry, Tony,' she said. 'I need more than fun at this point in my life.'

'Perfectly understandable,' he said. 'Would it be odd taking on a friend as a client?'

'Not at all,' she said. 'In fact, when we started the business we began by ringing up every unattached friend we had to beg them to sign up. There was a great deal of giggling in that first set of interviews, but there were some early successes, and we've been at it ever since. If you'd like to give it a try, it's five pounds to start.'

'And then what happens?'

'We interview you, get your goals and preferences, then search through our eligible females for the ones we deem most suitable and set you up for a first date.'

'How personal is this interview?' he asked.

'Personal,' she said. 'This isn't for a job. It's for marriage.'

'Is it confidential?'

'We don't have any legal confidentiality,' said Sparks. 'We're not lawyers or doctors. But otherwise we maintain it professionally.'

'So you can keep secrets,' he said.

'I can,' she said, looking straight at him. 'I can, and I have.'

'Well, sounds like five pounds is worth the risk,' he said. 'Do I make an appointment, or just show up?'

'Either,' she said, reaching into her bag for a card. 'Here's the number. And, by the way, that's also the number where you can reach me, even if you don't want our services. I want to renew the friendship more than anything else.'

That was true, she thought to her surprise and regret.

'I'll call tomorrow,' he promised.

'Wonderful,' she said. 'So, what else can I tell you? Did you hear about the fire at Heffer and Sons' Bookshop?'

'No!' he exclaimed. 'How bad?'

'They promised they'll reopen,' she said. 'Some poor nutter did it. They said he was also sending hand grenades through the post . . .'

And all she could think as they continued catching up was that Stage Two had commenced.

FOUR

She had to keep herself from pouncing on the telephone each time it rang the next morning, waiting impatiently for Mrs Billington to take the call in the next office. Gwen finally picked up the telephone and placed it on her own desk, ignoring each ring with a placidity that Iris found more and more irritating as the morning crawled along.

Finally, the intercom buzzed. Iris flipped the switch before it had even finished.

'Yes, Saundra?'

'There is a Mr Danforth on the line,' said Mrs Billington. 'He said he had spoken to you about coming in for an appointment.'

'He did,' said Iris. 'When would he like to see us?'

'Well, he can only break away during his lunch hour, and that's when the two of you usually take lunch.'

'Tell him to come in then. We can send out for sandwiches afterwards.'

'Very good, Miss Sparks.'

'But—' began Gwen.

Iris had already disconnected. She looked over at her partner, who appeared perturbed for the first time that morning.

'What?' she asked.

'I had a, um, lunch – appointment,' said Gwen.

'Nothing you couldn't break, surely,' said Iris. 'Duty calls, darling, and I really need you for this. In fact, I think you should take the lead in the interview, given my prior history with him.'

'No, no, you're right, this is what we . . . right, I'd better—,' said Gwen, reaching for the telephone and dialling a number.

'It's me,' she said softly. 'Sorry, something's come up at work, so I can't make it. No, tonight is still on. Yes, I'm sorry. I was looking forward to it, too. What were you—'

She lowered her voice. Iris studiously concentrated on reading through her index cards of possible candidates for Miss Ford, the switchboard operator from the previous week.

'Oh! Really?' continued Gwen, blushing deeply. 'That is a pity. That sounds . . . quite lovely, in fact. Keep it in the queue. I'll see you later.'

She hung up.

'I both don't want to know and want very much to know,' said Iris. 'Either way, sorry.'

'I'm sorry if I seem . . . eager,' said Gwen. 'I feel as if I'm making up for lost time.'

'Nothing to apologise for, darling,' said Iris. 'I'm happy for the both of you.'

'Anything in particular you want me to ask Mr Danforth about?'

'No, follow your instincts. It's all right to tell him that I mentioned him to you.'

'Of course,' said Gwen. 'Jump in when I'm floundering. Oh, that reminds me.'

'What?'

'Mr Lonsdale called after you left yesterday.'

'Oh? Was it about Miss Lowle?'

'I'm afraid so.'

'How bad was it?'

'He's given up on finding a match. He's leaving London and going back home.'

'That's unfortunate,' said Iris. 'Was it a very upsetting conversation?'

'It was for me,' said Gwen. 'I just had this awful feeling that we've hurt an innocent person in the service of this mission, no matter how small or well-meaning our involvement is.'

'Are you angry at me for suggesting him?'

'At you, and at myself,' said Gwen. 'I felt as if I should have been more forceful in my opposition to the idea. This is how they pull you in, I suppose. They prey upon your good intentions, and the next thing you know, someone else has given up on his life.'

'He might come back,' said Iris.

'We don't know that,' said Gwen.

'No. Nor do we know what's going to happen to Tony.'

'What are you hoping for?'

'His complete and absolute exoneration,' said Iris.

'But you still want to go through with this.'

'Yes, because that's the only way to get his complete and absolute exoneration, assuming he deserves one. The wheels for this were set in motion before we became part of it.'

'Very well,' said Gwen. 'I feel conflicted about him, and I haven't even met him yet.'

The clock ticked slowly towards the appointed hour. As the bells tolled noon outside, they heard the door to the building open and shut, then footsteps ascend the stairs. A minute later, they heard Mrs Billington greeting someone and a man's voice reply.

'That's him,' said Iris.

'And now he'll be filling out the application, then Mrs Billington will bring him over,' said Gwen. 'Just like every other client.'

Two minutes later, Mrs Billington appeared in the doorway, an application in hand.

'Are you ready, ladies?' she asked.

'We are,' said Gwen.

'Mr Danforth, if you'll come with me,' said Mrs Billington, coming in.

Shorter than I expected, thought Gwen as they rose to greet him. Nice-looking, though.

'Hello, Tony,' said Sparks warmly, coming over to kiss him on the cheek. 'Welcome to The Right Sort. This is my partner and friend, Mrs Gwendolyn Bainbridge.'

'How do you do, Mr Danforth?' said Mrs Bainbridge. 'Please take a seat.'

'Thank you, Mrs Bainbridge,' he said. 'Good afternoon, Miss Sparks. I trust you're none the worse for wear after our reunion?'

'Nothing I couldn't handle,' said Sparks with a grin. 'Yourself?'

'A bit of a head this morning, I'm afraid,' he said, smiling ruefully. 'Those slings may have been short a few ingredients, but alcohol certainly wasn't one of them.'

'Miss Sparks has told me all about you, Mr Danforth,' said Mrs Bainbridge as she sat behind her desk. 'She was so happy to find you were back in London, and even happier that you were coming to us. However, in the interest of giving you a more objective assessment, I am going to be conducting the interview, if that's agreeable.'

'Of course,' said Danforth. 'I'm quite curious to see what this is all about. Perhaps I'll learn a few things about myself.'

'Well, it isn't psychotherapy,' said Mrs Bainbridge with a smile. 'Let me peruse your application for a moment. Oh, you left your address blank.'

'I've just signed for the place,' he said. 'I haven't taken up residence yet.'

'When are you moving in?'

'This Saturday.'

'Why don't you add it, then?' she said, passing it back to him. 'We'd be addressing correspondence to you there, and if we come up with a good prospect for you in the next two days, we could always ring you at your office.'

'Certainly,' he said, filling it in. 'It's Grenville House, Flat 504, Dolphin Square, in Pimlico. I have to get used to saying that. You're the first people I've told. Very much bachelor's digs at the moment, so if you succeed quickly I'll have to move again to accommodate my new bride. I'm up on the fifth storey, and not on the side with the nice view of the Thames, so more a convenient location than anything else.'

'Easy walk to the Foreign Office, at least,' commented Mrs Bainbridge as he handed the forms back to her. 'Now, let's get to the business at hand. Education, we know about. You've been with the Diplomatic Service since 1939?'

'Yes,' he said. 'Went out to Singapore, tried my hand at teaching first, and found I didn't like children much. So I went hat in hand to the local consulate to beg for a job. They put me at a desk approving visas at first, but someone overheard me speaking Malay to the locals and I was moved up to something with more responsibilities. Then China in late '41, mostly

under George Kitson after he took over in Chungking. I put
in for the position here five months ago and my appointment
came through in May. And here I am.'

'Are you hoping to stay in London?' she asked.

'I'm hoping to move up the ladder as far as I can, whether
that leads to a higher post overseas or a bigger desk here.'

'So ultimately what?'

'Ambassador to Muckity-Muckistan or Grand High
Pooh-Bah,' he said, laughing. 'I have no idea what that top
level might be.'

'Would you go back to China?'

'Ah, doubt it,' he said, grimacing slightly. 'I'm done with
them, they're done with me.'

'What happened?' she asked.

'That would make for a very long and boring conversation,'
he said. 'Let's just say that I made certain recommendations
of policy that were dismissed out of hand, and by the time
they realise I was right, it will be too late. So I've come home
to strike a new path.'

'With a new wife.'

'Exactly so. Have you got any?'

'Maybe,' she said. 'What sort would you like?'

'Not sure,' he said. 'Never had one before.'

'Do you have specific requirements?'

'Two of everything where two is the normal number,
although a three-eyed woman would be fascinating, come to
think of it.'

'Let's be a little more serious about this, shall we?' said Mrs
Bainbridge. 'We'll go through the basics. Religion?'

'Immaterial,' he said. 'Although I may have to sham my way
through some church services now that I'm back.'

'Age?'

'Old enough to know better, but not old enough to know
better than me.'

'Education?'

'University, of course,' he said.

'That's the first answer you've given that wasn't flippant,'
she said. 'So her education is important to you.'

'I will be making my way through a world where conversation at social events may be at a very high level,' he said. 'I would like a woman who could hold her own at that level, while looking stunning enough to intrigue every man in the room.'

'Then her looks matter as well,' said Mrs Bainbridge.

'Presentation is all. She should be fluent in French, of course, and any additional language would be a plus.'

'What about children? You mentioned that you didn't like them as a teacher. Would you like them if they were yours?'

'I suppose I would have to,' he said thoughtfully. 'I hadn't really considered that aspect of marriage.'

'It does happen, you know,' said Mrs Bainbridge.

'To be sure,' he said. 'I would have to think about that. Children would be terribly inconvenient at the moment.'

'Speaking from experience, there is never a moment in which they are convenient,' said Mrs Bainbridge. 'But this is an area which matters to people, whether it's yea or nay.'

'Do I have to vote yea or nay from the outset?'

'Of course not. Just be aware that this is one of the criteria we use to match people.'

'Then put me in the undecided column— no, let's say no to children,' he said.

'Let me suggest that we stick with undecided for now,' said Mrs Bainbridge.

'It's just that—'

He stopped.

'What, Mr Danforth?' she asked.

'Fine,' he said. 'Undecided is my decision, he said decisively. For now.'

She looked at him, then put down her pen.

'Mr Danforth, may I speak freely?' she asked.

'Please do,' he said.

'You are not the first person I've met who uses humour or flippancy as a defence mechanism,' she said. 'In fact, I work quite closely with one on a daily basis.'

'A hit, a most palpable hit!' cried Sparks.

'She still does that, does she?' observed Danforth, smiling

at Sparks. 'You have my deepest sympathies, Mrs Bainbridge. It must be a living hell being here with her.'

'There are compensating factors,' said Mrs Bainbridge. 'However, the point of this interview is not only for you, Mr Danforth, but for the benefit of the woman with whom we set you up, whoever she may be. You've given us superficial require-ments for the most part, but your potential match didn't come to us merely to play-act a society princess to advance your career. She came here for the same reason everyone comes here: because they want to find someone. Someone with whom they can fall in love, or be happy with, or, at the very least, who will assuage their loneliness.'

'Ah,' said Danforth. 'That might be asking a great deal from me.'

'I don't think so, Mr Danforth, or you wouldn't be here,' she said. 'I have friends and family in the Diplomatic Service, so I know what life is like in that world. I have been to more than one embassy ball in my time, and have seen Diplomatic Service wives in action, smiling on behalf of their countries as they get their toes trodden upon by visiting dignitaries on the dance floor.'

'That is an occupational hazard,' agreed Danforth. 'I should add dancing as a requirement. Or armoured shoes.'

'But after all of that pretty artificiality, they still must return home with their husbands,' continued Mrs Bainbridge, 'and that is where the real marriage happens.'

'In bed, you mean.'

'Nothing so crude as that, Mr Danforth. I mean the act of living with another person at home, when all of the outer trappings and subterfuges have fallen away, and the two of you are confronted with the simple reality of being with each other as human beings.'

'Is that ever truly simple?'

'It can be,' said Mrs Bainbridge. 'And it should be if it's going to last. My question for you, Mr Danforth, is what do you want in a woman at the end of a day, when ambitions and artifice have been set aside but there is still the rest of the evening to fill?'

He seemed to deflate in his chair.

'I thought you said there wouldn't be any psychoanalysis,' he muttered.

'No, but there should be truth,' she said.

'At the end of the day, I want a friend and companion,' he said. 'Someone with whom I could drop my shields and be myself.'

'Any ideas as to what sort of woman could do that?' she asked.

'Make a duplicate of her, for a start,' he said, glancing at Sparks.

'What is it about Miss Sparks that you find appealing?' asked Mrs Bainbridge.

'Her intelligence, of course,' said Danforth. 'And her forthrightness. She's always been a straight shooter.'

'You overpraise me,' said Sparks. 'I don't think of myself that way.'

'You always have been with me,' he said. 'So someone who at the end of the day will be honest about how she feels, and call me out on my failures to do the same. It would be a heavy burden.'

'Some women might find it lighter than others' said Mrs Bainbridge. 'It would be up to us to find her for you.'

'Do you think you can?'

'There are no guarantees of success in our profession,' she said. 'But we've done well by our clients so far. And I think I have a sense of who you are now, Mr Danforth. Miss Sparks, do you have any questions?'

'I do not,' said Sparks.

'Moment of truth, Mr Danforth,' said Mrs Bainbridge. 'Would you like to sign up?'

'Gamble five pounds on a lifetime of happiness?' he asked, his smile returning. 'I've made worse bets. Yes, Mrs Bainbridge, I will place my marital prospects in your hands.'

'Then sign here,' she said, handing him the contracts.

He signed them, then pulled out his wallet, removed a five-pound note and handed it to her.

'I see there is a clause about the two of you not dating

clients,' he said as she countersigned. 'That wouldn't prevent Sparks and me from getting sozzled on a frequent basis.'

'It would not,' said Sparks. 'We could add an extra clause requiring us to.'

'Let's keep that non-contractual, if you don't mind,' he said, rising. 'Ladies, this was far more interesting and, I'm surprised to say, more hopeful than I thought it would be. How soon should I expect results?'

'We will come up with a candidate within the next two days,' said Mrs Bainbridge. 'That will give you time to move in to your new flat before your first date.'

'Astonishing,' he said. 'Thank you both. Sparks, call me when you're ready for some more catching up.'

'Will do,' she said. 'Goodbye, Tony.'

'Good day, Mr Danforth,' said Mrs Bainbridge.

They watched as he left. When they heard the door downstairs open and close, Gwen went to their office door and shut it.

'I'm exhausted,' she said, returning to her chair and collapsing into it. 'How did you manage to keep up pretences for an entire relationship when you were on that assignment?'

'I could drop the act when I wasn't with the target,' said Iris. 'I wasn't living with him, fortunately. God, I couldn't bear hearing Tony praise me for my honesty today when it was nothing but deception. Each word he spoke was another twist of the knife. I thought you did quite well, by the way.'

'It wasn't easy,' said Gwen. 'He's very likable.'

'He is.'

'Much of that is a pose, though,' said Gwen. 'He needs to be liked, so he becomes likable. He's concealing something. Any ideas as to what?'

'No,' said Iris. 'Deep-rooted communism, perhaps?'

'And now you're concealing something,' said Gwen. 'What's going on? Did something happen between you last night that you haven't told me about?'

'He sort of proposed to me,' Iris confessed.

'Sort of? What is a sort of proposal?'

'It was couched in a way that meant he didn't expect it to be taken seriously.'

'When a man who shows the world a frivolous face makes a frivolous proposal of marriage, it might be serious underneath.'

'That's too convoluted for me to figure out,' said Iris. 'In any case, I turned him down without further discussion.'

'Also frivolously?'

'Actually, quite seriously,' said Iris.

'Because that would have contradicted our assignment.'

'Right,' said Iris. 'And because I am not in the marrying mood at the moment. Even if I was, it wouldn't be Tony.'

'Why not, if you don't mind my asking?' asked Gwen.

'Because I do want children,' said Iris. 'I want to leave someone behind to make a better job of changing the world than I have. All right, we should contact Miss Lowle and have her come in to brief her.'

'Please tell me you don't want to do that this afternoon. She'd have to come in after office hours.'

'I've already deprived you of one hour with Sally,' said Iris. 'I won't take a single minute more. Tomorrow is fine.'

Gwen met Sally at Istanbul, a Turkish restaurant on Frith Street not far from his Soho flat.

'Ever eaten here before?' he asked as he opened the door for her.

'Not when it was this place,' she replied. 'I vaguely remember this location from before the war. Italian, perhaps?'

'Yes. Battaglia's was here. Istanbul opened in 1940, just in time for the Blitz.'

'They've stayed in business. Good for them.'

The restaurant couldn't have been more than eighteen feet wide, yet every available inch of space was crammed with tables packed with businessmen rehashing the day's deals over small plates of olives and mashed vegetables. A young Bengali man in a dinner jacket and bow tie presided over a long table in one corner covered with bowls of salads and rice dishes, while another waiter whirled like a dervish through the room, deftly distributing plates of various types and forms of meats on skewers. He looked at Sally with trepidation, the usual look inspired by a man of that height coming into any establishment that would be expected to feed him.

'Smells divine,' said Gwen.

'The owner used to be the chef at the Turkish embassy,' said Sally as they wedged themselves into a table for two across from the salad table. 'The ambassador wanted to take him back with him, but he had enough encouraging whispers from salivating Londoners to set up shop here.'

'What do you recommend?'

'Shish kebab if you like things ground and spiced, shashlik if you like them cubed and marinated. Or is it the other way around? Either way, you can't go wrong.'

They sorted out the differences with the waiter, who was accustomed to English ignorance of the menu.

'How was work?' Sally asked after they placed their orders. 'Any interesting lonely people wander in?'

'Actually, we have a new client whom you may know,' said Gwen.

'Really? Who?'

'Anthony Danforth. He was a year ahead of you at Cambridge, I believe.'

'Danforth?' he exclaimed. 'He came back?'

'Apparently so,' she said.

'I can't believe it,' he said, shaking his head in wonderment. 'Of all the bloody nerve.'

'You knew him, I take it.'

'He was a— well, I can't exactly say rival for my affections for . . .'

He stopped.

'For Iris, you were going to say,' she prompted him. 'It's all right to speak of that. I'm not jealous.'

'I only fell for her because I hadn't met you yet,' he said hastily. 'And I don't know that I can call him a rival when she never felt anything for me other than friendship.'

'Which has been considerable.'

'It has,' he agreed.

'Then what was Mr Danforth to her?'

'I never quite figured out the exact nature of it,' he said. 'She took lovers at Cambridge. She usually told me what was going on in her life at every moment, yet the details of Danforth were either vague or completely not forthcoming. Then she went silent about him, and that was rather disturbing.'

'Why do you say that?'

'When he left England, well, it was under a considerable cloud at the time.'

'Why?'

'There were some rather dark stories circulating about an incident that caused him to leave England abruptly.'

'What are you referring to?'

'When he went to Spain. In '36, along with the other idealistic idiots.'

'Idealism isn't idiotic.'

'It is when you go in at half-cock with insufficient training and equipment,' said Sally.

'It was courageous, at least.'

'Oh, no doubt,' said Sally. 'Idiocy and courage often charge side by side into the fray. But I don't think Danforth was an idiot, nor do I think he was all that courageous for going there. He went to Spain because he was running away from England.'

'Why?'

'I don't know the full story,' said Sally. 'I don't think Sparks does, either, although she must know more than most. Besides Danforth, the only others who would know are dead. Bruce Cater died in Spain, Kevin Pickard at Anzio, and Sauce, well, she was the reason they ran.'

'Sauce?'

'That's what people called her at Cambridge. She was at Newnham College, a year ahead of Sparks. Sad, I can't remember her full name any more. Nancy something, but everyone called her Sauce. She used to say it was because of her saucy nature.'

'She died as well?'

'She did,' said Sally. 'While still at Cambridge. A couple of rowers found her face down in the river early one morning.

The official ruling was death by misadventure, but there were some nasty rumours after.'

'What about?'

'There had been a party a month or so before. A select gathering of the favoured few at a mansion belonging to Pickard's family while said family were touring somewhere far away. The participants supposedly were invited based upon their willingness to shed their inhibitions and reportedly their clothing at the front door, but that may have been exaggeration or extrapolation after the fact. God knows there were plenty of stories floating about. The wildest one I heard mentioned a Roman theme, complete with togas and bunches of grapes, as well as everything into which a grape could be transformed, but that rumour was spread by someone who wasn't there on the good authority of someone else who also wasn't there.'

'You were not invited, I take it.'

'Good Lord, no. I was much too middle class, too physically freakish and too Italian to draw the slightest whiff of attention from that lot. But Sauce was invited as one of the pre-eminent party girls of the university, plus she was making a play for Pickard. But when she came back, by all reports she no longer merited her nickname. She became quiet, withdrawn. She started to miss classes. Meanwhile, whispers of her behaviour that weekend circulated which she vehemently denied when she became aware of them. But they persisted and multiplied, and the looks and comments when she walked about the colleges and town became more and more condemnatory. Sparks told me that she took to locking herself in her room, barely touching any food. And then they found her in the river.'

'Poor girl,' said Gwen. 'Was suicide suspected?'

'That's what everyone thought, but things were hushed up and misadventure was the official verdict. Best for all concerned, what? But then another rumour began spreading.'

'What about?'

'That she had left behind a letter detailing what had happened that weekend, naming names. And that suddenly became the explanation as to why Tony Danforth and Bruce

Cater dashed off to Spain to fight the fascists, while Pickard decided to take an extended tour of the world.'

'Who got the letter?'

'In one version, it was posted the night before her body was found, addressed to Pembroke College. Hutchinson, the Master of Pembroke at the time, retired a year later, which added fuel to that particular conspiratorial fire, but he died a few months after retiring. In another version it was sent to the Proctor, and in a third to the local police. In any case, if it existed, it never saw the light of day.'

'Nobody knows what it said?'

'No.'

'And Iris has kept quiet about all of this.'

'She has,' he said as their meals arrived.

'When she keeps quiet, it's usually about something serious,' said Gwen. 'She never mentioned anything about this when we discussed Danforth.'

'There was one thing I noticed about her at the time, though,' he said, picking up a skewer.

'What?'

'Have you ever wondered why Sparks took up martial arts?'

'She told me it was her mother's idea while she was still in her teens.'

'True enough,' said Sally. 'But since the idea came from her mother, her efforts prior to coming to Cambridge were haphazard and inadequate at best. It was only after Sauce's death that she quite methodically turned herself into the pint-sized warrior that she is today.'

FIVE

Gwen was ten minutes late to work the next morning, something that never happened. She was also wearing the same outfit she had had on the previous day, a Herschelle linen suit with a blue and white willow pattern. Both Iris and Mrs Billington noticed the repetition. Mrs Billington chose discretion and made no comment. Iris, on the other hand, stared at her partner in shock and tapped her wristwatch pointedly.

'What?' asked Gwen as she unpinned her hat and hung it up.

'Why, Mrs Bainbridge, how can we run a tight ship when you are so lacking in punctuality?' Iris demanded sternly.

'How many times have you been late?' retorted Gwen as she took her seat.

'I stopped counting long ago,' said Iris. 'But I make up for my missed minutes by my superior efficiency.'

'Of course you do,' said Gwen.

'Did you make up for enough lost time last night to stay through lunch again?' asked Iris.

'I did,' said Gwen. 'What's happening at lunch today?'

'Miss Lowle is coming in for a briefing.'

'Ah. Wonderful,' said Gwen with a grimace of distaste. 'How do we do that?'

'She asks us what she needs to know, and we tell her. Then we give her contact information to Tony.'

'And then we're done.'

'And then we're done.'

'Unless he's exonerated,' said Gwen. 'In which case, we have to make a genuine effort to find him a wife.'

'Right,' said Iris.

'You're sounding more dubious about that prospect today,' said Gwen.

'The idea of Tony settling down after his extremely adventurous life doesn't seem a likely possibility,' said Iris.

'People change,' said Gwen. 'He may be more realistic about his prospects now.'

'Or he's slithering his way up the ladder of authority, if the Brigadier is correct,' said Iris. 'We shall see.'

The Miss Lowle who arrived a few minutes after their lunch hour began was a different Miss Lowle from the one they had first met. Her manner was now almost brusque in her address and questions, and her accent could have passed for upper-crust London in its tones.

Is that her true voice, or another character being done for our benefit? wondered Gwen.

'So he took the bait?' Lowle asked.

'He signed up for our services,' said Sparks. 'We normally send a letter to the gentleman with the lady's telephone number. Do you want us to use your number at the ministry?'

'Yes, that would be best,' she said. 'I don't want my new landlady getting nosy about all this. How did Danforth seem to you about the idea?'

'Interested,' said Sparks.

'Ironic,' added Mrs Bainbridge.

'What do you mean by that?' asked Lowle.

'He is amused by what we do,' said Mrs Bainbridge. 'On the one hand, he seems genuinely interested in finding a partner in life. But on the other, he thinks finding one through a professional agency is strange.'

'Then I shall feel the same about it,' said Lowle. 'A mutual disdain for the norms, covering what? Some real loneliness underneath, right?'

'That's . . . that's actually good,' said Sparks, impressed in spite of herself.

'What about the war?' asked Lowle. 'Is that something he likes to talk about?'

'Not so far,' said Sparks. 'He didn't want to talk about Spain when he got back from that one, and he was fairly close-mouthed about China when I saw him the other night. Mind you, given the clandestine nature of his assignments there, he may not discuss it at all.'

'But he's been overseas for eight years,' she said. 'It would be natural for me to be curious about that, having never been.'

'Just don't pry,' advised Sparks. 'You're not going to get much out of him at first meeting. Your objective is to get a second date, then a third, and so on.'

'String him along, keep him interested,' said Lowle. 'Make him fall in love with me if I can. What sort of woman attracts him?'

The two partners didn't answer.

'Well, come on, then,' said Lowle irritably. 'I can't go into this blindfolded.'

'Someone like Miss Sparks,' said Mrs Bainbridge reluctantly.

'Really?' exclaimed Lowle, looking at Sparks in curiosity and disbelief. 'And here I was thinking I'd have to fake upper-class for him. What is it about you that he fancies?'

'My brain,' said Sparks. 'Can you fake one of those?'

'He read History and Classics at Cambridge,' she replied. 'I got top marks in both in Manchester. I can hold my own. What else?'

'He's looking for a diplomat's wife on the surface,' said Mrs Bainbridge. 'I take it you speak French?'

'Fluently. And German. And Russian. I wouldn't have got picked for this assignment if I didn't.'

'Can you dance?' asked Sparks.

'Ballroom or jitterbug?' asked Lowle. 'I can do both, as it happens. What did the two of you talk about when you were in school together?'

'Everything under the sun,' said Sparks. 'History, politics, books, films.'

'What sort of books? You made the recent connection at a bookshop. What was he buying?'

'A book of Asian languages and a copy of Thucydides.'

'Oh, God, do I have to read about the Peloponnesian War again? That was a slog and a half.'

'It would endear you to him immensely,' said Sparks.

'But don't be smarter than him,' said Mrs Bainbridge.

'That's true of every man on every date,' said Lowle with a laugh. 'You should have seen me asking that poor bloke about tying flies the other night. How did he like me, by the way?'

'He liked you,' said Mrs Bainbridge shortly. 'He was very disappointed that you turned him down after.'

'Oh, Lord,' she said, sighing with exasperation. 'Good luck with that one. You should probably marry him off to a fish.'

'In fact, he's decided to drop our services,' said Mrs Bainbridge.

'Has he?' she said with an absolute lack of surprise. 'Honestly, that's probably for the best. Right, so back to Danforth. You said he likes films, too?'

'Yes.'

'What kinds?'

'Romances, musicals,' said Sparks, thinking back. 'Costume epics, but he liked to point out all the errors and anachronisms.'

'So he likes to show off his big brain,' she said. 'Typical Cambridge type. Good, I think I've got a handle on him. Do you think he's a commie? Still a commie, I mean?'

'I don't know,' said Sparks. 'Maybe. Maybe not.'

'My job to find out,' she said. 'Well, it's back to the ministry for me, and then I get to spend my free time rereading Thucydides, eûge, eûge! I guess this is the last time we'll see each other. His Majesty's government thanks you for your assistance in this matter.'

'Did the Brigadier tell you to say that?' asked Sparks.

'No,' said Lowle. 'That was genuine. From me. I do take this assignment seriously, Miss Sparks. I was too young for the recent war, but I am going to fight this one with every breath in my body.'

'Good luck to you,' said Mrs Bainbridge. 'And be safe.'

'Thanks,' she said.

She opened the door, gave them a quick wave, then headed towards the stairs.

'I almost liked her for a moment at the end,' said Gwen. 'You're still competing with her, by the way.'

'I know,' grumbled Iris. 'She sets me off for some reason.'

'You can't see why?'

'I suppose you can.'

'She's doing what you used to do, and thought you would do well,' said Gwen. 'And despite the unhappy end to your adventures in espionage, you still miss it.'

'Maybe,' said Iris. 'You've given me a head start on my session with Dr Milford this afternoon. I'll have Saundra send a letter to Tony. What a week it's been! And it's only Thursday. What have you planned for the weekend?'

'I'm going out to the Bainbridges' estate to visit Ronnie and John,' said Gwen.

'Is Sally going?'

'Weekends are his busy time at the BBC, so we'll resume things Monday,' said Gwen. 'I told him about Mr Danforth, by the way.'

'Told him? Told him what exactly?'

'That he was now our client.'

'Nothing about the mission, though.'

'Of course not. Why would you think that?'

'Because he's a signatory to the Official Secrets Act as well as being your boyfriend,' said Iris. 'I'm not sure it was wise bringing Tony to his attention.'

'If he found out about him signing up with us later, he'd wonder why I hadn't said anything,' said Gwen. 'I thought this would be a natural way of letting him know.'

'How did he react?'

'He was surprised to hear that Mr Danforth had returned to England,' said Gwen. 'He mentioned something about him leaving amid a scandal of some sort.'

Iris said nothing.

'At Cambridge,' continued Gwen, watching her.

'Tony wasn't— that was a long time ago,' said Iris.

'But he was involved?'

'He was on the periphery, not in the centre,' said Iris.

'And you know this because?'

'Because I was on the periphery with him,' she said reluctantly.

'You might have said something before,' said Gwen.

'It had nothing to do with the current situation.'

'But a woman died as a result,' said Gwen.

'Sauce – Nancy, I should say – drowned. They never figured out the how or the why of it. But Tony wasn't the cause.'

'You sound quite certain about that.'

'He wasn't involved with her,' said Iris. 'I'm certain about that.'

'So he wouldn't present a threat to any woman we set him up with?'

'No,' said Iris.

But she knew from Gwen's expression that she hadn't convinced her.

She sat in the chair in front of Dr Milford's desk in his Harley Street office.

'You've stopped smoking,' she observed.

'Only in here,' he replied. 'I've had some complaints, and thought it would be fairer not to smoke in front of everyone rather than ask each individual for permission. Some of my patients might feel I'm putting undue pressure on them.'

'Go ahead,' said Iris. 'I like watching you smoke your pipe. You turn it into a little ritual every time.'

'I suppose I do,' he said, picking it up from its stand and tamping tobacco into it. 'It's a useful prop for stalling for time while I think of the next question. Why do you like watching me do it?'

'Is that the next question?'

'It is.'

'Well, Daddy didn't smoke, so it doesn't remind me of him,' she said. 'I can't think of any significant pipe-smokers in my history apart from my narrowboat neighbour, Casper, and I don't have any ambivalent feelings about him. If we extend it to older men who smoke . . .'

She stopped, frowning.

'Tell me what you're thinking,' he said, lighting his pipe and drawing in the smoke with a grunt of contentment.

'Another older man who smokes has reappeared in my life,' she said. 'My old boss.'

'From your Intelligence days,' he said.

'Yes.'

'And?'

'And he's roped me into an operation,' said Sparks.

'I thought you weren't going back to that line of work.'

'Unfortunately, I put myself and Gwen into harm's way last April, he being the harm.'

'Without going into details, how heavily involved are you now?'

'A minor cog in a great machine,' she said. 'He's found someone else to do the real dirty work. I just have to put her into position.'

'"Her."'

'Yes, "her". A new me. Younger, maybe better. And not at all conflicted about any of it.'

'You sound jealous.'

'I know, I know,' she groaned. 'Gwen said as much, too. My replacement father figure has a new favourite daughter, and that feeds into my general feelings that I am ageing out of all hope of accomplishment in my life.'

'You've accomplished quite a lot in the past year or so,' he pointed out. 'A successful business. Several criminal cases solved.'

'But this isn't what I saw myself doing when I was seventeen and starting at Cambridge,' she said.

'Most people don't end up doing what they expected at seventeen,' he said.

'That doesn't make it feel any better,' she said. 'I was supposed to be a world-travelling adventuress by now, alternating voyages into dark jungles to discover new species of beetles with shattering societal structures while clad in smashing, risqué frocks.'

'And it took an entire world war to thwart those dreams.'

'Yes,' she said. 'Only that could have had enough power to stop me.'

'You didn't embark on any jungle adventures when you got out of Cambridge,' he pointed out.

'No. I had already been to Berlin by that point. I put away my childish dreams for the more important grand adventure of saving the world from fascism. Then I cocked up my efforts in that.'

'Is that why you said yes to your old boss this time? To make up for your prior failures?'

'Maybe.'

'When he asked you to do this, could you have refused?'

'According to him, yes.'

'But you agreed.'

'Yes. And now I'm regretting it.'

'Why?'

'Because the assignment involves betraying an old friend.'

'Why didn't you refuse the assignment if that's what it was about?'

'Because he may be a traitor himself.'

'And that justifies it to you.'

'Well, there's also . . .'

He waited, puffing on his pipe, watching her through the small clouds of smoke obscuring her.

'In a way, he betrayed me before,' she said. 'And in doing so, caused me to betray someone else.'

'When was this?'

'At Cambridge. A woman I knew there drowned herself, either intentionally or accidentally, we never found out for certain.'

'What did this have to do with you and this man?'

'We could have stood up for her earlier. There was a situation – apparently an ugly one, although I never knew the specifics first-hand. And because I didn't know exactly what happened, I didn't take a side in it. I didn't take her side. And I should have.'

'And you blame this man for it?'

'In part. He did take a side. The other side.'

'And now he's back in your life, and the subject of your former boss's operation.'

'Yes.'

'It sounds like you're taking a side now.'

'Yes, it does,' said Iris. 'And I'm worried that I'm doing it out of vengeance rather than duty.'

'Interesting that you've never brought this man up before,' commented Dr Milford. 'Your relationship with Sally at Cambridge, we've discussed. But not this man.'

'No.'

'Why do you think that is?'

'He went to Singapore a few years later. I thought he was out of my life forever, and that I could forget that part of it.'

'But this woman's death was traumatic, wasn't it?'

'It was.'

'And we don't forget trauma, do we?'

'No. Not really.'

'If you feel that you're taking vengeance upon him,' he said, gesturing at her with his pipe, 'maybe you're not truly suited for this assignment.'

'Well, Doctor, I wish you had been around to tell me that before I accepted it,' she said.

The next afternoon, Gwen left The Right Sort at two, her portmanteau packed for a weekend in the country. Iris held the fort in case of any late Friday afternoon arrivals.

The telephone rang a little after four. Iris waited for Mrs Billington to field the call. A moment later, the intercom buzzed. She answered.

'It's Mr Danforth,' said Mrs Billington. 'Are you available?'

'Of course,' said Iris. She picked up the telephone's handset. 'Hello, Tony.'

'Greetings, my Cupid,' came his voice. 'You have impressed me. I had the afternoon off to start moving things into the new flat. I collected my postbox key, tried it out, and what do I find waiting for me as my first letter? A missive from The Right Sort containing my first date! Very exciting!'

'I hope you like her,' said Sparks.

'I find myself positively giddy at the prospect,' he said. 'Which leads me to a request: are you available for some sozzlement this evening? I need your advice.'

'Advice? On what?'

'It occurs to me— no, it's been consuming my mind ever since I came in for my interview with the two of you that I haven't gone out on a proper date with a proper Englishwoman since before the war. Hell, since before I left for Singapore. I need some tips on how it's done nowadays before I blunder in. Could I barter drinks for some guidance?'

Bad idea, Sparks, she thought.

But combined with drinks, so a much worse idea.

'Love to,' she said. 'But make sure I give you the advice before the second drink. The quality declines rapidly after that.'

'As will my ability to remember it,' he said. 'How about meeting me at the Barley Mow at six?'

'On Horseferry Road?'

'That's the one.'

'I'll see you there.'

After work, she walked south from Mayfair. Her route took her by Buckingham Palace. The betrothal of Princess Elizabeth to Lieutenant Philip Mountbatten of the Royal Navy had been announced the previous day, and crowds of people were gathering to launch cheers in the presumed direction of the happy couple and to leave bouquets of flowers at the gates.

Iris, remembering the small but significant roles she and Gwen had played in saving that romance the previous year, blew a kiss to the palace as she walked by. She wondered if they would receive an invitation to the wedding. She doubted it. That story was not meant for public knowledge.

Still, the ballyhoo over the wedding would undoubtedly drum up more business, she thought happily.

The weather was cool and cloudy, making the walk an easy one. Horseferry Road was in Westminster, running west from the Lambeth Bridge. The pub itself was in a corner building across the street from the Westminster Coroner's Court, ominously enough. She anticipated overhearing conversations involving causes of death and bodily decay, with morbid jokes that were only funny to the macabre sensibilities of those in the trade.

Tony was waiting for her inside, having secured a table for

two by a window on the Arneway Street side. The bar wrapped around the interior corner of the room with tables surrounding it throughout the L-shaped space, the dartboards in one corner already in heavy use.

'A pint of ale to start?' he asked.

'Sounds good,' she said.

He signalled a barmaid and placed their order.

'How goes the moving?' she asked.

'Didn't have a lot to move,' he said. 'I've got in all the basics: bed, bookcases, clothing. I'm living out of my steamer trunk for the moment. The hired furniture's coming in tomorrow, so tonight will just be me and my book of Asiatic languages.'

'You make that sound as if it's an ideal evening,' she said. 'This is why you need The Right Sort in your life.'

'I see that,' he said. 'What is this Miss Lowle like?'

'No, that's not how it works,' she said. 'I am not going to predispose you to her, nor give you an unfair advantage of knowledge before first impression. The playing fields at The Right Sort are even.'

'I hate even playing fields,' he said with a sigh. 'So all I have is her office number and home address. I guess showing up at her doorstep tomorrow first thing in the morning is out.'

'You try that, we will refund your fee and ban you from our services for life.'

'Duly noted. I won't call her until Monday. Should I ask her out for lunch then? Dinner Monday evening?'

'You really have fallen off your game,' she said. 'Do you think any woman will want to go out with someone with no time for preparation? Presentation is all, you said the other day. That goes double for us poor ladies. You need to give her a chance to agonise over what frock to wear, what hat to go with it, and which shade of lipstick will match them all.'

'Are hats so very critical?'

'Given that the styles of ladies' hats far outnumber those for men, I should think you would have known that. How much they conceal, how much they reveal, how much they distract, how much they draw attention to – why, it's taken me as long as half an hour to choose the right one for a first date.'

'Then I should be ready to insert "I like your hat" as soon as I possibly can in the conversation.'

'I wouldn't bring it up as the very first thing,' said Sparks. 'But mention it somewhere from third to fifth, and she shall be putty in your hands.'

'If I had known that women were this easy, I could have saved myself your five-pound fee,' he said. 'Very well. I'll call her Monday, but I'll suggest Tuesday evening. Will that be enough time?'

'If she doesn't decide to get her hair done, yes.'

'She could always wear a bigger hat if she doesn't.'

'Now, you're getting it.'

The pints arrived. They each ordered a light supper, then picked up their glasses and clinked them together.

'What else do I need to know about dating in this modern era?' he asked.

'Be yourself,' she said. 'Like Gwen said, that's who you are in the long run, so let her know who you are now.'

Easy, Sparks, she admonished herself. Don't push him too hard.

'I've never truly been able to do that on a first date,' he said wistfully. 'The closest I've ever got was that long lunch with you at the Whim. You were so open about everything that I couldn't help wanting to be the same. Are you still like that?'

'I've become much more reticent in my old age,' she said. 'I sometimes wish I could be like that bold young girl again. I've been burned a few times too many since then. But be open, Tony. Secrets cause damage. I've learned that the hard way.'

'You know I can't tell all my secrets,' he said quietly.

'Not on the first date, certainly,' she said. 'But if it goes well, sooner or later the walls must topple. For both of you.'

'Did your fiancé know everything about you?' he asked, glancing down at her ring.

'He knew a great deal,' said Sparks. 'I would have told him the rest, given time. We didn't have enough, unfortunately.'

'I'm sorry again, Sparks,' he said. 'Sorry I never got a chance to meet him and give you my blessing.'

'It would have been interesting seeing the two of you interact,' she said. 'You're from very different worlds.'

'Don't tell me he went to Oxford!' he exclaimed in mock horror.

'Oh, no,' she said, laughing. 'I still have some standards. No, his school was of the hard knocks variety. He was a spiv from the East End.'

'Really? Well, I guess I shouldn't be all that surprised. You grew up there as well, I recall.'

'Different part, but yes,' she said. 'We could speak the same language.'

'You can speak everyone's language everywhere,' he said. 'It surprised the hell out of us back then when we found out you weren't one of us.'

'Lucky for me you were so intent on destroying class structure back then,' she said.

'Maybe not so lucky,' he said. 'Here comes the food. And we're dry. Another pint?'

'Yes, please.'

As she looked up at the barmaid, she noticed a man sitting at the bar. He had been watching them, but turned away as she looked up, drawing her attention.

His hair was neatly combed now, and his suit fit in with those of the lawyers and clerks who had come in from across the street, but she immediately recognised him as the dock worker who had made contact with her on Edgware Road.

No surprise that the Brigadier would have a man tailing Tony, she thought.

Unless he was tailing her. Would they be doing that? She hadn't noticed anyone following after she left The Right Sort, but that didn't mean it wasn't happening. Or maybe their office phone was being tapped, which meant that this meeting had triggered the surveillance.

No, it must be for Tony, she concluded. He's the target. She wondered if he had picked up the tail.

'What about flowers?' asked Tony. 'Do I bring them as a first date offering? Or is that too much?'

'Depends on where you're meeting her,' said Sparks. 'Flowers are always welcome, but they have to be lugged around for the rest of the evening. That can become impractical, not to mention precarious to their lifespan.'

'And roses come with thorns,' he said. 'Flowers for a later date, then. One where I am picking her up at her flat, so they can be left behind, preferably in a vase with some water. Excellent coaching, Sparks. I shall become a romantic pragmatist.'

They concluded the meal with a third pint each. She was definitely feeling the effects by the end of it, rising unsteadily as he came around to hold her chair.

'I'm going to call you a taxi,' he said.

'No need,' she assured him.

'It's the height of the evening, and I have put you into a wobbly condition,' he said. 'I insist.'

'I surrender,' she said, taking his proffered arm.

She assumed the tail was still on the job as they walked out of the pub.

'What about a kiss?' he asked.

'At the end of a first date?' she replied. 'That depends entirely on how things go between—'

The kiss caught her by surprise.

Her first instinct was to shove him away. She quashed it before putting it into action and allowed the kiss to happen, letting her arms drop to her sides. He sensed her reluctance, and released her.

'Sorry,' he said. 'I shouldn't have done that.'

'It's all right, Tony,' she said, reaching for her handkerchief and dabbing her mouth. 'But please don't do that again. Why did you do it?'

'I'm out of practice,' he said. 'I thought I'd give it a go with someone I once kissed before I try it on someone new.'

'You would have been better off trying that when you saw me in Maggs Brothers,' she said.

'The two of us surrounded by old books,' he said. 'I remember. Lesson learned, Sparks. Here's a cab. What's the address?'

'Little Venice,' she said, as he held the door for her. 'I'm living on a narrowboat.'

'Sounds nice. As long as there aren't any typhoons.'

'So far, so good,' she said. 'Goodnight, Tony. Let me know how things go.'

He slipped some coins to the cabbie, then waved as she rode away. She gave a tentative wave back in response, then turned and watched through the windscreen without another backwards glance.

She had the cabbie let her off a street away rather than have him know her exact location, then walked to the *Cecilia*.

She wondered if there would be someone waiting for her already, but the narrowboat had no one there who shouldn't be. She went inside and immediately brushed her teeth, hoping it would reduce the smell of ale on her breath. Then she picked up her book of British water beetles, curled up in the overstuffed armchair in the saloon, and read, waiting.

She had almost drifted off when the knock came at the door. She put the book down, then picked up her cricket bat which she had placed leaning against the armchair. She walked over to the door.

'Who is it?' she called.

'It's Carruthers, Lollipop,' came a man's voice. 'Put your coat on. He's in the car, and he's hopping mad.'

SIX

Carruthers was the Brigadier's principal bodyguard and chauffeur since the early years of the recent war. He was tall and well-built, his usual black suit tight around the biceps. Sparks sometimes wondered how she would fare against him hand-to-hand. She thought she might be able to beat him, but only if she landed the first blow.

The Bentley was parked on the street by her boat. She followed Carruthers to it and got in the rear without protest when he opened the door for her.

'Good evening, sir,' she said as she sat down. 'To what do I owe the pleasure?'

'I was informed this evening that you met up with Danforth at an establishment in Westminster,' said the Brigadier, staring straight ahead, the Dunhill in his mouth burned down almost to the filter. More cigarette ends poked from the ashtray in the rear of the front bench.

'The Barley Mow. I recommend the ale.'

'I want to know every word that was said, and then I will decide whether or not to let you out of this car.'

'Your man didn't give you a full report?'

'He couldn't hear everything. But he informed me that the date ended with you kissing Danforth.'

'He kissed me. It wasn't my idea.'

'Why were you with him?'

'He asked me out for a drink.'

'And you agreed? Just like that?'

'He's still my friend,' said Sparks. 'He still thinks I'm his. It would be odd if I turned him down.'

'Yet you didn't alert us.'

'I was going to call afterwards, but I spotted your man. I figured I'd be receiving a visit tonight. That's why I'm not in my pyjamas as we speak.'

'I appreciate your keeping your clothes on for me, Sparks. Tell me about the conversation.'

She recounted it in as much detail as she could.

'Dating advice,' he said, shaking his head. 'He actually asked you for dating advice?'

'I do have some expertise in the field, sir.'

'But you kissed him!'

'As I said before, he kissed me,' she said. 'I wasn't expecting it.'

'You told me last week that the two of you weren't lovers.'

'We weren't. We're not.'

'Yet you allowed this.'

'I didn't think that punching him in the throat would have furthered the mission, sir.'

'What concerns me is the possibility that you have feelings for Danforth, and that they are going to compromise this operation.'

'Understandable.'

'Am I right to be concerned, Sparks?'

'The friendship, the fondness for him are still in me some-where,' she said. 'But I won't let them stand in the way. There's no reason for them to interfere. If I had given him the cold shoulder, it would have aroused suspicions on his part.'

'The kiss meant nothing to you?'

'It was quite off-putting, to tell you the truth,' she said. 'I don't like being used for target practice.'

'Do you think he has any romantic feelings for you, Sparks?'

'Not likely,' she said. 'I made it very clear that I was not on the market, neither now nor any time in the near future.'

'And yet—'

'And yet he kissed me, yes. It doesn't mean he loves me, or that I love him. I've kissed many men I didn't love. Hey, Carruthers! Want me to kiss you so I can prove my point?'

'No thanks, Sparks,' replied Carruthers.

The Brigadier finally turned to look at her as he finished his cigarette. She met his gaze steadily.

'I've gone out on a limb for you, Sparks,' he said. 'More than once. I cannot have you repay my trust and protection with this erratic behaviour. If someone else's man had seen the two of you together like that, you'd be a guest of His Majesty's prison system more quickly than you can blink.'

She looked at him for a long moment, then blinked.

'I'm still here,' she said. 'I guess that means you're releasing me back to the wilds of London.'

'If he calls you, if he sees you, if you bump into each other on the Tube, I want to know about it inside of five minutes,' he said. 'Is that understood, Sparks?'

'It is,' she said. 'I'm sorry I didn't call you straight away.'

'Apology accepted. Get out before I change my mind.'

'One more thing, sir,' she said, reaching into her coat pocket.

The two men tensed, but all she brought out was a folded piece of paper which she handed to the Brigadier. He opened it, scanned it briefly, then looked at her.

'That much for a book about bugs?' he asked.

'Water beetles are not bugs, sir,' she replied. 'They're Coleoptera, not Hemiptera. And yes, the book cost that much, but the plates are superb. May I remind you that I am not otherwise being paid for this assignment?'

He pulled out his wallet, extracted a few bills, and handed them to her.

'Thank you, sir,' she said. 'I owe you change. I left my bag on the boat, but I could run and fetch—'

'Get out of the car, Sparks, and don't come back,' said the Brigadier wearily.

'Yes, sir,' she said, as Carruthers unlocked the door with a switch in front. 'Goodnight, sir. Goodnight, Carruthers. You missed out on the best kiss of your life, by the way.'

'I'll live with it,' said Carruthers. 'Go home, Sparks.'

She got out and closed the door, resisting the temptation to slam it shut, then walked slowly and deliberately back to her boat, waving over her shoulder without turning to look when she reached it. She went inside and locked the door, listening as the Bentley roared into the night.

The still-open book of water beetles waited for her on her

armchair. She closed it, leaving a marker in place, and went to bed.

Lowle called on Monday at nine thirty, asking to speak to Sparks.

'He called me,' she reported. 'First thing. I had barely settled at my desk when the telephone rang. He sounded very eager to meet me. You must have done a good job selling me to him.'

'Not so much selling you as selling him on the general idea,' said Sparks. 'I didn't tell him anything about you specifically, so you are free to concoct your character as you see fit. When's the date?'

'Tomorrow night,' she said.

'Good,' said Sparks. 'I told him to give you some time to prepare.'

'Sound advice. I already got my hair done Saturday so it's just a question of what to wear. I guess I'll be needing some bulletproof lipstick. I heard he really nailed you Friday night.'

'He did.'

'So he's a masher, then.'

'Didn't used to be, but that was years ago.'

'Any good?'

'It was better when we were younger.'

'Most things are. I guess I should be expecting the same treatment now that he's got you out of his system. How does he like to be kissed?'

'He certainly took the initiative this time. It used to be the other way around. The element of surprise seems to be a factor.'

'Fine. I'll play it by ear. Wish me luck.'

'Good—' began Sparks, but the other woman hung up before she could finish the phrase. She replaced the handset and drummed her fingers on her blotter.

'What was better when you were younger?' asked Gwen from her desk.

'What?' replied Iris, turning towards her.

'The thing that you weren't expecting in which he took the

initiative. Tony Danforth, I'm guessing from your side of the conversation.'

'We went out Friday night after you left,' said Iris.

'Interesting. And?'

'And he kissed me at the end of it.'

'Did he?'

'He did.'

'Were you supposed to do that?' asked Gwen. 'Was this some part of the grand scheme I didn't know about?'

'Look, I was already called in for an official upbraiding. I don't need another one.'

'You were? By the Brigadier?'

'Yes.'

'When was this?'

'Later that night. He paid me a call at the *Cecilia*.'

'How did he find out so quickly?'

'He had a man tailing Tony. That dock worker who wasn't a dock worker. He saw us together.'

'Including the kiss?'

'Yes.'

'All of this on only one Friday night,' said Gwen in wonder. 'I leave you alone for less than two hours, and this is the trouble you get into. Anything happen on Saturday or Sunday I should be privy to?'

'Laundry on Saturday, narrowboat lesson with Casper on Sunday. Do you need details?'

'No, I do not,' said Gwen. 'Dear Lord, Tony proposed to you on Tuesday, then kissed you on Friday. Everything the two of you do is in the wrong order.'

'That has been the hallmark of our relationship,' said Iris.

Tony called in the afternoon.

'Any last-second tips?' he asked when he heard her voice.

'You're thinking too much,' she said. 'Just let things happen and enjoy the evening. She called us earlier – she sounded quite excited about the prospect of meeting you.'

'I thought you didn't tell the prospects anything about each other.'

'I didn't,' said Sparks. 'She just sounded generally enthused about having a date.'

'You're not fobbing me off on one of your rejects, are you, Sparks?' he asked suspiciously. 'Putting me through the romantic wringer for the pure sadistic joy of it?'

'Given what we do for a living, that would be a terrible business plan,' she said. 'I only torment the men in my personal relationships, Tony, not our clients.'

'Your mercenary motives have convinced me,' he said. 'I go forth to do battle on the Fields of Love, and will return either with my shield or on it.'

'Any man who goes into a date quoting Plutarch deserves a sound beating,' said Sparks. 'Do try and have some fun, Tony.'

'I'll give it my best, Sparks,' he said. 'I'll ring you up on Wednesday and give you a full report on the carnage.'

He hung up, and her smile faded immediately.

'I have to report to the Brigadier,' she said, rising and going to fetch her hat. 'I should be back in fifteen minutes.'

'I will be coming to rescue you in twenty if not,' said Gwen.

Sparks forced herself to slow down to a walk down the stairs. She went outside, found the phone box, and went through her calling protocol. It rang three minutes later.

'Report,' said the Brigadier the second she answered.

'He called just now to let me know he's having his first date tomorrow,' she said. 'Nothing of import otherwise.'

'Nothing?'

'He quoted Plutarch.'

'Plutarch had something to say about dating? I'm not familiar with that passage.'

'Sayings about war can be transposed to love quite easily,' she said. 'Too easily, now that I think about it. In any case, he said he'd call me on Wednesday for the post-mortem. It wouldn't surprise me if alcohol will once again be applied to that conversation. Do I have your approval for that?'

'Do you think you can restrain yourself from further oscula-tion, Sparks?' he said. 'Our operative doesn't need the competition.'

'She's probably a better kisser than me as well, isn't she?'

'I have no basis for comparison,' he said. 'Very well, go on with your contacts. We'll leave the rest of it to Miss Lowle.'

'Thank you for walking me home, Mr Danforth,' said Miss Lowle the following evening as she clung to his arm.

'Tony, please,' he said.

'All right. Thank you for walking me home . . . Tony,' she said, blushing slightly. 'May we stop here for a moment?'

'Don't you live further down?'

'I do,' she said. 'But my landlady is a busybody and I don't want her asking me questions about you.'

'Of course,' he said. 'There's a bench. Shall we sit for a moment, Miss Lowle?'

'I'd like that very much. And you shall call me Evelyn. No! Don't call me that!'

'Why not?' he asked, amused.

'Because only my gran calls me that,' she said. 'Please call me Evie, Tony.'

'I will.'

'And what I wanted to tell you before we got within earshot of my landlady is that I had a lovely time with you tonight,' she said, the words pouring out of her in a rush. 'I was gun-shy coming into it, because the last date they set me up with . . . oh, it was awkward. He was nice enough, but there was no connection there.'

'Do you feel that we have one?'

'I'm not saying we should find the nearest church and rouse the minister,' she said with a smile, 'but I do feel that there is something here, something worth exploring further. I'm being too forward, aren't I? Sorry, I'm told it's a fault of mine.'

'No, no, I find it refreshing,' he said.

'It's just that I came to The Right Sort thinking, well, this is either going to be a complete lark or an act of desperation, do you know what I mean?'

'I do, in fact.'

'And, um—'

She stopped.

'Go on,' he urged her.

'I've been so lonely since coming to London, and I think I've shut myself down after all this time,' she said, looking down for a moment. Then she looked back up at him shyly. 'But I've felt very comfortable talking with you.'

'I'm glad.'

'And I think what I'm trying to say is . . . I know, I know, I'm the female, and we're not supposed to take the initiative—'

'By all means, initiate,' he said, laughing.

'What I'm trying to say is if you are wondering what I would say to a request for another date, then the answer is yes,' she said, looking at him expectantly.

He didn't speak for a moment, his face suddenly serious.

Her face fell.

'Oh, God, you weren't going to!' she cried. 'I'm such a damn fool!'

He leaned towards her, placing his hands on her shoulders.

'I am definitely asking you for another date, Evie,' he said. 'What I was wondering is whether or not I should kiss you right now.'

'If you're seeking my input on the question—' she said.

'I am.'

'Then I would heartily endorse the idea.'

He closed the distance between them. The kiss was gentle and slow, and when they separated, she looked up at him, her eyes brimming.

'I'm awfully glad you did that,' she whispered. 'I'm very much looking forward to our next date.'

'I will ring you tomorrow,' he said. 'Now, let me get you back to your warder before the portcullis is lowered.'

She glanced around when they reached the door, then turned and kissed him again quickly before turning the key and slipping inside. The last glimpse he had of her was her turning to smile at him one last time through the diminishing sliver of the doorway before it closed entirely.

Promising start, he thought to himself as he turned and

headed to the Tube station. He took the underground to Pimlico, from where it was a six-minute walk to Grenville House. He went through the Grosvenor Road entrance, then, not quite trusting the lift, which had made some disturbing grinding noises when he had taken it in the morning, bounded up the stairs until he reached the fifth storey.

His flat faced Dolphin Square East, his view being of the rooftops of the houses separating Grenville House from St George's Square, a park beloved of the local dogs and their owners. He switched on the lights when he entered, wincing slightly at the bareness of it. He had the furniture deliverers coming in the morning, with luck. He had left the windows closed, and the place felt stuffy. He opened the parlour window and threw back the shutters. Then he went into the bedroom, turned on the overhead lamp, and repeated the process with that window as well, leaving the door between the two rooms open to provide some ventilation.

He turned away from the window and started heading towards the bathroom.

Which meant he had his back to the explosion.

Iris was distracted at The Right Sort the next day, twitching every time the telephone rang, waiting for the muffled tones of Mrs Billington next door to be followed by the news that it was Tony calling.

'He may be busy,' said Gwen. 'He does have a job, you know.'

'He said he would call,' said Iris.

'This may be a smaller matter in his life than it is in ours,' Gwen pointed out.

'I know,' said Iris. 'But the longer it takes, the more disproportionately grow my anxieties about it.'

'You said once we set him up with Miss Lowle we were done with this,' said Gwen. 'You weren't happy doing it, so don't make yourself more unhappy worrying over it.'

'Everything you say makes perfect sense. It follows that since I'm ignoring it all I am clearly not in my right mind.'

'Focus on the work,' suggested Gwen. 'We have real couples to match, remember?'

Around three o'clock, the telephone rang. Then the intercom buzzed. Iris answered it right away.

'It's Mr Danielli,' said Mrs Billington.

'I'll pass the telephone to Gwen,' said Iris.

'No, he wants to speak with you,' said Mrs Billington.

'Oh. Fine, put him through,' she said, picking up the handset. 'Hello, Sally. What's up?'

'Have you seen the *Evening Standard* yet?' he asked.

'No. I usually pick up the final edition on the way home. Why?'

'There was some kind of fire last night. An explosion.'

'What happened?' she asked, her heart sinking. 'Why are you calling me about it?'

'A man was badly burned, it says here,' said Sally. 'It was Tony. Tony Danforth.'

She clutched the handset, the room blurring for a moment.

'Where did they take him?' she asked as Gwen looked over in concern.

'St George's,' he said.

'Do they know how it happened?'

'Not as of publication time,' he said. '"Police are making enquiries," that vague cliché. But Gwen mentioned he was back in town and a client of yours, of all things, so I thought you should know.'

'Thank you, Sally,' she said. 'Do you want to speak to Gwen?'

'I can't, actually. I'm at work, but I broke away for five minutes to ring you.'

'All right. Thanks again.'

She hung up.

'He wanted to speak with you, not me?' asked Gwen. 'What's going on?'

'Tony Danforth was injured last night,' said Iris. 'Someone torched his flat.'

'Good God! Which hospital did they take him to?'

'St George's.'

'Let's go,' said Gwen.

The hospital was across from Hyde Park Corner, normally a twenty-minute walk from Mayfair. They did it in fifteen, Iris's nervous trot barely keeping up with the long, determined strides of her taller partner.

The hospital's current form dated from a massive rebuilding a century earlier, with a Greek colonnade over the entrance facing Grosvenor Place. Iris pulled up short as they came to the entrance.

'What's wrong?' asked Gwen.

'I haven't set foot inside a hospital since Archie died,' she said. 'I need a moment to steel myself.'

'If it's any comfort, I have a very happy connection to this place,' said Gwen. 'It's where I gave birth to Little Ronnie. Let me know when you're ready.'

Iris took a deep breath, then grabbed Gwen's hand.

'I'm not being rational right now,' she said. 'Thank you for bearing with me.'

'It's an insane situation,' said Gwen. 'Fortunately, I have much experience with those.'

'I'm ready,' said Iris.

They went in, Iris still clutching Gwen's hand. There was a line at the front desk. They waited patiently until they reached the receptionist.

'May I help you, ladies?' she asked.

'We're looking for a friend who was brought in last night,' said Iris. 'Anthony Danforth.'

The receptionist ran her finger down a ledger book.

'Yes, he's here,' she said. 'He's in the intensive care ward.'

'Still alive, then, thank goodness,' said Iris, sagging against Gwen in relief. 'May he have visitors?'

'Are you family?'

'Friends,' said Iris.

'Then I'm afraid not,' said the receptionist.

'Is there anyone we could speak with about how he is doing?'

'I'll see if either the surgeon or the matron is available,' she said, picking up her telephone. 'What names shall I give?'

'Miss Iris Sparks and Mrs Gwendolyn Bainbridge.'

'Very good. You may wait in the waiting room until they come down.'

They followed her directions to a room full of narrow,

wooden benches, filled with anxious and exhausted people. They found space for themselves and sat.

'This is a nicer waiting room than the one in London Hospital,' Iris observed, looking around. 'Is this where your husband waited while you were in labour?'

'I believe there is a separate room for the maternity ward,' said Gwen. 'In any case, he wasn't here for the birth. He was already in training with the Fusiliers. I had gone into labour before the due date, so there was no time to alert him. Harold pulled some strings and got him leave to visit two days later. I'd never seen Ronnie so happy as when he showed up, still in uniform, to meet his new son.'

'I wonder how long it will take to find out anything about Tony.'

It was twenty minutes before anyone came to see them, but it wasn't a doctor or nurse. It was a brown-haired man in his late forties, the grey in his temples matching the grey moustache, who appeared in a doorway, looking at them warily.

'Parham's here,' whispered Gwen, seeing him.

'Himself,' said Iris softly. 'We'd better be careful. The Act still applies unless we're given specific permission to reveal anything.'

Parham motioned for them to follow him with a quick nod towards the corridor. They got up and trailed him as he turned off to the right. There was an empty office. He beckoned to them, then closed the door.

'Miss Sparks, Mrs Bainbridge, I must confess I'm surprised to see you here,' he said, pointing them to a pair of chairs, then perching on the edge of the desk.

'As we are to see you,' replied Sparks.

'Surely you must know that this is a matter for the police. Why the surprise?'

'That it's you, Detective Superintendent, and not one of your subordinates,' she said. 'Why is that?'

'The victim works for His Majesty's government,' said Parham. 'There is a certain protocol for such affairs.'

'Not to mention your having a higher security clearance,' said Sparks.

'That as well,' he said. 'As the two of you are very much

aware given our previous history together. What is your connection to Mr Danforth?'

'He's an old friend from Cambridge,' said Sparks.

'And he signed up at The Right Sort,' added Mrs Bainbridge. 'When?'

'Last week,' said Sparks.

'Could you tell us how he's doing before we get any further into this?' asked Mrs Bainbridge. 'That is our immediate concern.'

'He was badly burned, I'm afraid,' said Parham. 'Mostly on his back. He was lucky to be facing away when it happened. Had it reached his lungs, this would be a homicide investigation. He spent several hours here in a saline bath. They're deciding now whether to proceed with debriding the burned skin immediately, or to stabilise him to the point where they can safely transport him to the burn facility in East Grinstead.'

'Oh, God,' whispered Mrs Bainbridge. 'The poor man.'

'How did it happen?' asked Sparks.

'A petrol bomb, thrown through the open window,' he said. 'What the tabloids like to call a Molotov cocktail. How well do you know him, Miss Sparks?'

'We were good friends at university,' she said. 'He went east to teach in Singapore before the war, then got caught up with events there. I hadn't seen him since he left, then bumped into him last week.'

'Where?'

'Maggs Brothers, the bookshop. We went out for drinks, and he decided to enrol with us.'

'I see. Do you know his family?'

'Never met them,' said Sparks. 'I think he was estranged from them, especially after being gone for so long.'

'What about his involvement with The Right Sort? Had he gone out with anyone there?'

'He had his first date last night,' said Sparks. 'With a Miss Evelyn Lowle.'

'Last night,' he repeated. 'I'll have to speak with her. You don't happen to have her contact information, do you?'

'Not with me,' said Sparks. 'We could call you in the morning if that's acceptable.'

'That should be fine,' he said. 'I'm going to stay here in case he says anything else.'

'Anything else?' repeated Mrs Bainbridge. 'You mean he's able to speak?'

'He's been drifting in and out due to the morphine,' said Parham. 'The one thing he said clearly made no sense whatsoever.'

'What was it?' asked Sparks.

'Something like "I forgot to praise her hat",' said Parham.

Sparks gave a sharp, quick laugh. Parham looked at her, an eyebrow raised.

'His date,' she explained. 'Sorry, that laugh was inappropriate, but it caught me by surprise. I had told him that women liked having their outfits admired. I can't believe that's what was on his mind.'

'Morphine will do that,' said Parham. 'Very well. Leave Miss Lowle's information with my secretary. You know the number.'

'We have it memorised,' said Mrs Bainbridge. 'If Mr Danforth wakes, please tell him that we were here, and that I will be praying for him.'

'Of course,' said Parham. 'Goodnight, ladies.'

They left and exited the hospital.

'He should know what's really happening,' said Gwen.

'I agree, but it's still an ongoing operation,' said Iris.

'Surely this must take precedence.'

'We end up in prison if we tell Parham without clearing it first,' said Iris. 'And there is one more problem.'

'Which is?'

'What if the Brigadier was behind this? What if our Miss Lowle learned enough to condemn Tony to immediate execution?'

Gwen turned pale.

'Do you mean to say that was a possibility when we embarked on this?' she asked softly.

'I didn't think so at the time,' said Iris. 'But I've been out of the loop for a few years. Things may have escalated since then.'

'How can we know?'

'Only one way to find out,' said Iris. 'Had you any plans for the evening?'

The Brigadier was reading a report as Carruthers drove him home. He looked up as the Bentley slowed to a halt some distance from the entrance to his house.

'What is it?' he asked.

'We may have a problem, sir,' said Carruthers. 'How would you like me to handle it?'

The Brigadier looked through the windscreen to see Sparks standing at his gate, glaring at the Bentley as if she were trying to stop it telekinetically.

'How do you think she knew your address?' asked Carruthers.

'She makes a point of knowing about things she shouldn't,' said the Brigadier wearily. 'Let's find out why she's here.'

Carruthers pulled up in front of the house, then got out.

'What do you want?' he asked.

'I want to talk to him,' said Sparks. 'Now.'

'You going to make a fuss, Lollipop?' he asked.

'Only if you get in my way, Carruthers.'

'Tell her to get in the car,' said the Brigadier from inside the Bentley.

'Not a chance,' said Sparks. 'I'm not putting myself in any situation where there are locks on the doors. You get out of that car and talk to me. Right here, right now.'

The Brigadier hesitated, then opened the door and stepped out.

'Do we need to frisk you for weapons, Sparks?' he asked.

'I'm carrying the usual in my bag,' she said. 'They'll be staying there. This will be a brief conversation. Sir.'

'Very well,' he said, approaching her as Carruthers stepped to one side. 'What do you want?'

'Did you do it?' she asked. 'Has the office sunk to this point?'

'Do you really think we did?'

'I don't think anything. I am asking you.'

'Then the answer is no, Sparks. We didn't make an attempt on Danforth's life. We needed to find out if he was working for the enemy. We still do. All Miss Lowle did was make the preliminary contact. She was not expected to do anything more than that, and you should know that is not how an operative would work in that situation.'

'No, but she's new to this,' said Sparks.

'Further reason for her to take things one step at a time,' said the Brigadier. 'And you should consider this: if we wanted him dead, he would be dead. We certainly wouldn't resort to such an inefficient mechanism as a petrol bomb. There is no guarantee of success, as you've already seen. Danforth lives on.'

'For the moment.'

'Yes.'

'You should speak to Parham. Or let me speak to him.'

'Absolutely not.'

'Why not? He's cleared specifically for these types of cases but he'll be working solo because of that. He needs all the help he can get, especially if . . .'

She hesitated, not wanting to complete the thought.

'Especially if Tony dies and it becomes a murder case,' she concluded.

'It's premature to be asking that,' said the Brigadier. 'Danforth isn't dead. And frankly, we hope that he survives. We wish to continue the operation until we know more. In fact, I would like you to arrange a visit to his bedside for Miss Lowle to encourage her continuing rapport with him.'

'He may not live through the night, and you're already plotting the next phase?' she asked in disbelief.

'If he dies, then it's a waste of a good cover story for Miss Lowle,' he said, shrugging. 'Valuable training for the woman, though. But we all hope he lives. Don't we, Sparks?'

She looked at him, then nodded slowly.

'Good,' he said. 'We're done here. And if I ever see you at my gate again, I shall direct Carruthers to shoot you on sight and bury you where you'll never be found. Understood?'

She nodded again, glancing at Carruthers, who smirked at her.

'Then I will bid you a good evening, Sparks,' he said. 'Go home. Report to me if you succeed in visiting your old friend in hospital.'

He turned, opened the gate to his house and walked inside.

'You wouldn't really shoot me, would you?' she asked Carruthers.

'Nah,' he said. 'It'd be more fun to break your neck, Lollipop. Now get out of here. I'll wait until you're gone.'

She turned and walked away. Carruthers watched as she vanished around the next corner, waited, then opened the gate and knocked on the Brigadier's door. It opened a moment later.

'Any further instructions?' he asked.

'Search Danforth's flat,' said the Brigadier. 'See what you can find.'

'Yes, sir. What about Sparks? Should we keep an eye on her?'

The Brigadier snorted.

'If I had three men capable of following Iris Sparks without losing her, I'd be running England,' he said. 'We'll leave her be for now. But let me know if she causes any more trouble.'

'Yes, sir.'

SEVEN

Gwen was waiting for Iris as she turned the corner.
'Were you able to get a good view of his face?' asked
Iris.

Gwen held up a pair of opera glasses, which she folded up
and placed in her bag.

'I've never tried to read someone from a distance before,'
she said. 'Good thing you had him under the street light. But
you planned that, didn't you?'

'I did. How much could you hear?'

'Not everything, but enough.'

'And?'

'And I believe he was telling the truth about not being behind
the attempt on Mr Danforth's life.'

'So do I,' said Iris, starting to walk.

'You almost sound disappointed,' commented Gwen, joining
her.

'It would have simplified things,' said Iris. 'God, I want a
drink right now. Several, to be precise. I need complete
obliteration.'

'Come back to my place,' said Gwen. 'I have the means
necessary.'

'So does the nearest pub, and I can get there sooner.'

'You shouldn't be drinking alone, and you shouldn't be
going to a pub to get soused right now,' said Gwen. 'You'll
either end up in a brawl or going to bed with a complete
stranger.'

'What if I get to know him first?'

'Come with me, Iris,' said Gwen firmly. 'You've been off
your stride ever since this mission was shoved into our lives.
We will delve into my personal supplies, and if you pass out,
it will be in my guest room, not a public house.'

'What if I get into a brawl with you?'

'I've been training,' said Gwen. 'I might be a match for you if you're drunk.'

'Doubt it.'

'So do I. But it's a better idea for you to be drinking with me, so come on. We'll pick up some dinner on the way home.'

'I have no appetite.'

'You will by the time we get there.'

They stopped by an Indian restaurant to pick up a couple of curries, then caught a cab to Maida Vale. It was past eight o'clock when they walked through Gwen's front door. Millie, her housekeeper, appeared from the upper landing.

'Good evening, Mrs Bainbridge, Miss Sparks,' she called. 'Do you need anything?'

'We're fine, Millie,' replied Gwen.

'But she may need help carrying me up the stairs later,' added Iris.

'I'll check back before I turn in,' said Millie.

'You don't mind eating in the kitchen, do you?' asked Gwen as they hung up their coats. 'It's more convenient and our conversation is less likely to travel upstairs.'

'Fine with me.'

Iris followed Gwen to the rear of the house, then sat at the small kitchen table while her partner busied herself fetching plates, bowls and spoons.

'I prefer G&Ts with my curry,' said Gwen, pulling a bottle of Gordon's from the refrigerator. 'Especially during the summer months. Will that do the trick?'

'As long as the ratio favours the gin,' said Iris.

'And look!' said Gwen holding up a precious lime. 'We will ward off malaria and scurvy simultaneously.'

She fetched a chunk of ice from the freezer, put it in a steel bucket, then handed it to Iris along with an ice pick.

'Take out your frustrations on this,' suggested Gwen.

Within seconds, Iris reduced the chunk to fragments, her face glistening from the spatter. Gwen scooped several pieces into a pair of tumblers, added a sliver of lime to each, poured the gin well past the halfway level, then added the tonic, pouring it over a bar spoon. She gave each drink a single stir, then placed one at each end of the table.

'To Tony Danforth,' she said, raising hers. 'May he live through the night, and long after.'

'To Tony,' echoed Iris, clinking her tumbler against Gwen's. She downed most of it on the first swallow.

'Pace yourself, darling,' said Gwen as she took a small sip from hers. 'We need your brain intact for this conversation.'

'The gin won't kick in for a few minutes,' said Iris.

'Have some curry,' said Gwen, ladling it into the bowls with some rice. 'I find that the burning sensation stimulates thinking.'

'I don't want to think right now.'

'Do you want to find who did this to Mr Danforth or not?' asked Gwen.

'Why is that our responsibility?' asked Iris as she spooned some curry into her mouth.

Then she made a muffled grunt and grabbed for her gin.

'I told you to pace yourself,' said Gwen, calmly swallowing one spoonful, then another. 'As to responsibility – Parham is hampered by having to work alone and in the dark. The Brigadier isn't going to lift a finger to help him. Which leaves us.'

'But we're working for the Brigadier and we can't tell Parham anything.'

'We can't tell Parham anything about the operation, or the Brigadier's suspicions about Mr Danforth. But what if the attack had nothing to do with the operation?'

'What else could it be?' asked Iris.

'You're empty,' said Gwen.

She took Iris's tumbler and mixed another, the gin nearing the three-quarter mark this time.

'Chin-chin,' she said.

'You can't toast Indian food with Chinese toasts,' protested Iris.

'I don't know any Indian toasts. Do you?'

'No, come to think of it. Cheers.'

She swallowed. Gwen sipped, watching her.

'What else could it be?' repeated Iris.

'It struck me that a Molotov cocktail is a particularly vicious method of attacking someone,' said Gwen. 'It's designed to cause a great deal of pain and not necessarily a quick death. It also has to be planned. One doesn't just happen to have a bottle of petrol concealed in one's coat pocket.'

'All that is true enough,' said Iris. 'What's your point?'

'That this was personal rather than political,' said Gwen. 'The attacker wanted him to suffer before he died. What if vengeance was the motive?'

'Vengeance for what?'

'What about that woman in Cambridge? Nancy something. Sauce, I believe people called her.'

'What about her?'

'Mr Danforth comes back in town for the first time in ages and this happens,' said Gwen. 'Someone could have been waiting for this opportunity.'

'After all these years?' scoffed Iris. 'That's a very lazy avenging angel. They should have hunted him down overseas.'

'They might not have had the means,' suggested Gwen. 'Or they might have thought that the wars would take their toll. As they did for the others – what were their names? Kevin something was one, Sally said.'

'Pickard,' said Iris. 'Kevin Pickard and Bruce Cater. Both were at Pembroke with Tony. The Unholy Trinity, they used to call themselves.'

'Why?'

'Oh, just some stupid nickname Pickard thought up. They had an act at parties, singing dirty satirical songs in three-part harmony, often bringing in the names of faculty members or fellow students. They thought they were amusing.'

'Were they?'

'More cruel than funny, in my opinion, but Pickard was hugely rich and very well-connected, so people would laugh to stay on his good side. Either I've burned away my taste buds or I'm getting used to the curry now.'

'I told you you'd be hungry. Was Nancy ever featured in one of these songs?'

'I never heard first hand, but there was gossip of a particularly vicious reference in one dedicated to the girls of Newnham sung at some secret club gathering. There was a fair amount of sniggering among the stupider sex afterwards.'

'Were you included in that one?'

'Maybe,' said Iris, shrugging. 'Probably. Who cares?'

'How long after that song was Nancy's death?'

Iris finished her glass.

'Not long,' she said, holding it out for another refill. 'I know what you're doing, by the way.'

'What's that?' Gwen asked as she mixed another and handed it to her.

'You're trying to get me drunk so I will reveal what you suspect is some dark secret I'm concealing from those times,' said Iris. 'Well, it won't work. I have been trained for just such an approach. My ability to keep mum is directly proportionate to my capacity for alcohol.'

'Iris, whoever tried to kill Tony may try again,' said Gwen. 'Surely that's crossed your mind by now.'

'Of course, it has,' said Iris. 'And I'm sure it crossed Parham's as well. He'll be having a constable guarding Tony's room.'

'That only covers the near future,' said Gwen.

'Yes, well, Tony ought to be on the alert now, don't you think?' snapped Iris. 'If this stems from . . . from anything in the past, then it's his responsibility to–to—'

'To do what? Defend himself from more petrol bombs?' finished Gwen. 'How does one do that exactly? And what if the next attack turns out to be more thorough and less defensible? Parham will either find this attacker soon, or he won't and will have to move on to the next priority, but Tony will be in a long, slow recovery, and no one is going to be guarding him full-time. But if his attacker is caught—'

'If we catch him, you're saying.'

'Yes. If we catch him, then Tony will be safe. I think that's worth doing.'

'How do we go about doing that?'

'I don't know enough about what happened to answer that – yet,' said Gwen. 'I need you to enlighten me.'

'The thing is, I don't know for certain,' said Iris.

'Why not?'

'Because I was sound asleep in bed with Tony when the screaming started,' she said. 'By the time we got to that part of the house, everything was over.'

Gwen looked across the table at her for a long time.

'I thought you said you weren't lovers,' she said finally.

'I said I didn't think that word applied to us,' said Iris. 'Not as it is generally defined.'

'But you went to bed with him. You said things never got that far.'

'I said— oh, hell, I am not going to provide you with details,' said Iris.

'No, I don't want any, thank you,' said Gwen. 'But I think you had better start at the beginning.'

'What was the beginning?' Iris mused aloud. 'It was the last weekend of April, Easter Term, 1936. A Friday afternoon. Bruce was driving. He had a Morris Twenty-Five, and five of us were crammed into it, plus too many valises and bags of food and booze for one weekend. Tony and I were in the rear seat, smashed together with some of the bags, and Kevin was up front.'

'And Nancy?' asked Gwen.

'She was on Kevin's lap.'

Cambridgeshire, 1936

'Stop!' Sauce cried, laughing as she playfully slapped Kevin's hands away. 'People will see.'

'I have to put them somewhere,' said Kevin as he wrapped his arms around her. 'Besides, it's for your protection. If there's a sudden halt, I will keep you from crashing through the windscreen.'

'There won't be any sudden halts,' said Bruce, whipping around a slow-moving lorry. 'I am a masterful driver.'

'How fast are we going, Catey?' asked Tony.

'Only seventy,' said Bruce. 'And don't call me that in front of the girls, or I will make it a point of taking Sparks away from you this weekend.'

'I might be able to squeeze you in for a dance or two,' said Sparks. 'It's too tragic that Gloria came down with the flu. She was so looking forward to seeing the legendary Pickard family manse.'

'We'll do our best to make up for her absence, won't we, Sparks?' said Sauce, leaning over to plant a kiss on Bruce's cheek.

She shrieked as the Morris swerved momentarily.

'See what happens when you distract me?' he said, grinning at her.

'She is quite the distraction, isn't she?' said Kevin, nuzzling her neck, drawing a delighted giggle in response. 'Who's got some booze handy?'

'Here,' said Bruce, pulling a flask out of his jacket and handing it to Sauce. 'Be a dear and give us a taste before Picky guzzles the whole thing.'

She uncapped it, took a healthy swig, then leaned over and planted her mouth on his, letting the liquor pass into it.

'Jesus, watch the road!' shouted Kevin.

The left wheels of the Morris caught dirt as the car veered off the pavement. In an instant, they were plunging through a newly sprouted barley field as Bruce frantically shifted gears and spun the wheel until he had regained control. He brought the car to a stop ten feet from a stone wall.

'Everyone intact?' he said, glancing around.

'A bit squashed back here,' said Sparks who had been thrown into Tony.

'I don't mind that at all,' said Tony, giving her a squeeze. 'That was fun. Let's do it again.'

'Maybe on the return trip,' said Bruce. 'We should get back on the road before some idiot farmer shows up demanding damages for his precious plants. But let's have one more while we are motionless, shall we?'

'All right,' said Sauce.

She took another sip, then transferred it to him again by the same method, lingering this time.

'Hey, now,' protested Kevin.

'I'm just being a good guest,' said Sauce as she pulled away. 'Here's some for you, darling.'

This time Kevin was the lucky recipient as she twisted in his lap to reach his lips, some of the whisky dribbling down his chin as she had trouble controlling her laughter by that point.

'I must say, I'm not missing Gloria much at all right now,' said Bruce as he put the Morris back in gear. 'Although if it turns out that you also have the flu—'

'Don't worry, alcohol sterilises everything,' said Kevin. 'Even Sauce.'

'Good thing we brought plenty,' said Sauce, settling back against him as the car pulled back onto the road. 'And good thing you had your arms around me, darling. You saved my life.'

'I will expect your gratitude to be expressed throughout this weekend,' said Kevin.

They passed through the town of Kimbolton, driving by the castle in the centre. Bruce slowed down and thumbed his nose at it as they passed by.

'You know them?' asked Sparks.

'Cousins,' he said. 'The Montagu family. A noble lineage fallen into disrepute as their castle falls into disrepair. The recent lords established a new tradition of marrying heiresses, spending their fortunes, then cheating on them with young, marginally talented actresses. Yet they get to keep the title, and are stuck with that historic monstrosity. I spent many wretched holidays there, pretending to be nice to them.'

'That's where— which one of the wives was it?' began Kevin.

'Catherine of Aragon,' said Sparks and Tony simultaneously from the back.

'Right, her,' said Kevin. 'That's where she finally ended up after the divorce. Died there, too. Ridiculous, all the fuss she caused.'

'She caused?' sputtered Sparks. 'How do you figure that?'

'She should've just quietly got on with her life once the king found someone younger and prettier,' said Kevin. 'She was lucky he kept her around for as long as he did.'

'Right, turn the car around,' said Sparks. 'I must protest on behalf of all the wronged women in the world. Especially the short ones.'

'You haven't been wronged by anyone,' said Kevin.

'But the night is young,' Tony murmured into her ear, and she smiled.

'How much longer?' asked Sauce as they reached the open road going west.

'Another twenty minutes,' said Kevin. 'Barring any detours through farmland. Think you can manage to keep on the road the rest of the way, Catey?'

'This part I can drive with my eyes closed,' said Bruce. 'Watch.'

He squeezed them shut. The Morris kept going.

'Yes, that's enough now, Bruce,' said Sauce.

He kept them shut, with the car inching ever closer to the ditch running alongside the road.

'I said enough!' she shouted.

'Come on, old chap,' Kevin said quietly.

Bruce opened his eyes and made a slight adjustment with the wheel, bringing them away from the brink.

'I told you,' he said.

Sparks looked over at Tony. He was grimacing in pain. She realised she had grabbed his hand and was squeezing it tightly. She relinquished it, and he made an exaggerated gesture of wiping his brow in relief.

They drove on in silence, passing farms and forests on both sides. Then an impressive gate came into view on the right.

'It's open,' said Tony. 'They anticipated our arrival.'

'It's been rusted open for years,' said Kevin. 'Maintenance is not the Pickard family's strong suit.'

The tree-lined drive was three-quarters of a mile long, ending in a circular gravelled driveway, beyond which was a mansion which Sparks and Sauce goggled at.

'So that's where all the bricks in England ended up,' said Sauce.

The house was massive, four storeys high and very Gothic, designed by some deranged late-Victorian architect with a fetish for an unnecessary number of towers and spires with spiralling brick patterns that made them look like some giant with access to a kiln had screwed the entire assemblage into the ground from above. Tall hedges flanked both sides with openings giving glimpses of stables to the left and a poorly pruned maze to the right that Sparks immediately decided she would spend time solving the next morning.

'We have this whole place to ourselves?' she asked as Bruce eased the Morris under the porte cochère in front of the main entrance.

'We do,' said Kevin. 'The parents are touring the subcontinent and my sisters are tanning, or more likely reddening, away in the Bermudas, so the place is more or less closed down.'

'More or less?'

'They left Mrs Dorter, the housekeeper, behind to keep things swept and dusted,' said Kevin. 'Couldn't be bothered to pay any other staff while they were gone. Someone comes in once a week to cut the grass and tend to the gardens.'

'Are there horses?' asked Sauce eagerly. 'I saw stables.'

'Imagine the dreary life of a stabled horse when no one is around to ride it,' said Kevin. 'The last one was sold off when I was sent away to Eton. Sorry, my dear, there will be no riding this weekend. Speaking of which, I will need you to vacate my lap now that we've arrived safely.'

'Dorty knows we're coming, doesn't she?' asked Bruce as he cut the motor.

'I called her a few days ago,' said Kevin. 'Give her a toot to let her know we've arrived.'

He opened the car door and unceremoniously shoved Sauce off his lap onto the driveway, then staggered after her, limping. Bruce honked the hooter a few times, then got out and came around to open the boot. Sparks and Tony emerged from the rear, stretching and silently giving thanks for surviving the journey.

'My leg's gone to sleep,' complained Kevin, rubbing his thigh. 'I think someone's been sitting on it. Right, everyone grab your valises. I'll get Dorty to load the grub and bub into the kitchen. And here she is! Hermia, my first love, how dost thou?'

This to a fortyish woman who had appeared at the front door, wearing a plain, dark frock with a wide white lace collar. Her grey-streaked hair was in a simple bun. She did not look pleased to see the party, even less so when Kevin bounded up the front steps to lift her up in a bear hug.

'Put me down, you rascal,' she said. 'Just because you fancy yourself lord of the manor while everyone else is away doesn't mean you don't mind your manners with me.'

'I stand rebuked,' he said, lowering her gently. 'Forgive me. Mrs Dorter, allow me to introduce our guests. You are already acquainted with the gentlemen.'

'Hello, Dorty,' said Bruce.

'Mrs Dorter, it is good to see you again,' said Tony.

'Mr Cater, Mr Danforth,' she said, nodding to each. 'Welcome.'

'And these lovely ladies are Miss Nancy Spurlock and Miss Iris Sparks. They're at Newnham College.'

'How do you do, Mrs Dorter?' Sauce greeted her.

'Hello, Mrs Dorter,' said Sparks. 'Thank you for having us.'

'Well, they're polite enough, aren't they?' said Mrs Dorter with a sniff. 'Shall I show you to your rooms?'

'I'll take them up,' said Kevin. 'You can fetch the provisions. Put a couple of bottles of champers on ice right away, would you? I'm parched.'

They followed him into the entry hall. Sauce whistled as she slowly spun around, taking in the massive oak stairs that curved up three storeys along the walls, banister-lined landings surrounding each level, a glass skylight surmounting it all. The floor was a tessellated pattern of black, white and green tiles, and the marble coving at the meeting of walls and ceiling was ornately carved with scenes of pastoral life alternating with hunting tableaux. Bronze statues of dubious taste but definite antiquity pointed various weapons at them from alabaster alcoves.

'I'm afraid we'll be roughing it tonight,' said Kevin. 'I hired extra staff to come in for the party tomorrow, but it's just us and Dorty right now, and she'll keep to herself once supper is laid out. This way if you please, my lords and ladies.'

They followed him up the stairs to the first storey.

He beckoned to Sparks and Tony.

'You don't mind sharing a wing, do you?' he asked as he took them to the east hall.

'We'll scrape by as best we can,' said Sparks.

'That's the old Newnham spirit!' he said. 'Fine, I'm putting you in sister Lucinda's room. You have your own bath, and everything should be sufficiently girly for you. Tony, you're taking my old room.'

'Where are you going to be?' asked Tony.

'As the momentary master of the house, I am taking the master suite,' said Kevin.

'Your father would have your hide if he found out,' said Tony.

'Which is exactly why I'm doing it,' said Kevin. 'Get yourselves settled. It's just us chickens, so no need to dress for dinner tonight. We'll rendezvous in the dining room in twenty minutes.'

'Kevin, I'm still standing here,' called Sauce from the other wing.

He looked at her, then back at the two of them with a wolfish grin.

'Make it thirty,' he said, then he scurried towards her.

'I think gratitude is about to be expressed,' commented Tony.

'He has put us in adjacent rooms,' observed Sparks. 'Far from the madding crowd.'

'He has,' said Tony.

'A girl might suspect a plan behind that,' she said, glancing at him coyly.

'A plan? By moi?' he replied innocently.

'Hmm. Go unpack, then let's take a quick stroll about the grounds while there's still some daylight. I want to see how the other one-half of one per cent lives before I return to my campaign of social revolution.'

'Doesn't this opulent adventure contradict that?'

'It's research, dear boy, nothing but research.'

'I am at your service, comrade.'

'Let me get this straight,' interrupted Gwen. 'This was a weekend of what sounds like typical young upper-crust debauchery at a country estate with you and Tony in adjacent rooms.'

'Yes,' said Iris.

'And you ended up sleeping in the same bed together?'

'Yes again.'

'That same night?'

'Still yes.'

'Yet, and again I don't require details, you didn't consider yourselves lovers?'

'No,' said Iris. 'The devil is in those details, but they will

remain in the dark. What mattered is that's where we ended up late that night, after dinner, after dancing to the gramophone for hours, after much, much champagne and risqué badinage and drunken flirtation, after we all retired to our respective wings. And Tony and I were fast asleep in sister Lucinda's bed when we snapped awake to the sound of Sauce screaming.'

Sparks sat bolt upright immediately, then shoved Tony a few times until he groaned groggily.

'What the hell is going on?' he said.

'It's Sauce,' said Sparks, jumping out of bed and grabbing her dressing gown.

She picked his off the floor and tossed it to him.

'Should we, I don't know, arm ourselves or something?' he asked as he threw it on.

'No time,' she said, tying her dressing gown and quickly stepping into her slippers. 'Come on.'

There were no lights on in the hall, but the moonlight came down through the skylight into the void separating the wings from each other. The last echoes of the screams faded as Iris ran towards the landing.

'Sauce!' she shouted. 'Where are you?'

There was no answer.

'Kevin! Bruce!' she called. 'What's going on?'

'Everything's fine,' said Kevin, emerging from a doorway on the other side, the lit room behind him putting him into silhouette.

'What do you mean "everything's fine"? She was screaming.'

'Well, she was upset at something, I guess,' said Kevin. 'She had too much to drink, and suddenly flew off the handle and turned into a banshee.'

'Where is she? I want to talk to her,' demanded Sparks, walking around the landing to reach his side.

'That may be a problem,' said Kevin. 'She's run off.'

'Run off? Where?'

'No idea,' said Kevin, looking up and down the hallway.

'We should go look for her,' offered Tony, who had come up behind Iris.

'Let her sulk the night away somewhere,' said Kevin. 'She'll be fine in the morning.'

'She is drunk, upset and wandering around in the dark in a giant house she doesn't know her way around in,' said Sparks. 'She could hurt herself.'

'It would serve her right,' said Kevin.

'She could also break something,' Tony pointed out. 'Something valuable.'

A fleeting expression of agony passed over Kevin's face.

'A valid point,' he said. 'Sparks, head down to the ground floor. I'll take this level. Tony, work your way up. Turn the lights on as you go.'

'Should one of us fetch Dorty?' asked Tony.

'My guess is she's already up and on the hunt,' said Kevin. 'Whoever finds Sauce first, bring her back to her room so she can sleep it off.'

Sparks immediately headed for the staircase, feeling her way with one hand on the banister, the other holding up the skirts of her dressing gown. Halfway down, it occurred to her that Bruce hadn't come out. She wondered about that, but given the amount of alcohol they had consumed it wasn't all that surprising.

She reached the bottom of the stairs, then felt around the wall by the foyer until she found a light switch.

'Sauce?' she called.

There was no response. She thought back through her hazy recollection of the last few minutes. She didn't think she had heard the front door open, so Sauce was probably still in the house somewhere. Unless she had escaped through the rear and was wandering the hedge maze like a lost, diaphanous apparition from a Victorian ghost story.

She made a circuit of the rooms they had been in, turning on lights as she went. The galleries, the parlours, the dining, reception and game rooms were all empty. From the floors above she could faintly hear the two men calling Sauce's name with no apparent success.

She saw a door leading from the dining hall. Towards the kitchen, she guessed. She opened it and nearly screamed herself as she came face to face with the forbidding visage of Mrs

Dorter, who regarded her impassively. She held a covered tray in one hand.

'I'm so sorry,' gasped Sparks. 'You gave me a fright.'

'What are you doing?' asked Mrs Dorter.

'I'm looking for my friend, Sauce,' said Sparks. 'I mean Nancy. Miss Spurlock. She was upset about something.'

'Screaming her bloody head off would be a more accurate description,' said Mrs Dorter. 'It's all right, Miss Sparks. I have her. I was just fetching something from the kitchen to soothe her nerves.'

'Oh, thank goodness,' said Sparks. 'Is she all right? I should go to her.'

'She doesn't want to see anyone at the moment,' said Mrs Dorter. 'She'll be fine. I'll take care of her. You and the gentlemen—'

There was something in her tone on that last word, thought Sparks. Something contemptuous.

'—should go back to bed,' continued Mrs Dorter. 'You have a busy day tomorrow.'

'But—'

'Goodnight, Miss Sparks,' said Mrs Dorter. 'Please be so kind as to extinguish all the lights you turned on. You're wasting the electricity.'

She passed by her, going through another door Sparks hadn't noticed before. Then Sparks heard her steps ascending.

A separate stairway to the servants' quarters, she guessed.

Her heart was still pounding, but she forced herself to retrace her path through the rooms to turn off the lights before she returned to the first-storey landing.

'Kevin! Tony!' she called. 'She's been found.'

Kevin appeared from the wing where she and Tony had been sleeping. Tony appeared a minute later, coming down from the second storey.

'Where is she?' he asked.

'Mrs Dorter found her,' said Sparks. 'She's taking care of her.'

'Good old Dorty,' said Kevin. 'Sauce is in good hands. Right, I'm turning back in.'

'Why does she need to be taken care of, Kevin?' asked Sparks.

'It's been a long night, Sparks,' said Kevin. 'Let's discuss things in the morning when we're sober and less frantic.'

'But—'

'Come on, Sparks,' said Tony, taking her hand. 'There's nothing more to do now.'

He pulled her hand. She resisted for a moment, then allowed him to take her across the landing.

'Oh, Tony?' called Kevin, watching them.

'Yes?' replied Tony, looking back over his shoulder.

'I noticed your bedclothes were undisturbed when I checked your room,' said Kevin.

'Did you?'

'Yes,' said Kevin, smiling approvingly. 'Good for you, lad.'

'Get some sleep, Picky,' said Tony.

Kevin disappeared. They returned to her room.

'I don't like this,' said Sparks.

'Whatever it is, we'll deal with it in the morning,' said Tony. 'I'm going to finish the night in my assigned bed, Sparks. Appearances and all that.'

'Appearances for whom?' she asked.

He smiled sadly, then left her, closing the door behind him.

She woke the next morning with a splitting headache. It took her a minute to identify her surroundings, then the events of the night before came back to her. She dressed quickly, then headed downstairs in search of Mrs Dorter. She found her in the kitchen stirring a pot of porridge.

'Good morning, Miss Sparks,' said the housekeeper.

'Good morning, Mrs Dorter,' said Sparks. 'How is Miss Spurlock?'

'Gone.'

'What? Where?'

'She decided that she would not attend the party after all,' said Mrs Dorter. 'She's taking the nine-twenty train to Kettering, then changing to a Cambridge train there.'

'Is she all right?'

'She said to tell you goodbye, and not to worry about anything.'

'Who is driving her to the station?' asked Sparks.

'Mr Danforth took her in Mr Cater's car.'

'Tony took her? Why not Bruce?'

'She preferred that Mr Danforth drive her,' said Mrs Dorter. 'Would you care for some breakfast? There are eggs and sausage in the breakfast room. I will bring out porridge momentarily.'

'Thank you,' said Sparks, who was still trying to absorb the information.

She went to the breakfast room, which had covered dishes and a tea service set on a sideboard by an oaken table, a bay window on the other side with a few of the gardens stretching out into the distance.

Kevin sat at the head of the table, the remains of his breakfast in front of him. He was sipping from a glass of orange juice which had been enhanced by a bottle of champagne standing by his plate.

'Ah, good, you're up,' he said. 'I thought Buck's Fizzes for this morning's hair of the dog. Care for one?'

'Care to tell me what happened last night?' she asked.

'Nothing happened last night,' he said, getting up to fetch a glass for her. 'Should be making these in flutes, I suppose, but I couldn't find any clean ones.'

'Why did she run off screaming if nothing happened?' asked Sparks. 'What did you do to her, Kevin?'

'You know how women get,' he said as he mixed her drink.

'I do, as a matter of fact,' she replied. 'Especially when they get like that. What happened? Why did she go back to Cambridge this morning?'

'You can ask her yourself on Monday,' said Kevin. 'She'll tell you the same thing.'

'I'll be certain to,' said Sparks. 'Why is Tony driving her to the station instead of Bruce?'

'Bruce still has a thick head from the evening's festivities. Tony was in the best shape of all of us,' he said. Then he leered at her. 'Of course, I expect you found that out for yourself last night.'

'Tony is the best man of all of you,' said Sparks.

'Debatable,' said Kevin. 'But you're not in any position to judge, are you?'

'Why not?'

'You're not really one of us, are you, Sparks?' he said, looking at her scornfully. 'The only reason you were invited is because Tony is besotted, or so he says, and you do seem like a lot of fun, although so far only he has been the beneficiary of that. But I hear you're ambitious, as well. Smart, they say. I'd like to see you act like a smart, ambitious woman now. Because if you do, things can go well for you.'

'And if I don't?'

'Then you'll find that there are influences in the tides of men that can swallow up the ambitions of even the smartest women,' said Kevin. 'A tenure at Cambridge is not guaranteed, and should old family forces intervene, you may never reach the finish line. So, that being said, I would like to throw a party tonight with a minimum of fuss and a maximum of fun. I'd rather see you on the fun side of that balance.'

He placed her drink in front of her, then held his up.

'Cheers,' he said.

She hesitated, then picked her glass up in salute and drank.

She was sitting on the front step when Tony returned. He got out of the Morris and walked up to her as she stood up, brushing the dust from her skirt.

'What did she tell you?' she asked him.

He looked at her, then over her through the doorway into the front hall.

'Let it go, Sparks,' he said. 'There's a party to set up.'

He walked past her and disappeared into the house.

London, 1947

'And then came twenty-four hours of nightmarish fun, which are all blurred together in a sort of Hogarthian haze in my memory,' said Iris, her hand pushing her tumbler forwards. 'On Sunday, we drove back to Cambridge.'

'Did you speak with Nancy about what happened?'

'I tried,' said Iris. 'She wouldn't talk to me about it. And that was it. Until they found her in the river.'

She started crying.

'Sauce couldn't swim,' she said. 'That's why she was on a bicycle when we raced the Bumps. She should never have—'

She cradled her head on her arms. Gwen came around and kneeled next to her, putting her arm around her.

'It wasn't your fault,' she whispered. 'None of it.'

Millie appeared in the doorway.

'Do you need any help, ma'am?' she asked.

'Miss Sparks will be taking the guest room tonight,' said Gwen. 'Will you get her other arm?'

'Right away,' said Millie, coming to help Gwen get Iris to her feet.

'I told you no one could make me talk if I didn't want to,' muttered Iris.

'I know, dear,' said Gwen as they guided her through the doorway. 'But you wanted to.'

Carruthers stood in the courtyard behind Grenville House, watching the lights go out in the various windows. When it was sufficiently dark, he went through the back door and climbed the stairs until he reached the fifth storey.

The door to Danforth's flat had been demolished by the fire brigade, but someone, he guessed the building's caretaker, had nailed several boards across the doorway. Carruthers did have identification on him that would have allowed him official entry had anyone poked their heads out of the nearby flats, but he preferred to make this visit as unofficial as possible.

He pulled a jimmy from inside his coat, then pried the bottom boards away. He was ready to flash the real-looking police warrant card if the noise roused the neighbours, but luck was with him. He shoved the boards into the foyer, then crouched down and crawled through. He stood once he was entirely in, pulled out a torch and flicked it on, playing the beam about the room.

The new furniture surprised him, stacked in the sitting room in their packing sheets, waiting to be unwrapped and set into place. Guess they came in after the investigations were done, he thought. Had to leave them somewhere. Nothing fancy, just what a bachelor would need to entertain cheaply. He noted the brands with an eye towards getting a piece or two for his own place, but work was calling.

There were scorch marks on the floor by the door leading to the bedroom. Must be where Danforth ended up, rolling to extinguish the flames before he passed out from the pain.

Carruthers walked through to the bedroom.

And there was the wreckage. Charred everything towards the window, water damage from the hoses, the wind coming in through the smashed windows. The remains of a bed burned down to charcoal. Some bits of books nearby, chunks of their corners left, the bindings now blackened and unreadable.

How the hell did Danforth survive this? he wondered.

But in the far corner away from the window was a steamer trunk nearly his own height. Badly singed outside, but relatively intact.

There didn't seem to have been much searching done. The fire brigade might have done a perfunctory investigation, looking for arson. And Scotland Yard might have done some poking around, but to them, Danforth was a victim, not a criminal.

To Carruthers he was a possible spy and a traitor, so he was going to be looking at the scene very differently. He popped the latches on the trunk and opened it. Danforth had been lucky in one sense: his clothes were untouched, albeit reeking of smoke. If he ever healed to the point of allowing wool or cotton to touch his skin, they were waiting for him.

It took him all of a minute to find the concealed compartment behind the suits, reinforced with thin steel plates, making it fireproof. He reached in and found a few sheets of paper. He held them up, shining his torch on them.

They contained arrays of handwritten numbers, all either two or three digits.

Code, he thought, and not one he recognised.

Well, well.

EIGHT

Iris woke up not recognizing the room she was sleeping in. It was not the first time that had happened, but there was no one else in the bed beside her, so that particular category of blackout adventure could be ruled out.

Her clothes from the previous day were neatly laid out on a chair by the bed, which further eliminated the possibility that she had allowed herself to be picked up by a man. She sat up, wincing as the hangover made its presence known, then swung her legs over the side of the bed.

The first clue to bring her back were the pyjama legs, which unrolled several inches past the bottoms of her feet.

Gwen, she thought. I'm wearing her pyjamas.

She rolled them up past her ankles, then lowered her feet to the floor. The windows were shuttered. She ignored the frantic warnings of the hangover and opened one. The view was of the rear gardens of Gwen's house with the greenhouse in one corner, beyond which a gate let out onto a common garden, available to the lucky ones who lived around it, hidden otherwise from the less fortunate denizens of the area. There were even birds singing, which she might have appreciated had not the hangover, already shrieking like a vampire in the daylight, begun to pound on the inside of her skull with one of those giant mallets from a high striker game.

It took a few seconds for the pounding to resolve itself into a gentle knocking on the door from outside.

'Come in,' she called.

Millie entered with a breakfast tray.

'Good morning, Miss Sparks,' she said. 'I've got aspirin and bicarbonate available should you need them.'

'Both, please,' said Iris. 'What's the hour?'

'Seven thirty. Mrs Bainbridge wishes to know if you would like to join her for her workout?'

'Not today, Millie. Thank her for asking.'

'Of course. There's a spare toothbrush on the dresser.'

Millie placed the tray on the bedside table, then slipped out, closing the door quietly.

The application of tea, toast and medicaments quelled the hangover down to a muffled sob. She grabbed the toothbrush and headed to the bathroom, then returned and changed.

My turn for the same outfit two days in a row, she thought. Serves me right for teasing her. And I didn't even have the fun to justify it.

Another rap on the door, a different rhythm this time and higher up.

'Yes, Gwen, I am alive and decent,' she called.

'Good morning,' said Gwen, opening the door. 'Do you need to borrow any make-up?'

'Let me take a look,' said Iris, stepping over to the mirror. 'No, I think I can pass for a human female today.'

'Do you want to swing by the *Cecilia* and change?'

'I don't want to be late,' said Iris. 'I'm setting you an example, after all.'

'I learn so much from you,' said Gwen. 'In that case, let's go.'

They headed downstairs, pinned on their hats, then walked out.

'How much did you learn from me last night?' asked Iris when they reached the relative anonymity of Edgware Road.

'Enough to consider a course of investigation,' said Gwen. 'If this were about avenging Nancy's death, then it would most likely be someone who was close to her. A family member, a friend, or a lover. Anyone come to mind?'

'I can't think of any man at Cambridge who would fit those descriptions,' said Iris. 'She wasn't in any serious relationships other than with Kevin, and that was over after that weekend.'

'What about women?' asked Gwen. 'Friends at Newnham?'

'She had friends, but there are regular friends, and there are the avenging-your-death sort of friends. I don't know that she had any of the latter at Newnham. Prior to Cambridge, I have no idea. Would you avenge my death if circumstances required it?'

'I would,' said Gwen with no hesitation. 'You?'

'Yes, darling. The difference being your method of vengeance would be to catch my killer and turn him over to the police, while mine . . .'

'Would be worthy of a Greek tragedy,' Gwen finished.

'I was leaning more towards the dinner scene in *Titus Andronicus*, but that's probably the hangover speaking.'

'I saw that play once,' said Gwen. 'The actress playing Lavinia was atrocious. We were all secretly relieved when they cut out her tongue.'

'And everyone thinks you're the nice one.'

'Hopefully, I'll keep on fooling them. All right, if it's not someone from Cambridge, then it may be someone from her family. Did you know them?'

'Not really. I met them a few times. They lived in Holland Park, but I don't know if they're still there.'

'Were they upper-class?'

'I think so, though I don't know where the money came from.'

'Then they may be out of town for the summer,' said Gwen. 'So there's her family to locate. And there are two other possible sources of information. One is Tony.'

'If he's up to speaking to me,' said Iris. 'Lord, an old friend is at death's door, and instead of offering comfort I need to inter-rogate him about an old tragedy while setting him up for further investigation as a possible spy. I am truly a despicable person.'

'Or you'll be saving him on two different fronts,' pointed out Gwen.

'Maybe. You mentioned a second possibility. Who?'

'The housekeeper at the Pickard house. Any idea if she's still there?'

'The Pickards loaned out the place during the war. It became a convalescent house for badly wounded soldiers. I don't know if she remained with it or not.'

'Well, I do have some connections to that area,' said Gwen. 'We stayed at Kimbolton Castle back in the thirties for a rather dreary ball or two. Thor, my brother, was friendly with Manchester's younger son from his first marriage, and—'

'Manchester?' interrupted Iris. 'Manchester's nowhere near Kimbolton.'

'I know, it makes no sense, but Lord Montagu was also the Duke of Manchester. I remember his second wife. Half his age, of course, and although she professed to have been an actress, I heard that her career consisted of exactly one small role in a West End comedy years before. She had come up as a tango dancer, though, and danced rather scandalously with one of the younger men while Manchester beamed proudly from the sidelines.'

'I wonder if Bruce Cater was at that party.'

'Maybe he was. Maybe I danced with him. Who knows? Manchester kept going in and out of bankruptcy, ending up in Wormwood Scrubs for pawning some jewels that actually belonged to the estate before the Lords of Appeal let him off. I heard he recently sold Kimbolton Castle for debts. In any case, let me do my aristocratic magic on the telephone and track down the Pickards. You said there was a sister named Lucinda?'

'Yes. I slept in her room.'

'Then that should be enough for me.'

As they turned off Oxford Street towards the building holding their offices, Gwen spotted a familiar figure standing by the doorway.

'That's Miss Lowle,' she said.

'I see her,' said Iris.

The younger woman waited for them, her expression perturbed.

'Miss Sparks, may I have a moment of your time?' she asked.

'Do you need me?' asked Mrs Bainbridge.

'No,' said Sparks. 'Go on up. I'll be with you soon.'

Mrs Bainbridge went inside. Sparks waited until the door closed, then turned to Miss Lowle.

'What is it?' she asked.

'Could we walk while we speak?' Lowle requested.

'Fine,' said Sparks.

Lowle no longer had the overconfident air of their previous encounters. Her face, despite the make-up, looked drawn.

'They told me you were going to ask Tony if he'd see me,' she began.

'You may refer to him as Mr Danforth with me,' said Sparks.

'Yes. I was told that last night. If I see him, I will make sure to ask him. Oh, and I had to give your name and number to the investigating detective, so expect a call from him today. Is that all?'

'Yes. Well, no.'

'What else?'

'Did we do this?' Lowle blurted out. 'I mean, did someone from–from our side do this to him?'

'I wouldn't know,' said Sparks. 'I'm not in that particular loop.'

'But do you think— is that the sort of thing that they would do?' asked Miss Lowle.

'"They"?' echoed Sparks. 'You're one of them now, remember? Yes, Miss Lowle, they are fully capable of doing something like this. Or even worse. And they may call upon you to do things of a similar nature. Was this not explained to you when you joined up?'

'Did you ever do anything like this?' she asked.

'What I did is classified,' said Sparks.

'You did do something, then,' said Lowle. 'How did you get through it? How did you live with it afterwards?'

'Who says I did?' asked Sparks.

'Miss Sparks, please,' said Lowle. 'I'm asking for your advice. As someone who's been there.'

Sparks looked at the younger woman. Lowle looked on the verge of tears. Sparks thought back to the disasters in her own career, how they had nearly destroyed her. And she had been about Lowle's age when they happened.

'Get through this assignment,' she said, relenting. 'The worst part has already happened, and it had nothing to do with you. When it's over, take a good, hard look at what you did, and whether it was worth doing. This fight will be fought whether or not you're going to be part of it, but you don't have to be the one sacrificing your happiness for it. Because that's what you'll be doing. And if you decide it's not worth the price, you're still early enough in your career to take a different path.'

'Thank you, Miss Sparks,' said Lowle, pulling out a handkerchief and dabbing at her eyes. 'I don't know if I'm ready for this.'

'No one is the first time,' said Sparks.

'I guess if it doesn't work out I've already signed up for you to find me a husband,' she said with a sad laugh.

'Mr Lonsdale may still be available,' said Sparks.

'Anyone but him,' said Lowle. 'Thank you, Miss Sparks. For everything. I'll await your call.'

She walked away. Sparks watched her, then turned and headed for The Right Sort.

Gwen was on the telephone when she got to their office. She waved Iris in.

'That's with two Ls?' she was asking, writing something down. 'And her husband is Jeremy? Got it. Thank you so much, Bella. Kisses to Henry and the girls.'

She hung up.

'I've located Lucinda Pickard, and it only took me three calls,' she said. 'She's Mrs Jeremy Kendall now and lives in Holland Park. Nancy Spurlock's family is still there as well, so we could kill two birds. Rather nice neighbourhood. You do know some fabulously wealthy people for an aspiring socialist.'

'Including you, darling,' said Iris.

'How did things go with Miss Lowle?'

'She was badly shaken by what happened to Tony,' said Iris. 'Her first time being blooded on the job. I almost got the feeling she was looking to me as a mentor.'

'She could do worse,' said Gwen. 'I hear someone coming up the steps. Let's continue this later.'

A moment later, Parham knocked on their door.

Mrs Bainbridge took one look at him and said, 'You need tea. Immediately.'

'I wouldn't say no,' he said as Sparks buzzed for Mrs Billington.

'Tea for three, please, Mrs Billington,' she said when their secretary appeared. 'Please sit, Detective Superintendent. You look like you've had a night and a half.'

'I had forgot what it was like to sit by a man's bedside all night, waiting to see if he'll wake,' he said, collapsing into the chair. 'It reminds me why I sought promotion: so I could sit in a more comfortable office and delegate that task to younger men.'

'How is he?' asked Sparks.

'He made it through the night,' said Parham. 'No telling how he'll do after that.'

'Did he say anything?'

'He did, finally,' said Parham. 'He didn't see the bottle coming. He had opened the window and was walking away when the explosion hit.'

'No idea as to who might have done it?'

'None, unfortunately,' said Parham.

'We've had one,' said Mrs Bainbridge.

'Have you?' he asked in surprise. 'Why would The Right Sort have any information on an attack on Danforth?'

'It's vague and tentative,' said Mrs Bainbridge. 'And it's more for Miss Sparks to tell than me.'

'What is it?' he asked.

'This goes back many years,' said Sparks. 'There was an incident at Cambridge.'

She gave an abbreviated version of the death of Nancy Spurlock and the events around it. Mrs Billington appeared with the tea tray a few minutes in and poured for the three, then left. Parham sipped his absent-mindedly while listening to Sparks. Partway through her narrative he pulled out his notebook and jotted a few things down, which she found encouraging. When she was done, he looked at his notes.

'Can you recall when her body was found?' he asked.

'Mid-May,' she said. 'I don't remember the exact date.'

'And the young men – did they leave England immediately?'

'No,' said Sparks. 'Pickard went on an extended holiday when the term ended. He had graduated, so there was nothing unusual about that. Bruce Cater and Tony Danforth left for Spain in September.'

'You mentioned the possibility of a letter left behind by this Miss Spurlock. When was that?'

'Rumours started circulating about it at the end of the term, but nothing concrete was announced by the police or the university.'

'In that case, it seems to me that had someone wished to

seek revenge on her behalf, they would have had time to do so back then,' said Parham. 'And whatever may have happened to her, and you still don't know what it was, I would think that Mr Danforth would not be a target, as opposed to the other two.'

'I agree with you on that last point,' said Sparks.

'I'll ring the Cambridge police, see if they have anything in that file, but it doesn't sound all that promising to me. I'm going to concentrate my efforts here.'

'Have you found anything else to go on?' asked Mrs Bainbridge.

'We've knocked on doors of the buildings across the street,' said Parham. 'But nobody was looking out their windows to see any shadowy figure heaving a flaming bottle at the time it happened. Mr Danforth could not think of anyone who might want to harm him. He did mention one interesting detail, though.'

'What?' asked Sparks.

'He had only just moved into that flat,' said Parham. 'He hadn't given his new address to the Foreign Office yet. Which means besides the building management at Grenville House, there was only one other place that knew it.'

'Where was that?' asked Sparks.

'He gave it to us, Iris,' said Mrs Bainbridge quietly. 'When we interviewed him.'

'Exactly so,' said Parham. 'Did either of you mention it to anyone?'

'No,' said Mrs Bainbridge.

'Absolutely not,' said Sparks. 'Why would we?'

'No idea,' admitted Parham. 'I will ask your secretary as well. Oh, and I'll need the contact information for the woman who had the date with him.'

'I have that here,' said Mrs Bainbridge, opening a file box on her desk containing the index cards for their female clients and pulling Miss Lowle's from it. She copied down her information and handed it to him.

'That's her office number,' she advised him. 'She's with the Ministry of Food.'

'Thanks,' said Parham. 'Did you happen to notice if your doors were unlocked in any of the mornings since you interviewed Danforth?'

'They weren't,' said Sparks. 'But these locks are not unpickable by any stretch of the imagination.'

'I happen to know you are speaking with some expertise on that topic,' he said. 'Very well. I'm going to grab a kip, then continue on. My higher-ups would like a quick result in this one. Oh, I almost forgot. Mr Danforth would be most grateful for a visit from Miss Sparks. I have placed your name on the visitors' list.'

'Thank you,' said Sparks. 'I'll go and see him later today.'

'Miss Sparks and I plan to keep looking into the Cambridge aspects,' said Mrs Bainbridge.

'Be my guests,' said Parham. 'Let me know if you turn up anything useful.'

'You're not going to tell us not to get involved?' she asked.

'When has that ever stopped you?' he asked. 'Thank you for the tea, ladies.'

He left. Iris buzzed for Mrs Billington, who appeared a minute later, the morning's correspondence in her hand.

'What's on the schedule for today?' asked Iris.

'There's a Mr Mellon coming in for an interview at eleven,' replied Mrs Billington. 'Other than that, nothing.'

'I can take Mr Mellon while you go to the hospital,' offered Gwen. 'Then call me when you're done, and we can go to Holland Park after.'

'Who's in Holland Park?' asked Mrs Billington.

'Some old ghosts,' said Iris.

'They must be old ghosts with old money,' said Mrs Billington. 'I'll keep the rest of the day's schedule clear, then.'

'Thank you, Saundra,' said Gwen.

The doors of the hospital lift opened on the floor holding the intensive care ward. The nurse at the desk consulted a list, then directed Sparks down a corridor. The room wasn't hard to spot. It was the one with the police constable standing by the door.

He verified her ID, matching it to a list of his own.

'I think he's awake, Miss Sparks,' he said softly. 'Be prepared. It's going to be a bit of a shock.'

'Thank you,' she said.

Then she took a deep breath and went in.

He was lying on his stomach, his back and legs a mass of bandages, more covering his head, leaving only the eyes and mouth free. A tube running from an intravenous bottle dripped fluid into one arm. Other tubes ran out of him for purposes she preferred not to know. Her mind immediately summoned up images of Archie lying on what turned out to be his deathbed in London Hospital, also a mass of tubes, but at least in that case it was still recognizably him. Here, it could have been almost anyone underneath all of that, were it not for the eyes, which were unmistakably Tony's.

And they were open and looking at her. One hand lifted from the mattress in a feeble half-wave.

'Hey,' he croaked.

'Hey,' she returned, pulling a chair over to his bedside and placing her hand gently on his.

'How do I look?' he asked.

'Like Claude Rains before he unwrapped himself in *The Invisible Man*,' said Sparks.

'Drat,' he said. 'I was going for Karloff in *The Mummy*. Thanks for coming, Sparks.'

'Of course,' she said. 'I tried yesterday, but you weren't receiving callers yet.'

'How'd you hear about it?'

'You made the afternoon papers. Sally Danielli rang me when he saw the article.'

'Danielli's still hanging about?'

'Very much so. In fact, he's dating Gwen now.'

'The Titan is dating your partner,' he said. 'That must be painful for you to watch.'

'Sometimes,' she said. 'Mostly, it's awkward. But let's not talk about me. How are you feeling?'

'Like I'm floating on a cloud of candyfloss,' he said. 'If I had known narcotics were this much fun I would have started using them years ago. I'm so glad you're here, Sparks. I wanted to apologise to you.'

'For what?'

'I was supposed to call you after my date with Miss Lowle. I was distracted from that task.'

'I was sitting by the telephone all day, you know.'

'Well, here is my report. I liked her.'

'I'm so glad,' said Sparks, keeping her tone light and smile bright. 'What about her did you like?'

'She reminded me of you in many ways, strangely enough.'

'That's why Gwen chose her,' said Sparks. 'She thought the same thing. I confess I don't see the resemblance, but self-appraisal has never been one of my better qualities. Miss Lowle came by the office this morning, by the way. She had heard about what happened. She was very upset.'

'I can imagine,' he said. 'I suppose this will take me out of the running for the near future. Please give her my regrets.'

'As a matter of fact, she wanted to come visit you,' said Sparks.

'I can't have her see me like this,' he said. 'Even if I pull through—'

'You will,' she said determinedly.

'Even if I do, God only knows what I will look like,' he said.

'Now, you listen to me, Tony,' she said. 'We have had many men as clients at The Right Sort who were injured by the war. You are not even the first burn victim. There are women among our clientele who look past mere appearances, and we have made successful matches with them.'

'Is Miss Lowle one of these superior women?' he asked.

'It remains to be seen,' said Sparks. 'If she isn't, I will make every effort to find you one who is. But she did ask to see you, already knowing this happened.'

'She does like to take the initiative,' he said. 'Tell her I'm not ready yet, but to be patient and wait for me. Tell her I need time to get my hair done and pick out a hat that will match this outfit.'

'I will,' promised Sparks, laughing. 'And I know you're going to recover because your sense of humour is still intact.'

He laughed briefly, which triggered a sudden coughing fit, which in turn must have caused him pain, for she could see tears running from his eyes, dampening the bandages.

'You poor thing,' she whispered. 'Who did this to you? Tell me, so I can hunt him down myself.'

'Will you? Have you become an avenging angel in your spare time, Sparks?'

'A girl needs a hobby,' she said. 'Any ideas?'

'None,' he said. 'It's all so bizarre. I survived Spain, I survived the world war, and I survived what I did in China, then I finally make it back to the peace and safety of London, and this happens.'

'I was wondering, and this will sound far-fetched . . .'

'What, Sparks?'

'Do you think it might have anything to do with what happened to Sauce back in Cambridge? Someone else's avenging angel, perhaps.'

He went silent. She waited.

'Oddly enough, that whole sad tale has been preying on my mind since I woke up here,' he said finally.

'Why?'

'I keep thinking about poor old Catey,' he said. 'He never really cared about the cause. He liked being rich. But he thought Spain would be some glorious adventure, maybe with a chance to redeem his soul.'

'So he thought he needed redemption,' she said. 'Do you think he found it in the end?'

'I know you're no believer, Sparks,' said Tony. 'But Catey— after Sauce drowned, he started quoting all the sermons from his childhood that he used to make fun of. The ones promising everlasting hellfire. When I suggested joining the fight, he jumped at it. Yet in the end, the fire found him anyway.'

'Excuse me, miss,' said a nurse standing at the door. 'We have to take him for another treatment.'

'I'll come back tomorrow,' said Sparks, patting his hand.

When she emerged from the lift, she saw the Brigadier's man in the reception area. He was wearing a hospital porter's outfit this time, but made no attempt to conceal himself, nodding as she noticed him. She raised an eyebrow in response, and he jerked his head over to a row of telephone boxes. She followed him.

'No kissing this time,' she said.

'I imagine that would have been fairly painful for him,' he commented as he stepped into one of the boxes. 'I'm here to make sure you report right away.'

He dropped a coin into the slot, then dialled a number, using his body to conceal the telephone from her as he did so. He waited for it to ring. A voice answered at the other end.

'I have her with me, sir,' he said. 'I'm putting her on now.'

He stepped out of the box and handed her the telephone. She stepped inside and closed the folding door. He walked away as she did.

'Sparks here,' she said.

'Did he agree to Miss Lowle's visit?' the Brigadier asked immediately.

'Not yet,' said Sparks. 'I did broach the subject, but he's in fairly bad shape at the moment. He wants a few days before he sees her.'

'A pity,' said the Brigadier. 'Morphine can be very helpful in these situations. Did he say anything else useful?'

'No. He doesn't have any idea about who did this. Sir, if we didn't do it, then maybe someone from the other side did, which would mean Tony isn't working for them. Have you considered that?'

'Of course, I have,' said the Brigadier. 'Why do you think I stationed a man in the hospital?'

'Am I supposed to believe that's for his protection, not to see who might try to contact him?'

'It's for both,' said the Brigadier. 'Another possibility to be considered is that Danforth had been a double agent, but quit. They might consider him either a loose end or a loose cannon.'

'Then wouldn't he come to us to tell us?'

'And risk life in prison? Hardly.'

'He could trade information for his safety.'

'We would be amenable to that discussion, Sparks,' said the

Brigadier. 'But I still think he's in league with them. Now more than ever.'

'Why so?'

'We found some coded messages in his flat,' said the Brigadier. 'Not in his handwriting. Our cypher team is going at them, but it appears to be a book code, and those are difficult to crack without the source. Miss Lowle suggested we try the copy of Thucydides that he purchased at Maggs Brothers, which was a smart idea, but it wasn't that, nor was it the language book he bought with it. Even so, there's no good reason for him to be in possession of those messages.'

'Won't he notice they're missing when he gets out?'

'We don't anticipate his release from medical treatment for some time, Sparks. We'll cross that bridge when we come to it. In the meanwhile, will you be visiting him again?'

'Yes, sir.'

'Get him to agree to Miss Lowle's visit.'

'I'll do my best, sir.'

He hung up.

He never asked me to try and get the information from him, she thought.

He doesn't trust me. Or he thinks I'm compromised.

Maybe I am.

She rang her office.

'Saundra, it's Iris,' she said. 'Could you put Gwen on?'

A moment later, her partner came on the line.

'How is Tony?' she asked.

'In bad shape,' said Iris. 'Not at death's door, but down the hall from it.'

'I'm so sorry, Iris,' said Gwen. 'How are you doing?'

'Distraught, aggravated, guilt-ridden – any number of horrible feelings jumbled together.'

'Is your head clear enough to investigate this?'

'I'll meet you at Marble Arch in twenty,' said Iris. 'We can take the bus to Holland Park from there.'

'On my way,' said Gwen.

NINE

'How do you want to approach this?' asked Gwen as they got off the Number 12 bus.

'You are going to be Deborah Lawrence,' said Iris.

'All right. Who is she?'

'Someone who was at Newnham with me.'

'Why is she here with you now?'

'We're organising a Newnham event. The real Deborah married an American soldier and is now living in the States, so no danger of her actually showing up. She wasn't close to Nancy, so the Spurlocks wouldn't know her.'

'I see. And who are you going to be?'

'I'm going to be me.'

'Why do you get to be you, but I don't get to be me?'

'They might recognise Deborah's name as a Newnham student even if they've never met her. It will give you more plausibility than being Mrs Gwendolyn Bainbridge, who has been in the newspapers solving murders occasionally.'

'As have you.'

'Yes, but I actually met the Spurlocks a few times back then, so they will more likely make the Newnham connection. I'll take the lead, you observe and pop in with any questions you come up with.'

The Spurlock residence was on Holland Villas Road. They passed one stately Victorian house after another, finally coming to one set back from a low brick wall with pillars placed at even intervals. There were covered holes along the top of the wall between the pillars, showing where the iron fence had been before it had been removed and donated to the war effort. The two women walked up the steps under the portico and rang the bell.

A minute later, a maid opened it.

'May I help you?' she asked.

'Good morning,' said Sparks. 'I am Miss Iris Sparks and

this is Miss Deborah Lawrence. We are with the Newnham College Alumnae Association. We were wondering if Mr or Mrs Spurlock was at home today.'

'May I ask what this is in reference to?'

'There is an upcoming event at Newnham, and we wished to speak with them about the remembrance portion.'

'Mrs Spurlock is in,' said the maid. 'Please come into the sitting room, and I will ask if she is able to see you.'

'Thank you,' said Sparks.

The sitting room was to the left. The furniture was old but well-cared for. The two women sat side by side on a sofa upholstered with a burgundy brocade, with cushions covered in an autumnal print of brown, orange and red leaves.

They rose as the maid returned, followed by a woman in her early sixties. Her grey hair was plaited unevenly and bound into an untidy bun. She was wearing a dark grey frock that stopped a few shades short of full mourning, but was funereal in appearance nonetheless except for a brilliant diamond brooch pinned over her heart.

'How do you do?' she said. 'I am Mrs Florinda Spurlock. Miss Sparks, I believe you were a friend of my late daughter, Nancy.'

'I was, Mrs Spurlock,' said Sparks. 'This is my friend and Newnham classmate, Miss Deborah Lawrence.'

'How do you do, Mrs Spurlock?' said Mrs Bainbridge.

'How do you do,' replied Mrs Spurlock. 'Were you also a friend of my daughter?'

'I was not,' said Mrs Bainbridge. 'I knew who she was, of course, but we were not close at the time. I regret not getting to know her better.'

'You were kind enough to attend the funeral, Miss Sparks,' said Mrs Spurlock. 'One of the few from Newnham, in fact.'

'I was, Mrs Spurlock,' said Sparks. 'Nancy was a good friend, and I miss her to this day.'

'Lottie mentioned something about a memorial.'

'Yes,' said Sparks. 'I don't know if you've been following events at Cambridge, but a report recommending that Newnham and Girton be given full status as colleges within the university was issued last month. We anticipate that the proposal will be put to a vote by the proctors before the end of the year. We are optimistic that it will pass, aren't we, Deborah?'

'Long overdue, in my opinion,' said Mrs Bainbridge.

'So we anticipate a formal celebration next year. Some of us were talking about all the Newnham girls who sadly did not live to see this, and it was suggested that there be some form of memorial established in their honour. I thought of Nancy, of course.'

'Why?' asked Mrs Spurlock.

'Because of her passing, and—' began Sparks.

'Why should that wicked girl's memory be prolonged any further?' said Mrs Spurlock, her expression darkening.

There was a moment of awkward silence.

'I never thought of her as wicked,' said Sparks, recovering.

'No, I expect you wouldn't,' snapped Mrs Spurlock. 'You were very much the same way.'

'We were young,' said Sparks.

'You were supposedly intelligent, though. Weren't you? Smart enough to think that the world couldn't ruin you.'

'We were smart enough to think that we needed an education to change it,' said Sparks.

'A fat lot of good that did you,' said Mrs Spurlock. 'The world is still decaying by the minute. Not that I think for a second that improving it was ever my daughter's goal.'

'What were her goals back then?' asked Mrs Bainbridge.

'To leave the course of protection and tutelage that I had arranged for her, and to go to a place with no limits and no proper supervision,' said Mrs Spurlock. 'I told her father over and over that university was no place for a girl, but she was the apple of his eye and could do no wrong. She needed to stretch her wings and soar, he said. And, as I predicted, she flew too close to the sun and fell. I should have stopped her from going, but I didn't have the courage to stand up to him. I failed her. She died, and I have lived with that failure ever since.'

'Perhaps we could speak to Mr Spurlock if this is too upsetting for you,' said Mrs Bainbridge.

'He is away,' said Mrs Spurlock. 'He has been away for some time. He's in Guiana, working for the Booker Group.'

'I'm so sorry,' said Mrs Bainbridge. 'You must be lonely here.'

'I have the Good Book and my faith to sustain me,' said Mrs Spurlock. 'I pray for my daughter's soul every day, as well as my own.'

'Is there anything you could tell us for the memorial?' asked Sparks. 'I would like to pay some tribute to her. She was my friend, after all.'

'She died in shame,' said Mrs Spurlock. 'You may engrave that upon your plaque if you wish.'

'That was never established,' said Sparks. 'It may have been an accident. The coroner's verdict—'

'The coroner's verdict was what we and the authorities wished it to be,' said Mrs Spurlock. 'But I know the truth. She drowned herself.'

'Do you know why?' asked Mrs Bainbridge.

'Because she carried the fruits of her sinfulness within her,' said Mrs Spurlock.

'She was pregnant?'

'She was, and will burn in everlasting hellfire, all because she wouldn't follow the true path that the Lord set before us.'

'Did she say who the father was?'

'She said nothing to us. We only learned of her condition after the autopsy. It wouldn't have mattered. It was God's justice.'

'You had no interest in justice for her?' asked Sparks.

'Vengeance is mine, I will repay, saith the Lord,' she replied. 'I would not be so arrogant as to usurp His will. My daughter reaped what she sowed. So you see, ladies, why I have absolutely no interest in keeping any memory of her alive any longer. Let her story die with me. I am sorry you wasted your time. Lottie! You may show them out now.'

'Once again, I am sorry for your loss, Mrs Spurlock,' said Sparks as she got to her feet.

'You and your daughter will be in my prayers tonight,' added Mrs Bainbridge.

Mrs Spurlock nodded to them briefly, then left the room without saying anything further.

Lottie, the maid, walked them to the front door. She looked quickly around the hall to make certain that her mistress was out of sight, then whispered, 'Please know that despite your reception, I'm sure she appreciated your visit. She doesn't get many visitors any more. Not since Mr Spurlock left her.'

'It's like that, is it?' said Sparks.

'They say he has another woman in Guiana,' she said. 'And another daughter with her. The new apple of his eye.'

'Then may God have mercy upon all of them,' said Mrs Bainbridge. 'I will come visit again. Thank you.'

They left, waiting until they had gone past several houses before speaking again.

'There were no brothers or sisters?' asked Gwen.

'None,' said Iris. 'They put all of their hopes and dreams on her. She told me once that the pressure was almost unbearable.'

'Did you know she was pregnant when she drowned?'

'No,' said Iris. 'I did not.'

'I can understand how, having betrayed her father's trust and her mother's faith, the poor girl felt she had no other recourse,' said Gwen.

'There were other options available,' said Iris. 'She never looked for them.'

'If she was with child, I would think she would have at least confronted the man responsible,' said Gwen.

'Maybe she did,' said Iris. 'Maybe his refusal to help or accept responsibility sent her into the river.'

'Do you suppose he could have pushed her in himself?' asked Gwen.

'It's a thought, isn't it?' replied Iris. 'It's crossed my mind more than once over the years. But if Kevin or Bruce did it, they're gone beyond the reach of any justice, earthly or otherwise.'

'And Mrs Spurlock seems content to let justice rest in God's hands, while the father has moved on to greener plantations across the seas. Which, if smiting there be, doesn't explain the recent hellfire visited upon Tony.'

'It doesn't sound like it came from this quarter, in any event. Fine. Let's continue on.'

Gwen looked back at the Spurlock house for a moment, a sad, compassionate expression on her face.

'What is it?' asked Iris.

'I was thinking how rattling around a big place by yourself could turn a woman into what Mrs Spurlock has become,' said Gwen. 'That could be me once Ronnie has grown up and taken over as Lord Bainbridge.'

'It could be worse,' said Iris. 'She could be rattling around in a much smaller place with no money and no servants. And you, if anything, are getting progressively saner as you get older.'

'I hope so,' said Gwen.

The Kendall home was a smaller affair on St James's Gardens, down from the church. It was a three-storey townhouse, more in proportion with the number of people living in it which included several small children, if the number of small bicycles leaning against the railings of the front steps was any indication.

'This time, I will take the lead,' said Gwen. 'And I am going to be me. I rang earlier for an appointment. You may still be you, though.'

Lucinda Kendall, née Pickard, answered the door herself. She was somewhere in her late thirties, but clearly took great pains to conceal that fact from the casual observer. She was wearing a black rayon bijou dress with floral borders that looked both stylish and comfortable. She herself looked flustered, the cause most likely being the high-pitched screams and ongoing mayhem that echoed from somewhere in the depths of the house. She looked at the two women blankly for a moment, then her face lit up in recognition.

'Mrs Bainbridge, right?' she said. 'You called earlier. Sorry, many distractions, forgot all about it. Do come in.'

'Is this a bad time?' asked Mrs Bainbridge as they were showed into the front sitting room.

'There are no good times, and God knows I could use the break,' said Mrs Kendall. 'Let me tell nanny to chain the little beasts inside the playroom and I'll be right back.'

They sat where she directed them, listening as they heard her indistinct shouts followed by a chorus of protests, finally muffled by the closing of a door.

'Why exactly do you want more children?' asked Iris.

'Not every moment is like this,' said Gwen.

Mrs Kendall reappeared.

'Forgive me, they have a load of friends over, and they are re-enacting the Charge of the Light Brigade, complete with horses,' she said with a laugh. 'I've sent Kitty to fetch us some lemonade from the kitchen. Unless you want something with more of a kick? Please tell me you do.'

'Whatever you're drinking is fine with us,' said Mrs Bainbridge.

Mrs Kendall got up and leaned into the hallway.

'Kitty!' she shouted. 'Cancel the lemonade and bring a bottle of whatever's cold and white, would you?'

There was a distant acknowledgment of the change, and she returned, sinking into an armchair.

'Thank God you're here,' she said. 'It gives me a reason to be social. Either of you have children?'

'One son,' said Mrs Bainbridge. 'He's in the country with his grandparents at the moment.'

'Lucky you,' said Mrs Kendall. 'My parents have a place, a huge one, in fact, but it's on loan to His Majesty at the moment. I know you from somewhere, Mrs Bainbridge, don't I? Before the war? What was your family name?'

'Brewster.'

'I was right! You're Thor's little sister, aren't you?' said Mrs Kendall. 'I may have dated your brother once or twice back then, I can't recall. Good-looking man. Still with us?'

'He is.'

'Still good-looking?'

'A sister is never the one to ask that, but others seem to think so,' said Mrs Bainbridge.

'Glad to hear it,' said Mrs Kendall. 'I say, aren't you the one who cracked up and got sent away?'

'When my husband was killed in the war, I went through a difficult period,' replied Mrs Bainbridge evenly.

There was a loud crash from upstairs, followed by multiple wailings.

'That must have been nice, actually,' said Mrs Kendall, glancing upwards. 'I wouldn't mind having a holiday in the country lolling about in my pyjamas all day.'

'It wasn't as much fun as it sounds,' said Mrs Bainbridge.

'No, I suppose not. Oh, goodness, I haven't properly introduced myself to your friend, have I? Forgive me, I'm Mrs Jeremy Kendall, but please call me Lucinda.'

'How do you do?' replied Sparks. 'Miss Iris Sparks, and thank you for seeing us.'

'Not at all, it's lovely to be speaking to some fully grown humans at this time of day,' said Mrs Kendall.

A housemaid came in with an opened bottle of Riesling in a silver ice bucket along with three wine glasses. Mrs Kendall filled the glasses and handed them around.

'To adult conversation,' she said, then she took a long sip and sighed contentedly. 'I believe you said on the telephone that it was a personal matter, Gwen?'

'I did. A mission of mercy for a friend.'

'That sounds rather serious,' said Mrs Kendall, looking back and forth between the partners.

'I'm afraid so,' said Mrs Bainbridge. 'He recently returned from a long sojourn overseas, but unfortunately met up with a severe accident. He's in extremis, I'm sorry to say, and was hoping to be reunited with some of his old friends while he still may. I've been trying to locate them. Iris was a classmate of his, and recalled that one of his friends had some older sisters, which led us to you. We were hoping that you might know where we could find your brother.'

'My brother?' exclaimed Mrs Kendall. 'Do you mean Kevin?'

'Yes,' said Sparks.

'You mean you haven't heard?'

'Heard? Heard what?'

'Oh, dear, I could have saved you the trip,' said Mrs Kendall. 'Kevin died at Anzio back in '44.'

'Kevin's dead?' cried Sparks. 'Oh, no!'

She burst into tears as Mrs Bainbridge turned to her in alarm. 'Iris, are you all right?'

'Sorry, sorry,' sobbed Sparks, pulling a handkerchief from her bag. 'I didn't know about Kevin. We were friends in Cambridge. More than friends briefly.'

'Ah,' said Mrs Kendall, nodding sympathetically. 'One of those. He cut quite the swathe through the female populace for a while.'

'God, I had no idea I would react like that,' said Sparks, wiping her eyes. 'It was rather a torrid— no, I shouldn't say it. You're his sister.'

'No, it's all right,' Mrs Kendall assured him. 'I've heard many such stories about my baby brother. I consider your tears a tribute to his, ah . . . let's say his virtues.'

'I still remember sitting across the breakfast table from him at your house, thinking what a gorgeous man he was,' said Sparks.

'You were at our house?'

'Oh, yes,' said Sparks. 'He threw a party, when was it? Spring of '36, I think. He had the whole massive place to himself.'

'Oh, you were at *that* party?'

'You heard about it?'

'Not in great detail,' said Mrs Kendall. 'But word reached Daddy, and there was quite the to-do when he came back.'

'Sounds like it must have been some bash,' said Mrs Bainbridge. 'Were there frequent parties back then?'

'Oh, Kevin took full advantage of being a Pickard while the parents were away, which was a frequent occurrence, thank God,' said Mrs Kendall. 'We all did, I suppose. They weren't particularly concerned with our upbringing once they had us, especially when they finally manufactured a son and heir after the disappointments of two daughters, so we had free rein back then.'

'Why do you think this particular party drew your father's ire, then?'

'You know, I never really heard the full story,' said Mrs Kendall, sipping her wine. 'We heard Daddy roaring in his study, then Kevin emerged from that little father–son tête-à-tête with his beaten-puppy expression and didn't say a word. The next day, he packed his trunk and was off on an extended world tour.'

'Um, my name didn't come up by any chance, did it?' asked Sparks.

'Not that I've heard,' said Mrs Kendall. 'I don't believe I ever knew your name before today. In any case, that was years ago, and he's no longer around with any reputation to besmirch, so you're quite safe.'

'I'm relieved,' said Sparks. 'Gosh, I should write your parents a note now that I know about his passing. Do you have their current address?'

'I'll get it for you,' said Mrs Kendall.

'Is that housekeeper of yours still there?' asked Sparks. 'I'd like to write to her as well.'

'Mrs Dorter? No, she's not with the family any more. I'm surprised you remember her.'

'She was very kind to me that weekend,' said Sparks. 'And she made a wonderfully effective hangover cure. I'd love to get her recipe. Hangovers are still a regular part of my existence. Where is she now?'

'She's running an inn somewhere,' said Mrs Kendall. 'Daddy helped set her up with it, in fact.'

'Very generous of him,' said Sparks.

'Yes, uncharacteristically so,' said Mrs Kendall. 'But she'd been with us forever, so I guess he felt he owed it to her. It was that same year, now that I think of it, towards the end of the summer. She was tired of keeping that enormous place ready for whenever one of us showed up. Can't blame her, really. I was surprised Daddy let her go, she had been with us for ages. Wait here, I'll be back in a sec.'

She left, and they listened to her footsteps ascending the stairs.

'How long after Nancy's death did Kevin leave England?' asked Gwen.

'Beginning of the summer,' said Iris. 'So maybe a month or two after.'

'I wonder what happened in the interim to trigger that decision,' said Gwen. 'It had to have been more than just his father's anger over a party. Hold that thought. I hear her coming.'

Mrs Kendall returned with a piece of paper, which she handed to Sparks.

'There's Mummy and Daddy's current address, no idea if they're home or travelling,' she said, pointing to the top. 'And there's Mrs Dorter's inn. It's outside of Bradford-on-Avon, which is outside of Bath. Middle of nowhere, really, but I imagine it's nice and quiet.'

A series of crashes emanated from the upper floor. Mrs Kendall glanced upwards.

'I could use some quiet,' she said, refilling her wine glass. 'Maybe I'll book a month there and let her take care of me again. I must thank you for this lovely interval, ladies. It was very much needed. Oh! You never told me who your friend in hospital is.'

'Tony Danforth,' said Sparks. 'He was great friends with Kevin.'

'Tony's back? I had no idea. I haven't seen him since he and Bruce Cater took off to Spain together. Poor Bruce! Well, break it to Tony about Kevin, and give him my best, would you?'

'We will,' said Mrs Bainbridge. 'Thank you for seeing us.'

A cacophony of shrieks sounded from upstairs, then every child in the building began to cry.

'Mrs Kendall, I could use some assistance,' called the nanny.

'I'd better go check for casualties,' said Mrs Kendall, downing the remainder of her wine in a single gulp, then getting to her feet. 'I guess that makes me Florence Nightingale in this scenario. Please show yourselves out, would you?'

'Good luck,' said Mrs Bainbridge.

They parted in the hall, Mrs Kendall dashing up the stairs. A moment later, they heard her shout, 'C'est magnifique, mais ce n'est pas la guerre!'

'Maybe not that many children,' said Gwen, looking after her thoughtfully. 'Let's go.'

It was late afternoon when they regained the street. Gwen glanced at her watch.

'No point in going back to the office,' she said. 'I told Saundra to close at four. Shall we walk to Dr Milford's? We can compare notes along the way.'

'Fine,' said Iris. 'What did you think of our new friend, Lucinda?'

'She doesn't seem overly mournful over her brother,' said Gwen as they headed north. 'Of course, it has been over three years since she lost him, and people react to loss in different ways, as we both know too well. That was quite the performance you put on in there, by the way. I wasn't expecting tears. How do you do that?'

'Part of my Intelligence training, oddly enough,' said Iris. 'They brought in an acting coach to work with us. The theory for women was if information came out of us while we were sobbing uncontrollably, it would be more likely to be believed. Now, I can cry on cue with the best of them.'

'This was training for being interrogated?' asked Gwen.

'Yes,' said Iris. 'And tortured.'

'My God, Iris,' said Gwen, taking her hand and squeezing it for a moment. 'I remember you telling me about the women you knew who were tortured and killed by the Nazis after their capture. They had this training as well?'

'They did,' said Iris. 'Not a single one of them gave up a single thing.'

'You were crying last night when you told me what happened at the Pickard place,' recalled Gwen. 'Those tears were real.'

'They were,' said Iris. 'You were right, I needed to get that off my chest. The gin helped.'

'I hope you'll forgive me for that,' said Gwen.

'For what? For plying an alcoholic with drinks? It's what we live for. If anything, you probably kept me from drinking even more last night.'

'That was part of my thinking. It doesn't make me any less complicit.'

'Work it out at church or with Dr Milford,' said Iris. 'I personally absolve you. So, what else have you figured out?'

'I am very interested in the fact that Mrs Dorter was set up in a very nice situation by Mr Pickard shortly after his son either fled or was banished from England,' said Gwen. 'The generosity of the gesture and its timing are curious, to say the least. It sounds like her silence was purchased.'

'And if it cost that much, she must have known something of consequence,' said Iris. 'Have you ever been to Bradford-on-Avon?'

'No. It sounds lovely. I think we should visit.'

'If it's on the Avon, maybe we could take my boat there,' mused Iris.

'Which would also be lovely if there were no urgency to our quest,' said Gwen. 'Come back to my place after our appointments and we'll consult the train schedules. We're off to the country for the weekend. My treat.'

TEN

The next morning, Iris packed her small suitcase for the two-day trip. She thought about their cover stories, then added her binoculars and the water beetle book.

She had planned to stop by the hospital to see Tony before meeting Gwen at Paddington station. She spotted the Brigadier's man as she checked in at the visitors' desk, monitoring the area once again in his porter's outfit. He made no signals, so she continued on to the lift to the intensive care ward. A different constable was standing guard outside Tony's room. He checked her ID and waved her in.

Tony was awake, though his eyes were somewhat unfocussed this morning. Still, he saw her and immediately lifted his hand in greeting.

'Good morning, my angel,' he said hoarsely. 'How goes the avenging? And why the suitcase?'

'I'm off to the country for the weekend,' she replied, pulling up a chair next to his bed.

'Because of me?'

'Even Vengeance needs to go on holiday once in a while,' said Sparks. 'I'll be refreshed and ready for more bloodthirsty pursuits come Monday. How are you feeling?'

'They're not letting me feel much of anything, yet,' he said. 'I dread the eventual reawakening of my nerve endings. It will be like opening a stack of unanswered letters, each containing a scream of pain saying, "Hello, remember me?" Oh, speaking of which, I received a lovely note from Miss Lowle. She said she knows the worst, but doesn't care. She wants to see me. The nurse who read it to me has quite taken her side in this. She's already cast Wendy Hiller in the movie version.'

'Hiller's too old,' said Sparks. 'You need a fresher face.'

'I'm sure anyone's face would look fresher next to mine at the moment,' he said. 'In any case, I'm thinking of relenting and giving the poor girl a chance. If she doesn't flee screaming from the room when she sees me, then I might consider charging the general public admission to the one-man freak show.'

'I think you'll find she's tougher than she looks,' said Sparks.

'Again, she resembles you in that.'

'Oh, I'm plenty tough,' growled Sparks. 'I could take you in a fight.'

'At the moment, a four-year-old could take me in a fight,' said Tony. 'So, where is your weekend adventure?'

'Off to the west to look at some beetles,' said Sparks.

'Anywhere in particular?'

'A group of ponds in the Cotswolds. I hear they have a good selection.'

'Have you got a bottle of chloroform and a stack of specimen boxes in that suitcase?'

'There are specimen boxes in there,' she said. 'The chloroform bottle I carry in my bag at all times. You never know when it might come in handy.'

'You really are a tough one,' he said. 'Thank you for visiting. Have a restful respite this weekend. And thank Miss Lowle for me. Tell her that I think I might be up to seeing her by Tuesday. They're scheduling me for some debriding over the next day or two.'

'I will,' she said. 'Good luck with that. I'll be thinking about you.'

'Hey, it's no skin off your back, Sparks.'

'Ouch. When the jokes get worse, I know you're getting better. Goodbye, Tony.'

She risked a light kiss on the bandage covering his cheek. She doubted he could feel it, but she hoped he'd appreciate the gesture.

On her way out, she veered towards the Brigadier's man.

'Lowle can visit on Tuesday,' she muttered.

'Good work,' he replied.

Gwen and Mrs Billington arrived at The Right Sort at the same time.

'Good morning, Mrs Bainbridge,' said Mrs Billington as she unlocked the reception room door.

'Good morning, Saundra,' said Gwen.

'Off to the country this weekend?' asked Mrs Billington, noticing Gwen's suitcase.

'I am, but a different part of the country,' said Gwen. 'Miss Sparks and I are going to be travelling together, and we'll be leaving early. I'd like you to stay until two to take calls, then close up the shop.'

'Oh? Is this a business trip?'

'Not quite. We're looking into a criminal matter for a client of ours.'

'Oh dear, not another investigation,' said Mrs Billington. 'Those never pay anything.'

'We've been paid for a couple of them,' said Gwen. 'In fact, one led to our being able to afford a second office and you.'

'Well, in that case, good luck, and I hope you turn a profit on this one.'

Not likely, thought Gwen.

She spent the early part of her morning answering letters and paying bills. Then the telephone rang. A moment later, the intercom buzzed.

'It's DS Parham,' said Mrs Billington. 'Are you available?'

'Of course.'

A moment later, the call was put through.

'Good morning, Detective Superintendent, it's Mrs Bainbridge,' she said. 'How may I be of assistance to you today?'

'No assistance needed, Mrs Bainbridge,' he replied. 'I wanted to let you know that I interviewed your Miss Lowle yesterday.'

'How did that go?'

'She's in the clear as far as I'm concerned,' he said. 'Her landlady verified the time of her return from her date with Mr Danforth, and that she remained in her room for the rest of the evening. I believe her landlady. In fact, I would put that landlady on guard for the Crown Jewels with her talent for vigilance. Miss Lowle herself was quite distraught over what happened to Mr Danforth, I must say. Professionally speaking, I think your firm may have made a connection there.'

'That's what we do,' said Mrs Bainbridge. 'I'm glad she's not on the suspect list. Any luck otherwise?'

'Not yet, I'm afraid,' said Parham. 'I did put in a call to the Cambridge Police. There was nothing in their file for Miss Spurlock's drowning indicating that she had left any note behind.'

'Isn't that unusual?'

'Not particularly. In any case, it was one of the reasons for the verdict of death by misadventure as opposed to suicide. There wasn't much else of interest. It sounds like a dead end to me.'

'Miss Sparks and I are still following up on a few aspects of it,' she said. 'We will let you know if we turn up anything useful.'

'I appreciate it, Mrs Bainbridge,' he said. 'I'm afraid I can't reciprocate, given the delicate nature of Mr Danforth's employment, but I wanted to let you know that Miss Lowle was in the clear in case you wished to set her up for any other matches should things with Mr Danforth not work out.'

'Thanks again, Detective,' she said. 'Good luck to you.'

She hung up.

Should things with Mr Danforth not work out, she thought. A nice euphemism for his death.

She shuddered at the thought, then glanced at her watch. She collected her hat, umbrella and suitcase, and left The Right Sort.

They boarded at Paddington and found an empty compartment. Gwen put her suitcase up on the overhead rack, then turned to her shorter partner and held out her hand.

'Do you think I've never done this before?' asked Iris as she easily tossed her suitcase onto the rack next to Gwen's.

'What about getting it down later?' asked Gwen.

'I've been known to make helpless eyes at tall, attractive men in just that situation,' said Iris. 'Otherwise, there are some gymnastics involved.'

'I picked up a travel guide for the area,' said Gwen, pulling a book from her bag.

'Bradford-on-Avon rates a travel guide?'

'Well, no, it's for Bath, Bristol and environs,' said Gwen, flipping through the pages until she reached a bookmark. 'But there are a few paragraphs on Bradford-on-Avon. I thought we should be conversant with the local points of interest.'

'Are there any?'

'Oh yes,' said Gwen, perusing it. 'It says it's very much like a smaller version of Bath, only without the, you know—'

'The baths.'

'Yes. But there's supposed to be a Saxon church dating from the eleventh century—'

'Still an atheist.'

'And what is described as a stunning and massive tithe barn from the fourteenth century. Its threshing floors are still intact. How do you feel about threshing?'

'I do like a good thresh every now and then.'

'I'm not sure you're using the word correctly.'

'I'm a city girl, forgive me. Fine, we'll visit the tithe barn. But you have to go beetling with me in exchange. That's my cover story for the expedition.'

'Speaking of which, I made the reservation under Mrs Bainbridge and companion,' said Gwen. 'I wasn't sure if you wanted her to recognise your name.'

'I've been thinking about that,' said Iris. 'She only met me the one time, and it was over eleven years ago. But it was a memorable occasion.'

'I doubt that you've changed in appearance that much since you were eighteen.'

'That is very kind of you,' said Iris. 'I always think I can still pass for a teenager until I meet actual teenagers and realise what war and the ravages of time have done to me.'

'Wait until you experience motherhood,' said Gwen. 'What name will you be using?'

'I'll go with Mary McTague,' said Iris, pulling a pair of black-rimmed glasses from her bag and donning them. 'I still carry that ID for special occasions. That way, Mrs Dorter won't have advance notice of my presence until we come face to face.

That should give me some advantage, and maybe the spectacles will throw her off.'

'Very well, Mary,' said Gwen, settling back in her seat. 'I am going to continue to study up on Bradford-on-Avon. I'll leave the beetles to you.'

The trip from Paddington took some three and a half hours with a change to a local train that stopped at a station in the part of the town south of the river. When they got off the train, Gwen consulted her directions.

'It says we need to go to an establishment called the Three Horseshoes on Frome Road,' she said. 'There's a telephone there from which we can ring the inn to send someone to pick us up.'

'Is there a pub inside where we can purchase refreshments while we wait?' asked Iris hopefully.

'There will always be a pub so long as there is an England,' said Gwen, picking up her suitcase. 'Shall we?'

The Three Horseshoes was a two-storey stone building with a black tiled roof. There was a gas street light in front, not yet lit. They went inside to find a low-ceilinged room with walls of thick, irregular stones, exposed beams running overhead and smaller rooms off to each side. There were a few tables, mostly occupied by older men smoking pipes or quaffing pints. They took in the sight of the two women appearing in their midst with interest.

There was a small, rectangular bar at the rear of the room with casks of beer and ale behind it, a red and white shield on the wall over them with USHER'S OF TROWBRIDGE – FINE ALES emblazoned upon it. The bartender looked them over expectantly as they approached.

'Good afternoon, ladies,' he said. 'Welcome to Bradford. Something to wet down the dust?'

'What's available?' asked Iris.

'Do you know Usher's?' he asked.

'No, but I'm ready to learn,' she replied.

'We have golden ale, bitter ale and oatmeal stout,' he said.

'And do I spy some fizzy lemonade over there?' asked Gwen.

'Yes, ma'am,' he said.

'One of those, please.'

'I'll have a bitter,' said Iris. 'A half-pint, please.'

'Where are you staying?' he asked as he drew a half-pint of the ale, then opened a bottle of the lemonade and placed the drinks in front of them.

'At Dorter's Inn,' said Gwen. 'I was told that you could ring them to come pick us up.'

'You're staying at Dorty's place?' called a man seated at a nearby table.

'We are,' said Gwen, turning to face him.

'That's funny,' he said. 'You don't look like witches.'

The men with him broke out into laughter. Gwen looked at them and smiled sweetly.

'The last man who said something like that to me is living quite happily on a lily pad now,' she said to the man. 'You have been warned, sir.'

He grinned and lifted his glass in appreciation.

Iris paid for the drinks while the bartender went over to a telephone by the till and dialled a number.

'What names shall I give them?' he asked.

'Mrs Bainbridge and Miss McTague,' said Gwen. 'They should be expecting us.'

He waited a moment. Then someone answered.

'Hello, it's Stan over at the Three Horseshoes,' he said. 'We got a couple of ladies just off the train for you. Mrs Bainbridge and Miss McTague. Very good.'

He hung up.

'They're sending a cart over,' he said. 'Should be half an hour.'

'Thank you,' said Iris.

They carried their drinks and suitcases over to an empty table.

'Did he say cart or car?' asked Iris.

'Cart,' said Gwen.

'Oh dear.'

'You staying long?' asked one of the men hopefully.

'Just a couple of days,' said Gwen.

'You know, long enough to get the coven together, dance

around the bonfire at midnight and make offerings to the Goddess,' added Iris.

'Now, don't get upset by Tom's little joke,' said the man. 'Dorty's all right. She just likes to keep to herself when she's not running things there.'

'I hear it's nice out there,' added another. 'A good place to go when you want to be nowhere at all. But if you're looking for something more lively, there's a band coming in here tomorrow night. There'll be dancing.'

'We'll see,' said Gwen. 'No promises.'

The door opened some twenty minutes later, and a young man poked his head in.

'Are the ladies for Dorter's Inn here?' he asked.

'That's us,' said Gwen.

'Good afternoon,' he said. 'I'm Timothy. I've come to take you to the inn. Are those your bags?'

'They are.'

He grabbed them, then held the door for the ladies. He couldn't have been more than sixteen, but he was tall and lanky with a thin face and nose.

There was a one-horse trap waiting for them outside. He lifted the rear bench up and placed the suitcases in a compartment under it, then closed it and helped each of them up.

'Hang on tight,' he advised them as he climbed onto his seat. 'Barney's feeling frisky today.'

'How far is it?' asked Gwen.

'A mile and a half,' he said. 'Shouldn't take us more than ten minutes.'

He guided the cart to a central circle from which several streets radiated, and took the next spoke out. The houses were almost all built from the same light-hued stone that made up the walls of the Three Horseshoes, with the rare brick building occasionally interrupting the pattern. The buildings quickly gave way to fields as they reached the outskirts of the town.

'That's the canal,' he said as they reached a bridge.

Iris nudged her partner. There was a narrowboat slowly making its way underneath them.

'I told you we could have come here by boat,' she said.

'It would have taken us a week,' replied Gwen.

'Do you know how long it would take to reach London by narrowboat?' Iris called to Timothy.

'I don't know that you can get to London that way,' he said. 'The canal goes from Reading to Bristol. We have some rowing boats if you want to take one out. The Inn is pretty close to it, and we have our own dock.'

'Any ponds nearby?'

'There's a decent one out back,' he said. 'You can go swimming if the weather gets warm enough. We're coming up to the drive now.'

They turned onto a track to the right. The driveway curved through a stand of trees, which then gave way to reveal a broad, stone grange house with some outlying barns and other buildings attached. There were several cars parked to the side.

'And here we are,' said Timothy, pulling the trap up to the front door. He hopped down, then came back to hand each of them down to the ground. 'I'll bring you in, then my sister Pam will take over while I unharness Barney.'

'You did very well, Barney,' said Gwen, coming over to rub the horse's neck. 'Thank you.'

'And thank you, Timothy,' said Iris as she handed him a tip.

'Thank you, miss,' he said, touching the brim of his cap. 'Let me know if you want to take a horse out for a ride tomorrow, and I'll get one saddled up for you.'

He carried their luggage inside.

Pam was waiting for them in the front hall, her hands folded in front of her. She must be his twin, thought Gwen. She was not nearly as tall, but had the same narrow face and cheerful expression.

'Good afternoon, ladies, and welcome to Dorter's Inn,' she said. 'I'm Miss Pamela Torrance. I will be checking you in and showing you to your room. Will you come this way, please?'

She picked up their suitcases and motioned for them to follow her to a sitting room with a small counter at one end with a large opened ledger book resting on top next to a call bell. A small collection of wine and spirit bottles stood on shelves behind the counter.

'You're sharing a twin room for two nights, correct?' she asked as she stepped behind the counter.

'Correct,' said Gwen.

'Payment in advance, please.'

Gwen produced a cheque for the fee and handed it over. Pam turned the ledger to face her and handed her a pen.

'We'll need both of you to sign,' she said. 'I don't believe I know your companion's first name, Mrs Bainbridge.'

'Forgive me,' said Gwen as she signed. 'This is my friend, Miss Mary McTague.'

'How do you do?' said Iris as she signed her name under Gwen's, glancing at the rest of the guest list as she did so.

'Welcome, Miss McTague,' said Pam. 'I'll take you to your room now. Dinner is at seven, and breakfast will be available in the morning from seven thirty to eight thirty. You're on your own for lunch, but we can pack sandwiches if you wish, and there will be tea set out in the parlour here in the afternoon. There is a reading room and a game room on this level. Timmy can provide you with boats and horses, and we have croquet and badminton sets available in the rear. Feel free to visit the barns, stables and coops. The animals are all very friendly. If there is anything you would like to know about the local attractions, please ask. One of us usually makes a run into town around ten in the morning if you'd like a lift, but you'll find the walk to be quite pleasant.'

'How are you fixed for birds, butterflies and beetles?' asked Iris.

'Ah, the three Bs. There's a decent variety right now. We have a resident family of teal at the pond. The ducklings are nearly full-grown, and quite entertaining. Butterflies like the meadows here, and beetles are . . . beetles. I confess I haven't paid much attention to them.'

'You're missing so much,' said Gwen.

'Anyhow, I would try the pond for them, then take one of the footpaths through the wood.'

'We'll get up early and take a walk before breakfast,' said Iris.

'Oh goody, that does sound like fun,' said Gwen. 'Now,

would it be possible for us to pay our respects to our hostess before dinner?'

'Mrs Dorter is busy in the kitchen right now,' said Pam. 'But you should have a chance to say hello at dinner. No need to dress up, by the way. We're away from all that. Let me take you to your room.'

She took a pair of keys out from under the counter and gave one to each of them, then picked up their suitcases and led them up a narrow wooden staircase to the first floor. This let out on a long central hallway with rooms on both sides.

'We have bathrooms at each end,' she said, indicating them. 'Please keep your baths under five inches of water, as the hot water is limited. The stairway and hall lights are on timers, so be sure to press the switch each time. You're in room four. And here we are.'

She opened the door to reveal a small but cheerfully appointed room with two single beds across from each other, separated by a shared bedside table under a wide window. The walls were covered with a cream-coloured wallpaper with burgundy stripes decorated with a paisley pattern. There was a small basin set into the wall by the cupboard, with a dressing table and chair next to it.

Pam placed the suitcases on small cedar chests by the foot of each bed, then stepped forwards to draw some muslin curtains and opened the window. The room looked out over a vast meadow beyond a fence. The pond was visible fifty yards or so behind it.

'We finally got in some screens so the insects won't get in,' she said. 'Unless Miss McTague would prefer them open so they could visit her instead of the other way round.'

'No, thank you,' said Iris, laughing.

'We don't have alarm clocks in the room, as you may have noticed,' said Pam, 'but Early Ernie will take care of that.'

'Early Ernie?'

'He is our resident rooster and very reliable,' said Pam. 'We will see you at dinner, ladies.'

She closed the door behind her as she left.

Gwen pulled a folding travel alarm clock from her suitcase and tossed it to Iris.

'Set it for the beetling hour, just in case Ernie decides to sleep in,' she said.

'Thanks,' said Iris, winding it. 'I wonder how the twins fit into the household.'

'Maybe relatives, maybe locals,' said Gwen. 'Let's have a wash and go down to dinner.'

The other guests were all couples who greeted the two women cordially, the men casting surreptitious and admiring glances, and the other women sizing them up as potential competition as the admiring glances of the men were not as surreptitious as they had thought. Pam circulated through the room, taking orders for cocktails, then left them to mingle and converse.

Iris and Gwen found themselves separated over the course of the cocktail hour as the men herded them into opposite corners of the room and took the lead in the conversations. Gwen was repeatedly sounded out as to her relationship with Iris, or Mary as she remembered to call her, and her repeated insistences that they were merely friends and travelling companions were met with knowing glances and raised eyebrows.

To her relief, Pam finally reappeared in the doorway.

'Dinner is ready, ladies and gentlemen,' she announced. 'This way, if you please.'

Pam led them into the dining room which had a long, rough-hewn table covered with a simple linen cloth. They took their places, Iris sitting on the side of Gwen away from the kitchen door, hoping to shield herself from view. Pam picked up a small dinner bell and rang it. A moment later, Mrs Dorter entered and stood at the head of the table.

Her hair had been transformed from a grey-streaked bun to an elaborate, brunette coif, Iris noticed. Her frock was of a dark-green velour with white laced trim, and her nails were perfectly manicured and painted a deep red. This was a different woman than the severe, dour servant Iris remembered. This was a woman who reigned over her domain, with a smile that exuded confidence even before she had uttered a single word.

'Good evening, and welcome to Dorter's Inn,' she said. 'I

am Mrs Hermia Dorter, your hostess. We welcome you to what we hope will be a restful and revivifying experience, and the first step towards that will be tonight's feast. We will be serving an apple and cress salad with a herb dressing, with all the ingredients gathered fresh from our gardens and orchards. There will be a selection of local cheeses, followed by a red mullet soup, then trout béarnaise with asparagus. We make our own scrumpy, and will finish if you still have any room left with Knickerbocker Glory for pudding. Bon appétit!'

With that, Pam rolled in a trolley with salad plates and a large bowl. Mrs Dorter began serving, keeping the conversation going as she did so. She managed not to delve too deeply into people's personal lives, noticed Gwen, sticking to local politics and gossip in Bath and Bristol.

'We have two Londoners with us, I hear,' she said as the soup was brought in. 'Mrs Bainbridge and Miss McTague, you are most welcome. What do you do there?'

'As little as possible,' replied Gwen. 'And we're completely exhausted as a result.'

'Hopefully this will be a restorative,' said Mrs Dorter. 'How did you chance to hear about us?'

'Oh gosh, who was it?' said Gwen, turning to Iris.

'One of your friends put us on to it,' said Iris. 'Lucy something, I think you said?'

'Oh, yes, Lucinda,' said Gwen. 'Our children were at the same birthday party, and we escaped to the drinks cabinet together. She said you were their housekeeper or something back in the day.'

'Ah, that would be Mrs Kendall,' said Mrs Dorter, smiling fondly. 'I was their housekeeper many years ago in Cambridgeshire. It was kind of her to remember me.'

'That must have been quite the place to manage,' said Gwen. 'She said she and her brother and sister ran pretty wild back then.'

'They were rich and rambunctious,' said Mrs Dorter. 'I cleaned up after them. But eventually, they all grew up and left. Now, here I am, in another big house in the country. Only this one is mine, which makes quite the difference.'

'How so?'

'Now, when I'm cleaning up after people, I know that what remains belongs to me, and I put more effort into making things perfect again,' she said.

'Well, the inn is lovely and the dinner is marvellous, so here's to perfection achieved,' said Gwen, raising her glass.

'You're very kind,' acknowledged Mrs Dorter.

The trout course arrived and was duly consumed and praised by all present. The conversation was taken over by the guests, with the men pressing Gwen and Iris for details of their lives which they fended off with grace and skill.

Yet once the Knickerbocker Glory had been demolished and the guests had repaired to the game room, the onslaught of the males continued.

'The name's Norris,' said one of them to Gwen.

'How do you do?' she replied. 'Mrs Bainbridge. Is Norris a first or last name?'

'The last seems to be Smith at the moment,' he said.

'Quite of few of you Smiths here tonight, if the register is any indication,' she remarked. 'Is there a family reunion going on?'

'Not exactly,' he said. 'Although there may be a fair amount of reuniting happening. You two came all the way from London, eh?'

'We did.'

'Interesting.'

'How so?'

'London folk go to Bath to get away from London,' he said. 'People in Bath go to Bradford to get away from Bath and Londoners. And this place is outside of Bradford. Getting Londoners here is unusual. You must really have wanted to get away from things.'

'The air is fresh, and there is ample opportunity for exercise and good food,' said Gwen.

He snorted.

'Exercise will be had,' he said, glancing about the room. 'Although I doubt that much of it will take place outside.'

'Oh?'

'One of the attractions of Dorter's Inn is its remove from the hustle and bustle,' he said. 'Another is the discretion of its staff.'

'I see,' said Gwen.

'In fact, should you fancy a respite from the fresh air, give us a knock,' he suggested. 'I'm in room seven.'

'Wouldn't your wife have some objections to that?'

'No doubt,' he said. 'But she's in Gloucester at the moment. Susie, who's here with me, won't mind at all. She'll either be grateful for the break, or want to join in.'

'I'll pass, but thanks for the offer,' said Gwen.

He left her for a card table where a game of whist was in progress. Gwen sidled up to Iris.

'I'm not sure what we've stumbled into here,' she whispered. 'But I think I was just propositioned.'

'I'm certain I was,' Iris whispered back. 'By two of the men and one of the women. Let's stick together this weekend.'

'Our hostess has vanished,' observed Gwen.

'Back to the kitchen for the washing up,' speculated Iris. 'It's a small staff here.'

'Let's go give our compliments to the cook,' suggested Gwen. 'See if we can speak with her.'

But they were met at the door to the kitchen by Pam, who was pushing a trolley into the dining room to collect the dessert plates.

'May I help you, ladies?' she asked.

'We wanted to meet and thank the kitchen staff,' said Gwen. 'See where the magic happens.'

'I'm sorry, but Mrs Dorter doesn't permit the guests in there,' said Pam. 'She's very protective of her recipes.'

'Of course,' said Gwen. 'Would she be able to come out for a moment?'

'I'm afraid not,' said Pam. 'After-dinner clean-up is a busy time, I'm afraid, and she is very particular. I will pass your compliments on. Will there be anything else?'

'Not at the moment,' said Gwen. 'Thank you.'

They went back to the game room. Two of the men were playing billiards. Gwen eyed the table speculatively.

'Step away,' whispered Iris, noticing her. 'We don't want any lemon games getting us kicked out before we find out anything.'

'A pity,' said Gwen. 'I'm pretty sure I could take them. It would pay for the trip. Well, in that case, what say we turn in? I'm exhausted by both the travel and the unwanted male attention, and I don't see us making any further progress this evening.'

'Agreed,' said Iris. 'Fresh air and beetling in the morning.'

'You're really going to be doing that?'

'How often do I get the chance nowadays? Will you be joining me?'

'Will there be mud involved?'

'Oh, yes.'

'No thanks. Come back and wake me for breakfast.'

They headed back to their room. The cool air coming through the window was refreshing. They changed into their nightdresses and turned out the lights. Iris looked out of the window. There was a new moon, so the stars were more visible, especially now that the two of them were away from the lights and smoke of London. Other tiny lights emanated from the meadow.

'Look, Gwen,' she said. 'Glow-worms! Lampyris noctiluca, the fires that shine at night. So pretty!'

'Why do they glow?' asked Gwen, coming to look over her shoulder.

'For the same reason we do,' said Iris. 'To attract mates. The females are the brighter ones.'

'Naturally,' said Gwen.

They watched and listened. An owl hooted somewhere in the distance. Then their reverie was interrupted by some amorous noises from the room adjacent to theirs.

'I believe some other species have attracted mates,' commented Gwen. 'I'm going to turn in.'

'You can sleep through that?' asked Iris.

'It's not my first time in a country inn,' said Gwen, settling into her bed. 'I don't think I'll have any problem. Goodnight, Iris.'

'Goodnight, Gwen,' returned Iris, getting into her own bed.

Sure enough, Iris heard her partner's soft snores within minutes. Those, combined with the distant hooting, their neighbours' increasing passion, and the travel alarm clock, whose ticking seemed to echo more and more loudly as she tried to ignore it, put her into a state of restlessness. Finally, she got up, threw on her dressing gown and crept softly out of the room.

She thought she would see if she could sneak down and grab a nightcap to help calm her. She didn't want to turn on the hall light and disturb any of her fellow travellers, not that she necessarily believed they were capable of distraction at the moment, so she tiptoed through the darkness until she reached the door to the staircase.

She felt for the wall and made her way down slowly and carefully. As she reached the bottom, a glow lit the doorway. Then a candle appeared abruptly as a woman turned into it, and Iris found herself face to face with Mrs Dorter, who looked at her in surprise.

'Sorry, didn't mean to startle you,' said Iris.

'Likewise,' returned Mrs Dorter, holding the candle up to view her. 'It's Miss McTague, isn't it?'

'Yes, it is.'

'Do you need something?'

'I was having trouble sleeping. I thought I'd see if I could get something to settle my nerves.'

'I'm so sorry, but we don't serve alcohol after midnight,' said Mrs Dorter. 'And our stoves are wood-burning and out for the night, so warm milk isn't available, either.'

'Goodness, is it that late? I'm so sorry to have disturbed you.'

'I was up, so no apologies necessary,' said Mrs Dorter. 'I'm sorry I cannot remedy your restlessness. I suggest some deep breathing. Let the country air work its wonders.'

'There's plenty of deep breathing happening about our floor,' said Iris. 'No one seems to be tiring from it.'

'Give them time,' said Mrs Dorter with a throaty laugh. 'They'll wear out eventually.'

'I'll get back to my room, then. Goodnight.'

'Goodnight,' said Mrs Dorter. 'And Miss McTague?'

'Yes?'

'You should be more careful.'

'About what?' asked Iris, eyeing the other woman warily.

'Wandering about in the dark like that,' said Mrs Dorter. 'Especially since you've forgotten to put on your spectacles. I'll light your way up.'

'Thank you. I appreciate it.'

She turned and climbed the stairs, Mrs Dorter two steps behind. Iris's shadow preceded her, jouncing in the candlelight. When they reached the guest floor, Mrs Dorter stood in the doorway to illuminate the hallway until Iris reached her room. She turned to wave at their hostess. Mrs Dorter merely nodded and turned to go to the upper floor, the candlelight fading away.

Iris was mildly irritated by the encounter as well as her lack of success in obtaining a nightcap. Blessedly, the noises from the next room had subsided, as had Gwen's snoring, so she was finally able to fall into an uneasy sleep with only the ticking of the clock breaking the silence of the night.

The clanging of the alarm jolted her awake just before sunrise. She stopped it quickly and sat on the side of her bed. Across the room, Gwen's eyes fluttered open.

'Breakfast?' she mumbled.

'Not for another two hours. Last chance to go beetling with me.'

'Promise me that's true, then go away,' said Gwen, closing her eyes.

Iris dressed quietly, finishing with her wellies and a broad-brimmed hat. She remembered to include the spectacles this time. She grabbed her binoculars and the beetle book, then headed downstairs and out the back door. The faint glimmerings of the sun appeared behind her, and as she reached the gate to the meadow, she was startled by a raucous cock-a-doodle-doodling to her right.

She looked to see a large brown and white speckled rooster with cream-coloured legs and feet and a bright red comb and wattle. It looked at her suspiciously, then tilted its head back and sounded the dawn again.

'Good morning,' she said. 'I presume you are Ernie. Well done, and thank you for your service.'

Ernie clucked at her. She chose to interpret the sound as cordial, and nodded affably before opening the gate and slipping through it, making sure to secure it firmly behind her.

There was a well-trodden path through the tall grasses. In the distance, she heard some low quacking. The path took her into that direction, and a few minutes later she came to large, irregularly shaped pond. As she did, a muddy brown-coloured duck paddled across, the splash of green on its wing giving away its identity. Behind it, four ducklings, about three-quarters the size of their mother, followed behind in a line, stopping to dabble amid a clump of weeds whenever she did.

Some movement out of the corner of her eye drew her attention, and she squatted by a yellowed stalk to see a small, narrow beetle climbing it. Its back had an almost beaded appearance with a thin, green stripe running up the centre.

Zircon reed beetle, she thought happily, pulling out a small notebook and jotting it down.

There was a group of beetles skating along the surface by a cluster of weeds at the edge. She made her way over to them to get a closer look.

'Once again, you should be more careful, Miss McTague,' came a voice nearby.

She looked up, startled, to see Mrs Dorter standing ten feet away, a large straw basket partly filled with herbs in one hand, and a rather sharp-looking blade in the other.

'Or should I say,' continued Mrs Dorter, smiling coldly, 'you should be more careful, Miss Sparks?'

ELEVEN

'W as that meant to be a threat?' asked Iris. 'Because I don't respond well to those.'

'Where you're standing,' said Mrs Dorter, pointing with her blade. 'You shouldn't be in that patch. That's spurge. It's an irritant. Get any of the sap on your skin and you'll be very sorry you did. I recommend you scrub those boots before you go back into the house. There's a pump over by the barn with a brush hanging from it you can use. Then leave them in the boot room when you come in.'

'Ah,' said Iris, stepping away from the weeds. 'Thanks for the warning. I'm not as up on my irritants as I should be. So. You called me Miss Sparks just now. How long have you known?'

'You looked familiar when I saw you at dinner, but I couldn't place you,' said Mrs Dorter. 'It wasn't until I bumped into you at midnight that I recognised you. It was seeing you in the doorway like that that jogged my memory, just like that night at the Pickards' mansion, although I still couldn't remember your name. I had to dig up my diary from back then to find it.'

'I'm impressed that you went to all that trouble.'

'You showed up at my establishment under an alias.'

'As do most of your clientele.'

'But I know all of their real names,' said Mrs Dorter. 'It guarantees my privacy and theirs. If you and Mrs Bainbridge were merely here to have a liaison away from the prying eyes of London society, then I couldn't care less. But you brought up that ludicrous connection to Lucinda Pickard, and that raised my suspicions, Miss Sparks. Why are you here?'

'To speak to you about that night at the Pickards' mansion. To find out what happened to Nancy Spurlock.'

'Why? Why now, after all this time?' snapped Mrs Dorter.

'She's long gone. So is Kevin, so is Bruce. Who cares about any of them any more?'

'Three other people were there that night,' said Iris. 'You. Me. And Tony Danforth.'

'Tony went off to Singapore sometime in the late thirties,' said Mrs Dorter.

'He came back recently,' said Iris. 'And someone tried to kill him almost immediately. It may have had something to do with what happened to Nancy that night. You're the only one who can tell me about it. That's why I'm here. This is as private a place and time as any. Nobody else is around. Tell me.'

'You're still the same silly little self-important girl, aren't you?' sneered Mrs Dorter. 'You think you can show up out of nowhere at my house and make demands? All dressed up with your fake specs like you're something out of a girls' detective novel. I bet if I knocked those stupid glasses off your face you could see just fine.'

'And I bet that if you tried you'd be floating in that pond before you ever connected,' Iris replied. 'Let's keep things peaceful, shall we? I only came to talk to you.'

'How did you know I'd be out here this time of day?'

'I didn't,' said Iris, holding up her book. 'I was looking at the neighbourhood beetles. It's a hobby of mine.'

'Beetles?' replied the other woman incredulously.

She looked down by her feet, where a brightly metallic one was crawling along.

'What's that one?' she asked, pointing at it.

'Oh, that's a nice one,' said Iris. 'A jewel beetle. Aphanisticus emarginatus. It's fairly common around—'

She stopped as Mrs Dorter stepped forwards and crushed it with the toe of her boot.

'All these years here, I never knew what any of them were called,' she said. 'Nor do I care.'

'That wasn't necessary,' said Iris.

'No, it wasn't,' said Mrs Dorter. 'Nor is this conversation. This is my property and I'll do as I damn well please on it. Now, I'm going to finish collecting my herbs and greens. Breakfast is at seven thirty, Miss Sparks, or Miss McTague, if you wish to continue the charade. It makes no difference to me.'

She turned and walked away, stopping abruptly to bend down and savagely slice off a clump of greens and throw them into her basket before disappearing into the woods nearby.

I hope those aren't poisonous, thought Iris.

She looked down at the lifeless beetle, then trudged back to the house. She stopped by the pump and rinsed off her wellies, scrubbing them with the brush as well as she could. She saw Ernie watching her dolefully from the ramp leading to the coop.

'You could have warned me,' she said to him.

He didn't reply, which she was beginning to see as the theme to the trip.

She tossed her wellies into the boot room, then padded up the stairs to her room. Gwen sat up in bed as she came through the door.

'Breakfast?' she asked hopefully.

'Soon,' said Iris. 'But I may have scotched everything in the meantime.'

'You've accomplished that before breakfast? While I was still sleeping?'

'Apparently.'

She recounted her conversation with Mrs Dorter while Gwen dressed and brushed her hair.

'I agree, that doesn't sound very promising,' said Gwen.

'Any ideas?'

'Not at the moment. Let's see if I can do better on a full stomach.'

But breakfast, while filling, was not enough to inspire either of them.

'I doubt that she will take kindly to being accosted by the both of us,' said Gwen afterwards. 'How would you feel about my distracting her while you sneak into her room and find her diary?'

'We're not in London, so I don't think we can rely upon the local constabulary to be as sympathetic to my trespassing with intent to snoop if I get caught,' said Iris.

'Well, if we hang about looking for opportunities, we'll only put her on higher alert,' said Gwen. 'So I suggest we engage in some normal touristy behaviour. You've had enough beetling for the moment?'

'My mood for that was spoiled.'

'Then let's walk into town, see the sights and perhaps an idea will strike us. If none does, then maybe we should embrace our failure and return home empty-handed. Or empty-brained.'

Half an hour later, they stood on the threshold of the Tithe Barn. Gwen consulted her guidebook while Iris peered inside.

'Who did this belong to?' she asked.

'The nuns of Shaftesbury Abbey originally,' said Gwen. 'Most of this area was given to support them.'

'Ten per cent of the local crops to support nuns,' marvelled Iris. 'For which the peasants received what? Prayers? Divine intervention?'

'I suppose,' said Gwen. 'And a place to send their superfluous daughters. It might have been my fate had I lived then.'

'You would have been plucked from your cloistered life to wed the local lord,' said Iris, stepping inside and looking up. 'While I probably would have been burned at the stake for some minor misunderstanding or other. I do like that vaulted ceiling, I must say. I wonder how much of it is original.'

'It says they started restoring it during the Great War,' read Gwen. 'They've replaced most of the rotted beams. It belongs to the Ministry of Works now. They've been renovating it over time, depending on when the funds come in. There's a collection box over there for contributions.'

Iris walked over to the stone threshing floor and stomped on it experimentally.

'Nothing but chaff this trip,' she said. 'I'm sorry I've wasted our time and your money.'

'Nonsense,' said Gwen. 'I've rather enjoyed spending a weekend with you. Do you realise this is the first time we've travelled together?'

'So it is,' said Iris. 'Maybe we could try it again when there isn't some crime involved.'

'I'd like that,' said Gwen. 'Let's go into the town proper. There's something I want to check.'

She dropped a couple of shillings into the collection box. Then they walked to the centre of the town, stopping to view the Town Bridge across the river. Gwen made certain to photograph the Bradford Gudgeon that surmounted the weather vane on top of the old two-cell town lockup. Iris expected her to hunt for souvenirs for Ronnie, but instead her partner stopped in front of the estate agents and perused the listings pinned to a bulletin board behind the front window.

'You're not thinking of buying a place here, are you?' asked Iris.

'Not at all,' said Gwen. 'There. Look at this.'

She pointed to one for a grange house with buildings and grounds.

'Not my style,' said Iris. 'And well beyond my means.'

'I know,' said Gwen. 'It looks to be a similarly sized property as our inn. Now, say you had been working as a housekeeper for twenty years or so. Do you think you'd be able to save enough to afford a place like this on that salary?'

'I don't know how much housekeepers get paid.'

'I do,' said Gwen. 'I'm paying for one now, and I'm paying her well. Yet even if the Pickards paid Mrs Dorter even more handsomely, I would still guess that this inn would have been too costly for her.'

'She would have bought it in '36 or '37,' Iris pointed out. 'The slump would have made things more affordable back then.'

'Even so, the place has been renovated extensively,' said Gwen. 'The furniture and the decor are first rate. Money has been spent. And you know as well as I do that the banks are not exactly forthcoming with loans for a new business when a woman is running it.'

'You think she knew enough about what happened to blackmail the Pickards?'

'I think it's a plausible explanation.'

'Very plausible,' said Iris. 'But it doesn't solve how we're going to get the information out of her.'

'No, but I think we're on the right track. We'll have to come up with a more effective approach.'

'You don't suppose a simple bribe would work, do you?'

'I didn't bring bribe money with me, alas. Let's get some lunch.'

Unfortunately, neither lunch nor further exploration of the attractions of Bradford-on-Avon stirred any further ideas for prying the information out of Mrs Dorter. They wandered through the Shambles, then headed back to the inn in time for tea. Mrs Dorter once again presided over dinner, managing to exclude Iris from any conversation without being obvious about it. At its conclusion, she stood to address the company.

'Game Night will be held in the game room as is customary,' she said. 'Pamela will be in attendance for those who require snacks and drinks. I myself will be retiring early, I'm afraid, so I will bid you all an enjoyable evening.'

With that, she departed the dining room.

'And that's our last chance,' muttered Iris.

A woman named Alice, half of one of the illicit couples staying there, leaned across the table.

'If you're looking for something more entertaining tonight,' she said, 'the ladies are going out dancing at the Three Horseshoes while the men waste the evening playing cards. We have room in our car for two more.'

'What do you think?' Iris asked Gwen.

'Sounds like fun,' said Gwen. 'I'm game.'

'Splendid,' said Alice. 'We'll change shoes, then rendezvous in the front parlour.'

Iris's wellies had been placed by the door of their room. She picked them up and went inside, then contemplated the two pairs of shoes she had brought for the trip.

'I packed for walking, beetling and dinner,' she said. 'I didn't expect dancing.'

'I'd recommend the walking shoes,' said Gwen. 'Just in case our ride is too drunk to get us back after.'

'I'm hoping to get too drunk as well,' said Iris as she put on her Oxfords. 'You remember my continuing curse: men who dance with me meet violent ends.'

'You'll be dancing with locals tonight,' said Gwen. 'I doubt the curse will be bothered.'

'The Curse Takes a Holiday,' said Iris. 'There's a title for something.'

'It's odd how a religious sceptic like yourself believes in a curse,' commented Gwen as she slipped on a pair of slingbacks.

'Recent evidence does support the idea,' said Iris.

'Or maybe dancing with gangsters and murderers increased the likelihood.'

'There is that,' admitted Iris.

Alice was waiting for them with another woman named Renee.

'The others have gone on ahead,' she said. 'The men have disappeared into a cloud of cigar smoke. You can smell it from here.'

'Unfortunate,' said Renee. 'I really don't like that scent permeating a man. But let them have their fun. We'll have ours. Come, ladies.'

Alice drove, while Renee turned and leaned on the back of her seat to talk.

'We've been trying to figure out what you two are,' she said. 'You're not lovers, and you're not on the prowl for men.'

'Not any of the ones here, certainly,' said Gwen.

'Oh, it's not such a bad selection this month,' said Alice with a laugh.

'I take it you're not here with your husbands,' said Iris.

'We are, in fact,' said Renee.

'Really?'

'Really,' she said. 'Only I'm with hers and she's with mine. We left Bristol amid a haze of respectability in separate cars, then stopped for lunch along the way and made the switch. Then on to Dorter's Inn for a weekend of Smith-ing, and we'll return to our regular lives Sunday night with some spicy memories to share.'

'Goodness!' exclaimed Gwen.

'"Goodness had nothing to do with it", as Mae West once said,' laughed Renee. 'But there is a small coterie of similarly minded people who are in the know about this place, so we were surprised to find you both here and unaware of what was going on.'

'We're just two good friends having a mildly rustic getaway,' said Iris. 'Explore the sights, see Nature, red in tooth and claw. Or mandible and claw, in my case.'

'I must say you're being quite open with us about all of this,' said Gwen.

'Neither of you seemed particularly taken aback by what's been going on,' said Alice. 'We appreciate that. The fact that Gwen didn't run screaming from the room when Norris made a pass at her was a relief.'

'And refusing him was excellent judgement on your part,' added Renee. 'We've all run screaming from Norris at one time or another.'

They parked down a few buildings from the Three Horseshoes and walked to the pub. Alice and Renee disappeared through the door immediately. Iris hesitated, hearing the sounds of frivolity within. She glanced at Gwen.

'Are you ready for this?' asked Gwen.

'Absolutely not,' replied Iris. 'After you, Mrs Bainbridge.'

'No, after *you*, Miss Sparks!' replied Gwen, pushing her through the doorway.

Inside, several of the tables had been cleared out to make space for the dancing, which was already in progress. Iris and Gwen, who had been expecting something along the lines of a rustic local band with a fiddler and a guitar, were pleasantly surprised to see a four-piece swing combo in from Bath where they must have played afternoon tea dances. Here, however, freed from the more genteel restraints of those tourist resorts, they were cutting loose, and the local crowd, already fuelled by the hardworking barman in the back, was trying with varying degrees of success to replicate the jitterbug moves that they had seen in newsreels and American films.

Fortunately, slower dances were brought into the mix, and the local men were by no means shy about asking the visitors to join them. Iris danced, reluctantly at first, but soon eased into the spirit of things. No violence occurred to any of her partners, with the exception of the occasional foot getting trod upon as the room became more and more crowded. She changed partners after every dance with an eye towards not encouraging anyone more than they should have been. Still, a few tried.

'You wouldn't want to go out back and look at the stars with me, would you?' asked one red-cheeked hopeful several years her junior as the sax player crooned 'The Stars Will Remember' in a passable impression of Steve Conway.

'Sorry, no, but that's a good line,' she replied. 'It's bound to work on some lucky lass sooner or later.'

Around eleven, Alice collected them.

'We need to get back while we still have some energy left,' she said.

They piled back into the car and drove back to the inn. Once inside, they went to the game room. As they passed the dining room, Gwen noticed that the dessert dishes from dinner had only been partly cleared, still stacked on the trolley near the door to the kitchen. Sloppy, she thought.

When they reached the game room, only the mismatched husbands of Alice and Renee were still there, playing gin rummy.

'Goodness, we shouldn't have left you stranded like that,' laughed Alice, coming over to kiss each of them in turn. 'Did you clean out the others?'

'Um, they've stepped outside for a smoke,' said one of them, smirking slightly.

Gwen looked at him, then turned to Iris so the men couldn't see her speak.

'Something's wrong,' she muttered to Iris.

'What?'

'They were all smoking away in here when we left, so no reason to go outside to do it. The dishes at the dining table haven't been cleared. And I don't see Pam in attendance.'

Iris immediately turned and grabbed a poker from by the fireplace.

'Excuse me for a moment,' she said.

She walked quickly through the dining room and opened the far door, Gwen following her as she went through a connecting pantry to the kitchen.

The kitchen was a huge one, with a large central table where meals for twenty could be prepared and copper pots that had escaped requisitioning during the war hanging from the walls.

It was on the tabletop that she saw Pam, struggling against the grip of one of the men staying at the inn while Norris attempted to climb on top of her.

'Stop squirming, you stupid girl,' he snarled. 'There's money in it for you when we're done. Hold her down, Elster!'

Her cries were muffled by the other man clamping his hand over her mouth.

'Hello,' said Iris from the doorway. 'I hope I'm interrupting something.'

The two men turned in surprise.

'You can walk away right now,' said Norris. 'This is none of your concern.'

'Oh, but it is,' she said, stepping into the room.

'I warn you, I am not without influence in these parts,' he said. 'I can make things very difficult for you.'

'Once you've recovered from your injuries, you are welcome to try,' she said, holding up the poker.

'Here now,' he said, sliding off the table on to his feet. 'There's no need for that.'

'There isn't, in fact,' she agreed. 'I'm perfectly capable of crippling you both without it. But this isn't my house, and this is a lovely kitchen, so I'd prefer to restrict the damage to just the two of you. We could take things outside if you'd prefer an old-fashioned bare-knuckle brawl. I like those as well.'

The man called Elster released Pam and stood in front of the table, his fists clenched. He had at least a foot and three stone on Iris. She looked up at him and smiled.

'Did you want to go first?' she asked sweetly.

Pam rolled off the table and grabbed a long knife from a rack. Iris held up her hand.

'No, dear,' she said. 'You don't want to be hauled in for murdering the guests. It might be a deterrent to repeat business. I'll handle this. Now, sir, as to you. You may either stand down or make the first move. But if it's the latter, I guarantee I'll be making the last one.'

'Come on, Norris, there's two of us,' urged Elster.

'And two of us,' said Gwen, slipping into the room behind Iris.

'You must be the muscle,' sneered Norris as he sized her up.

'Actually, she is,' said Gwen. 'She really doesn't need my help. But I've been practising, and I'm improving.'

'What is the meaning of this?' came Mrs Dorter's voice from behind them.

'Oh, good,' said Iris, stepping aside to let her in. 'I was hoping you'd show up.'

'Mrs Dorter, these two drunken harridans have been making some absurd threats and accusations,' said Norris smoothly.

'Have they?' said Mrs Dorter, coming forwards into the room. 'Of what nature? And what are you doing in my kitchen?'

'We came to look for Pam,' he said. 'She had left her station for a long period of time, and we were concerned that something had happened to her.'

'What had happened to her was the two of them,' said Iris. 'We found them trying to force themselves on her.'

'That is a vile slander!' shouted Norris. 'I demand that you—'

'Pamela, speak,' said Mrs Dorter, looking at the girl, who still held the knife.

'They attacked me,' she whispered. 'Here. They had me pinned on the table, and that one had his hand over my mouth. I don't know what would have happened if Miss McTague and Mrs Bainbridge hadn't come in.'

'I do,' said Iris.

Mrs Dorter looked at each of them in turn, then fixed her gaze on Norris.

'Pamela,' she said, her eyes never leaving him, 'go wake your brother. Tell him to fetch the shotgun. Rock salt only.'

'Yes, Mrs Dorter,' said Pam, edging past Elster, then scampering out of the room.

'The two of you should know better,' she said to Norris. 'Whoever you want to bring here, whatever arrangements you make with the other guests, that's up to you. But my staff are off limits.'

'This is nothing but a pack of lies!' sputtered Norris.

'You are to vacate your rooms immediately and leave the premises,' continued Mrs Dorter. 'Timothy will escort you to your autos and make certain that you do. If there is any sign of you twenty minutes from now, he has permission to switch to birdshot.'

'Do you know who we are?' shouted Norris.

'I know exactly who you are,' replied Mrs Dorter. 'As well as who the ladies are who you brought here. I will be happy to make that information known far and wide should any further trouble come from either of you. The twenty minutes began one minute ago, so I suggest you not waste any more time and get packing.'

The two men glanced at each other. Then Timothy appeared at the door, holding a double-barrelled shotgun pointing down.

'Goodbye, gentlemen,' said Mrs Dorter. 'There will be no refunds.'

They hesitated. Then Timothy stepped forwards, raising the weapon.

'Rock salt still hurts,' he said.

'We're going,' said Norris.

The two men stormed out of the room. Timothy followed them, keeping the shotgun levelled.

Mrs Dorter turned to Iris and Gwen, then noticed the poker.

'I'll take that,' she said, holding out her hand.

Iris gave it to her. She rested it against the wall by the stove.

'The fire is still lit,' she observed. 'I'm going to warm up some milk and sweeten it with a little rum. Would you like any?'

'Please,' said Iris.

Mrs Dorter bustled about the kitchen, pulling up three chairs that were stacked in a corner, then fetching a bottle of milk from an icebox in a small room off the far side. She poured it into a small pan, then set it on the stove top. As the milk began to bubble they heard two car engines roar to life, then the screeching of tyres. Then quiet.

She poured the milk into three cups, then added a healthy pouring of rum to each. Timothy appeared in the doorway, the shotgun broken open and unloaded.

'They're gone,' he reported. 'They didn't leave a tip.'

'That was to be expected,' she said. 'You did well, Timothy.

Get some sleep while you can. Tell Pamela to do the same. I'll clean up down here.'

'Yes, aunty.'

'Timothy.'

'I mean, yes, Mrs Dorter,' he said. 'Goodnight, ladies.'

'Goodnight, Timothy,' said Gwen. 'Don't worry about the tip. I'll make it up to you.'

'That won't be necessary,' said Mrs Dorter. 'They paid through Monday morning, so fewer meals to prepare.'

Timothy left. Mrs Dorter placed the cups and saucers on the table, then sat down.

'They call me their aunt, but they're my cousin's children,' she said. 'Their father ran off when they were young. My cousin came here with them to help me run this place, but the tuberculosis took her six years ago.'

'I'm sorry,' said Iris.

'I've never had children of my own,' she said, holding up her cup and blowing on it. 'So these two are quite special to me. Timothy was too young for the war, fortunately, and Pamela . . . well, I was hoping she'd remain out of danger as well, especially with her brother around to keep an eye out for her. But they're growing up. I want to protect them, but it isn't always possible. So I'm grateful for what the two of you did just now. Grateful and surprised.'

'Why surprised?' asked Iris.

'I'm surprised that you'd step up and put yourself in danger for some girl you don't know and have no responsibility for.'

'I know her,' said Iris shortly.

'Maybe you do,' said Mrs Dorter, looking at her, considering. 'Or maybe you have changed since we last met. Saving one girl doesn't make up for failing another one, though.'

'I know,' said Iris. 'All I can do is try to save who I can.'

'Which is why we're here,' added Gwen. 'There's still a man who needs saving back in London. And you can help us do that.'

'Saved, lost, it doesn't matter much in the end,' said Mrs Dorter.

'But it's not the end yet,' said Gwen. 'Not for you, not for him, and certainly not for Pamela. Hopefully, she can move on from this without too much of a scar.'

'I'm keenly aware that she's at the same age I was when my innocence was lost,' said Mrs Dorter.

She finished her cup, then refilled it, making the rum's contribution larger.

'Or more accurately, when it was taken from me,' she said.

'By whom?' asked Gwen.

'Who do you think?' asked Mrs Dorter. 'I grew up as a servant in a servant family in a large house set away from civilization, and Lord Pickard watched me grow up and waited, licking his chops, until he couldn't wait any more. I had no say in the matter, and my parents were too beholden to make any fuss about it.'

'What about Mr Dorter?' asked Gwen. 'What happened when he came along?'

'There never was a Mr Dorter,' she said. 'When Mum and Dad grew too old and were pensioned off, I took over, and the Pickards called me that to give me some respectability. There were no men on the staff who were brave enough to try to pry me away from Pickard's grasp, and the few in town who knew my situation considered me damaged goods, so I was trapped there, kept at his beck and call. And it became even worse.'

'How?' prompted Gwen, guessing and dreading the answer.

'When Kevin turned fourteen, his father decided he needed proper instruction in manly behaviour, and why take the lad to a bawdy house in the city when good old Dorty was right there for the taking?'

'How horrible,' said Gwen.

'Yes, well, Kevin didn't stick with me for long,' she said. 'Once he was up and running, the rich pretty boy became accustomed to the local girls falling for him. And fall they did, one after another, but he tired of them quickly. I became accustomed to sobering up many a confused girl after she would wake there, not sure where she was or what had happened. And I turned away more than a few tearful discards when they would show up on our doorstep, begging to see him again, hoping for another chance. He was a precocious little monster, was our Kevin. And when he brought Bruce into his orbit, the two of them became even worse.'

She sighed.

'I say all of this to give you an idea of the hellish situation I was trapped in,' she said. 'Not to justify what I did, but to explain it.'

'What you did?' repeated Iris. 'You mean to Nancy? You did something to her?'

'I saw her as my means of escape,' said Mrs Dorter. 'She was different because she came from outside the world ruled by the Pickards. And she was a Cambridge girl, so I thought maybe that meant she had more to her than all those frightened local girls. So when the opportunity came, I used her.'

'How?'

'She showed up at my door that night, sobbing and hysterical. Instead of telling her to go crawl into a room, lock the door and sober up until she could think straight again, I took her into my own room and comforted her. I didn't even know I was capable of giving comfort to another person, but somehow I managed with her, and she responded. She told me what had happened to her, that she had been violated and wanted to go to the police. I told her that nothing could be done right then, that the only constables who would be on duty wouldn't give a fig about a girl who went willingly to the Pickard house to drink and spend the night, then complain about what happened. But I told her there was one honest policeman in Kimbolton I could go to. I told her to write down everything that had happened and that I would protect her for the night, get her to safety in the morning and then bring the letter to him and see that she got justice. She believed me. She wrote the letter, I witnessed it, then I let her sleep in my bed while I went to collect her belongings from the master suite.

'I woke her early the next morning. The only person she would trust to drive her to the railway station was Tony. I roused him, told him that she had an emergency and was called away, and that he was the only one sober enough to drive her. I told him to keep quiet as the others were sleeping off the previous night's drinking.

'I told Nancy that I would take her letter to the policeman after the weekend. Only I didn't, of course. I saved it for myself, to use when I saw fit. She called a few times, asking what happened, why they weren't doing anything. I told her to be patient, that these things took time. But finally, I told her the truth: that there was no possible way that the police would act on the word of a silly little minx like her against the local lords and masters, and that she should have known better.'

She glanced over at the stove. The fire had burned down. She got up, took the poker and prodded the remaining embers until they fell apart.

'I didn't know that she'd go and throw herself in the river after that,' she said. 'But that ended up working out better for me, didn't it? I had to wait for the father to come back from his travels. It was too late for the dead girl, but that letter could still ruin his precious son and heir.'

'So you blackmailed Lord Pickard,' said Gwen.

'Pickard? No point in going to him about it,' said Mrs Dorter bitterly. 'If it was Kevin she would have happily gone along with everything, wouldn't she? She thought she had a chance with him, just like they all did at first, until he got bored and sent them packing. No, it was the other one.'

'Bruce,' said Iris.

'Yes, little Brucie, who usually got the leavings from Kevin, only he didn't want to wait that night. His girl had begged off from that particular party, hadn't she? So there he was, all alone, and his best friend wasn't about to let him go without. So Kevin gave her to Brucie. Held her down when she didn't want to go along with it. Held her down while his best friend satisfied himself with her, then they took turns, and when they were both spent, that's when the screaming started. Maybe it started before that, but with two of them it was easy enough to stop her screams. Every detail of what happened to her was in what she wrote. When I read it, it sounded like one long scream. And it sounded that way to Bruce's father when I brought it to him later that summer.'

'My God,' whispered Gwen.

'He paid for my silence and my escape here. I told everyone

it was Lord Pickard's generosity after my years of devoted service that allowed me to retire to a life as an innkeeper.'

'You could have saved her,' said Iris.

'So could you,' said Mrs Dorter.

'I didn't know what had happened.'

'You knew,' said Mrs Dorter. 'Kevin told you by not telling you when you sat with him the next morning in the breakfast room.'

'You were listening.'

'I was listening. So were you. And you stayed. You stayed, and you ate his food and drank his liquor and danced all night with him and his friends and all of you pretended to worship him.'

'I tried to talk to her as soon as I got back,' said Iris.

'How did you get back?' scoffed Mrs Dorter. 'In Bruce's car, with Kevin in the front seat? Did they hold the door open for you when they dropped you off at your fancy girls' college? Like proper gentlemen should? Did you give each of them one last kiss goodbye while Nancy watched you from her window? Are you surprised that she failed to confide in you?'

'You traded her life for this place,' said Iris. 'Was it worth it?'

Mrs Dorter stood and walked to the back window.

'They used to drown women they suspected of being witches in that pond in the meadow,' said Mrs Dorter, looking out into the darkness. 'Sometimes, I look out there at night. I think about her. How she gave herself to the water. I watch the water here, and wonder if she will rise from it, pointing at me. The water took her, the fire found Bruce and the guns took Kevin. And I'm still trapped in an isolated house in the country.'

She turned back, her face haggard.

'That's all of it,' she said. 'Now you know what I know. Go up to your room and get some sleep. I have to clean up around here.'

They left as she began shovelling the ashes from the stove.

TWELVE

Iris hadn't set the alarm clock, so she was surprised when it went off early Sunday morning. She was even more surprised upon opening her eyes to see Gwen getting out of bed.

'Arise and shine, partner,' said Gwen as she began dressing.

'What's going on?' Iris replied groggily.

'It's our last day here,' said Gwen. 'We should get some beetling done.'

'We?' said Iris, throwing off her covers. 'You actually want to go with me?'

'It would be a pity to have come all this way without having seen what else this place has to offer besides depravity and misery,' said Gwen. 'Besides, after hearing you rattle on about beetles so often, I confess that you've aroused my curiosity.'

Iris dressed quickly and grabbed her beetle book and her binoculars. The two went downstairs and out the back door unchallenged by anyone except for the rooster, which was emerging from the coop. He looked at the two resentfully.

'You must be Ernie,' said Gwen. 'I'm Gwen. How do you do?'

Ernie did not respond.

'I think he's angry because we've beaten him to the punch,' said Iris. 'This way.'

They went through the gate. Behind them, Ernie greeted the dawn.

'That's the pond,' said Iris.

'Oh, there are ducklings! How cute!' exclaimed Gwen, approaching it.

'Watch out for that patch over there,' Iris warned her.

'The spurge?'

'Of course, you knew that,' said Iris.

'I grew up on a country estate,' said Gwen. 'Our grounds-keeper taught us all about what plants to avoid. Big brother

Thurmond, of course, ignored his instruction and frequently came back covered with welts, which reinforced the lessons for me.'

She gazed into the murky depths of the pond pensively.

'I wonder if they really did drown witches here,' she said. 'If their bones still rest buried in the mud at the bottom while the teal paddle overhead, blissfully unaware. There should be some kind of marker set up in their memory. The witches, I mean, not the teal. Hang on – are those some kind of beetle skating about?'

'Whirligigs,' said Iris, coming over to look. 'They feed in groups like that.'

'And that one?' Gwen asked, pointing to a larger, somewhat menacing creature skimming along the surface.

'That, my dear, is the great diving beetle, Dytiscus marginalis, the terror of the pond. A predator to be feared, if you happen to be smaller than it.'

Gwen watched as the fearsome predator suddenly disappeared below the surface.

'Hence the name,' she commented. 'How do they breathe?'

'They can make an air bubble and clutch it to their abdomens as they dive,' said Iris.

'To think they've known how to do that for thousands of years, and mankind has only figured out scuba-diving this century,' said Gwen. 'I shall never underestimate the humble water beetle again.'

'Is this a full conversion, or are you only being nice to me?'

'I'm still going to church after breakfast,' said Gwen. 'You are welcome to join me.'

'Sorry, darling,' said Iris. 'I'll stay here and commune with Nature until you return.'

'Do you find Nature to be more or less forgiving than God?' asked Gwen.

'I can't compare the two since I don't believe in one of them,' said Iris. 'I think that if I did believe in God, I'd be even angrier at the world than I already am.'

'Would you be angrier at yourself?'

'It would be hard to be angrier at myself than I already am,' said Iris. 'OK, that one over there is a crescent water scavenger beetle. They go through dung and decayed vegetation searching for nutrients, and in doing so break them down into useful components for the soil. Very valuable creatures. More so than me at the moment, and I've dug through worse.'

'Iris, after what we learned last night, I am still of the opinion that what happened to Nancy wasn't your fault,' said Gwen.

'I should have helped her more than I did,' said Iris. 'I keep coming back to that.'

'You tried. She refused to be helped.'

'I should have done a better job of convincing her,' insisted Iris. 'Maybe I could have persuaded her to go to the police herself. Or to a doctor.'

'She did what she did because of who she was, how her parents raised her, and most importantly because she was raped by Bruce Cater and Kevin Pickard,' said Gwen. 'Nothing you did, or didn't do, caused any of that. Including her suicide, which we both believe it was. I think she did that because she felt betrayed by Mrs Dorter and was terrified of what would happen when her parents found out she was pregnant.'

'That still doesn't explain why someone tried to kill Tony,' said Iris.

'Not directly,' said Gwen.

'What do you mean?' asked Iris, looking at her sharply.

'My original thought was that this had been vengeance for Nancy,' said Gwen. 'But now that we have a more detailed account of what happened to her it seems unlikely that someone would want to punish Tony for it.'

'Why is that?'

'Because they could have gone after him when he came back from Spain, for one thing. But also because they haven't come after Mrs Dorter – or you. And both of you have been in England the entire time.'

'Maybe they considered us unimportant or uninvolved compared to the others,' argued Iris.

'Then why would Tony have been any more significant? He wasn't involved in the rape.'

'No, he wasn't,' admitted Iris.

'I think that the attack on him was because of something else. Remember when I said that the choice of a Molotov cocktail was to make him suffer before he died?'

'Yes.'

'There was something that Mrs Dorter said about Bruce Cater that struck me. About his death. "The fire found Bruce." Not that he died in battle, or in a hail of bullets or from a shell, but that the fire found him.'

'Tony said something similar,' remembered Iris. '"And in the end, the fire found him anyway." I had thought he was talking about everlasting hellfire. Maybe it was literal? How odd that an atheist like me would choose the religious meaning over the secular.'

'I still think the choice of a petrol bomb was meant to send Tony a message,' said Gwen. 'We should make it back to Paddington Station by mid-afternoon. We can go directly to the hospital and ask him.'

'Do you think this was about Bruce?'

'I'm beginning to,' said Gwen. 'We haven't spoken to his family yet.'

'That may present some difficulty,' said Iris.

'Why?'

'They won't speak to me. His parents came to visit at Cambridge several times and were quite clear about me not being good enough to consort with the likes of them. And when I attended the memorial service for him a few years later, they completely cut me dead.'

'Hmm. If it's merely a matter of upper-class snobbery I should be able to pass,' said Gwen.

'Good for you, milady,' said Iris. She glanced at her watch. 'Breakfast soon. I don't think any of our commandment-breaking fellow guests will be attending church, but maybe the twins will be going and can take you. Let's get packed now. Wait!'

'What? Did you think of something?'

Iris squatted down and gently plucked a tiny round-bodied creature from the edge of a pond, then held it out for Gwen to see it crawling across her palm.

'Simplocaria semistriata,' she said. 'The semi-striated pill beetle. That's a life-list find for me.'

'Good,' said Gwen, peering at it cautiously. 'I'm glad the trip hasn't been a complete waste of time.'

Their breakfast was augmented with lardy cakes and Bath buns, two local delicacies that they found on their plates, offered with a shy smile by Pamela. Then Gwen attended services with the twins while Iris wandered through the outbuildings and made friends with the animals.

When the time came for their departure, Pamela appeared in their doorway to carry their bags downstairs. Before she picked them up, she quickly stepped forwards and embraced Iris.

'I cannot thank you enough,' she said softly.

'These are all the thanks I need,' said Iris.

Timothy was waiting outside with Barney harnessed to the trap. He said nothing during the ride to the station, but after bringing their suitcases to the platform he solemnly shook their hands before leaving.

The local train came twenty minutes later. After they transferred to the London-bound train, Gwen once again placed her bags on the overhead shelf, then stood back to let Iris heave hers beside it.

Only this time, the bag caught the lip of the shelf and tumbled back. Iris frantically caught it, hugging it to her chest with both arms.

'I am losing my touch,' she said with chagrin.

She tossed it again, this time with success, then stared at it thoughtfully.

'What?' asked Gwen.

'An idea,' said Iris.

'This must have been what it was like when the apple conked Newton,' said Gwen. 'I am honoured to be present at the occasion.'

'You know he was a Cambridge man, don't you?'

'Oh, we are so lucky that a Cambridge man discovered

gravity!' cried Gwen. 'Why, if it had been an Oxford man sitting under that tree we'd all still be floating about, untethered to the earth!'

'I'm fairly certain that's not how it works,' said Iris.

'Well, what do I know? I've never been to university.'

'Another thing that's not my fault,' said Iris.

'Are you going to tell me your idea?'

'Not yet,' said Iris. 'I need to ask a few people some questions first.'

The taxi taking them from Paddington Station to the hospital arrived just after four in the afternoon. They went inside, still carrying their luggage.

'I'll mind the bags while you go and see him,' said Gwen. 'I'll be in the waiting room.'

'Thanks,' said Iris.

Tony, to her annoyance, was asleep when she came to his room. She pulled a chair up next to his bed and contemplated where she could poke him without causing undue pain or further damage. She couldn't think of any.

She leaned forwards and whispered, 'Tony. Wake up.'

It had no effect. She repeated the phrase, increasing her volume until he finally made an indecipherable snorting noise and opened his eyes. He looked at her in confusion for a few seconds, then they regained some semblance of clarity.

'Hello, Sparks,' he said. 'Catch any beetles?'

'A few,' she said. 'They're carnivorous. I released them under your bedclothes before waking you.'

'I hope they like their meat well done,' he said. 'I didn't think I'd be seeing you until tomorrow.'

'I had a question for you,' she said.

'Something to do with the vengeance quest?'

'Yes. Were you with Bruce Cater when he was killed?'

His eyes went wide, then distant.

'I was,' he said. 'It was horrible.'

'What happened?'

'We were low on ammo, and needed a distraction so we could slip away,' he said. 'Bruce made up a petrol bomb. The idea was he was going to heave it into one of the trucks at their encampment and beat it back to us, but as he was running towards them he tripped and the bloody thing went off where he fell. He was covered in flames in an instant. I heard him scream for a few seconds as he rolled around in the grass, but then he stopped. We got our distraction, all right. We left him there and ran.'

'Any chance he could have survived that?'

'None,' said Tony. 'You didn't see it, Sparks. He was halfway consumed by the time we picked up and ran. Were you thinking he had returned from the very depths of hell to bring me back with him?'

'No, of course not.'

'Mind you, if he had, I would have gone with him,' said Tony. 'Even to the very depths of hell.'

'Stay with us a little longer,' said Sparks. 'I still owe you a few drinks.'

'I'll take you up on that someday,' said Tony. 'Then you can tell me what the hell this is all about.'

'As soon as I know, I will,' she promised.

'Bruce Cater burned to death,' she reported to Gwen in the waiting room. 'He tripped trying to throw a Molotov cocktail.'

'That confirms that theory,' said Gwen. 'Do you know where the Caters live?'

'In Cambridgeshire. Outside of Kimbolton.'

'Good,' said Gwen. 'I'll see if Sally can drive me tomorrow. He's off on Mondays.'

'Sally? Why Sally?'

'I have an idea as to how to gain entry,' said Gwen. 'I need to call in a favour first. Shall we head home?'

'There's one more person I need to talk to here,' said Iris. 'Wait for me.'

She walked out into the entrance hall. Sure enough, the Brigadier's man was lingering about. She wandered past him, ignoring him while heading towards the telephone boxes. He gave her a few seconds, then turned and followed her.

'You have a good holiday, Sparks?' he asked.

'Was the firm keeping track of my whereabouts?' she asked.

'No,' he said. 'But you weren't here yesterday, and you're coming in late today with luggage, so I figured you were off somewhere. Lucky you.'

'You've been on surveillance the entire time?'

'Trading twelve-hour shifts,' he said. 'One of the more boring jobs I've had. Essential, but boring. Looks like I'm stuck here for the duration.'

'It's like that sometimes, isn't it?' said Sparks. 'Tell you what, when this is all over we should go out for drinks.'

'Yeah?'

'Why not? I might as well confine my social life to the firm since I don't have any privacy anyway. Give me your name and number and I'll ring you.'

'I'm not supposed to do that,' he said dubiously.

'You'll find that "I'm not supposed to do that, but here we go" is my motto,' said Iris with a grin. 'Especially after a couple of drinks.'

'If the Brigadier finds out—'

'You can tell him you were conducting some independent surveillance, acting on a hunch. He likes initiative.'

'He doesn't, you know,' he said, thinking it over. 'But we're both working for him, yeah? My name's Carlton. Carlton Edwards. You got something to write on?'

She produced her notebook and a pencil and handed it to him. He scribbled down a number and handed it back.

'How long do you think this assignment's going to last?' she asked

'No telling,' he said.

'Well, I'll ring you either way,' she said. 'Nice to finally have a name to put to the face. Which is a nice face, by the way.'

'Likewise,' he grinned.

She smiled, then walked back to Gwen.

Men are such idiots, she thought.

'That porter,' said Gwen as Iris rejoined her. 'He's the dock worker who first contacted us, isn't he?'

'Yes. He's been monitoring Tony here.'

'Did you just pick him up?'

'I did. I have his number in the same notebook I used for beetling.'

'Another life-list acquisition?'

'Hopefully not,' said Iris. 'Let's go home.'

The taxi pulled up by the *Cecilia* by six.

'Are you sure you don't want to have dinner?' asked Gwen as the cabbie fetched Iris's suitcase from the boot.

'Sorry, there's one more thing I need to look into,' said Iris. 'I'll see you tomorrow. Thanks for the weekend, darling. Next one is on me.'

She got out, collected her suitcase, walked across to her boat and waved before going in. She watched out of the window as the cab drove off with Gwen, then immediately dropped her suitcase on her saloon table and went back out.

Forty minutes later she stood in front of Grenville House, watching people go in and out of the entrance from the other side of Grosvenor Road for a while. Then she walked around to the side of the building and looked up.

Five storeys up, she saw one window that had been boarded up from the inside. She could see scorch marks around the window frame.

Sixty feet up, give or take, she thought.

She stood under the window, then turned and stood with her heels against the wall of the building. Then she paced across the narrow street until her toes bumped up against the building opposite.

Maybe twenty feet, she estimated.

She looked up at the building across from Tony's flat. The roof was set back another ten feet from where the lowest level hit the pavement.

She looked around until she saw a pebble lying on the ground. She picked it up, tossed it in the air and caught it a few times, getting a feel for its weight. Then she drew her arm back and threw it as hard as she could at the boarded-up window. It fell short by about ten feet, banging off the top of the window frame of the flat below.

Right, she thought.

She walked away quickly in case anyone in the lower flat would be looking to see who was throwing stones at them.

Avery Conley sat at his desk in his office at the BBC in Alexandra Palace on Monday morning, going over his list for the day's broadcasting schedule. They were going to be sending out a live performance of *The Barber of Seville* from the Cambridge Theatre in Seven Dials that evening, and the process of transporting and setting up the bulky cameras and sound equipment was proving to be a logistical nightmare.

But each logistical nightmare was a learning experience, he thought with more assurance than he truly believed. He hummed as he went through everything, then wondered at the tune.

Ah, 'Blue Blood' from *Iolanthe*. That had the lyric with 'Seven Dials' in it somewhere. Must have been what prompted it.

His intercom buzzed, and he pressed the lever to connect him to his secretary.

'Yes, Imelda?'

'There is a Mrs Bainbridge on the line wishing to speak with you,' she said. 'Are you available?'

'Mrs Bainbridge? How curious. Certainly, Imelda. Put her through.'

A moment later, his telephone rang.

'Avery Conley here,' he said.

'Good morning, Mr Conley,' came a woman's voice. 'It's Gwen Bainbridge. I hope this isn't a bad time.'

'Not at all, Mrs Bainbridge,' he said. 'It's an unexpected pleasure to hear your voice again. How may I help you?'

'I was wondering if I could ask a rather large favour of you.'

'Name it. I owe you one after what you and Miss Sparks did for us last spring.'

'I find myself pursuing another matter of a, shall we say, delicate nature.'

'Another criminal matter?'

'Well, yes. We are unofficially assisting Scotland Yard, and

I'm afraid I cannot tell you any more details, but I am going into a situation where I will be posing as something that I am not, which is awkward, to say the least, and I would like to use your name and number as a reference should I need confirmation.'

'Posing as what, specifically?'

'As an employee of the BBC.'

'Interesting,' he said, leaning back in his chair. 'What are you planning to do with this new career?'

'I'm going to interview someone,' she said. 'Would you mind terribly letting me pretend for a day or two?'

'I can do better than that,' said Conley. 'I have just hired you as a research assistant, starting immediately. I'll fire you as soon as you're finished doing whatever it is.'

'That is extraordinarily decent of you, Mr Conley. Thank you.'

'Will you tell me what this is all about when you're done?'

'I may not be able to,' she said. 'As I said, it's unofficial.'

'I understand. Good luck with whatever it is, then.'

'Thanks again, Mr Conley. Good day.'

'Goodbye, Mrs Bainbridge.'

He hung up, then buzzed Imelda on the intercom.

'Yes, sir?' she answered.

'Imelda, please add Mrs Gwendolyn Bainbridge to our list of freelancers,' he said. 'And if anyone calls, confirm that she's doing some research for me.'

'Yes, sir. Shall I alert Personnel as well?'

'Not necessary, my dear. We'll let them know when she signs her contract.'

'Very well, Mr Conley.'

He hung up, then went back to work, singing softly to himself, 'Spurn not the nobly born with love affected, Nor treat with virtuous scorn the well connected . . .'

'Got my cover story set up,' said Gwen as she hung up.

'You're a BBC reporter?' asked Iris.

'Nothing so grand or public,' said Gwen. 'Merely a researcher doing advance work. A plausible entry-level job for a well-connected socialite with no particular skills, wouldn't you agree? I'm hoping the Caters will.'

'Sally's going with you for this?'

'Yes, he's driving me. I telephoned the Cater house last night and made an appointment with Mrs Cater for this afternoon.'

'Before you knew you had your cover set? Pretty nervy.'

'I learned that from you,' said Gwen. 'Any progress with your gravity experiments?'

'My initial forays raised some ideas,' said Iris. 'I will be following up on them.'

'How?'

'I'm going to visit Parham later.'

'Oh? What for?'

'I have some questions about fire.'

Gwen emerged from the building at eleven to find Sally waiting by his Hornet, which was parked by the kerb. She gave him a quick kiss, then got in. He closed her door, then got behind the wheel and drove off.

'I like that we're a publicly acknowledged couple,' he said. 'It makes for more opportunities to kiss you.'

'I appreciate your donating your day off to helping me,' she said.

'Spending a full Monday with you is a delightful prospect, no matter what the objective,' he said. 'What exactly is the objective? I know we're heading towards Kimbolton, but why?'

'I'm going to interview Bruce Cater's parents.'

'Cater? Good Lord, why?'

She looked over at him, thinking carefully about how to phrase what she was about to say.

'Sally, I know that you're bound by the Official Secrets Act from going into much detail about what you did in the war,' she said. 'Just as Iris is for what she did.'

'Yes,' he said, glancing at her cautiously. 'Although I think we've both dropped our guards around you on more than one occasion.'

'You have,' she said. 'So I signed it myself recently.'

'You what?' he exclaimed. 'Why did you become a signatory?'

'Because of Iris. It seems that I have learned more than I should.'

'That woman,' he said hotly. 'She had no right—'

'She had every right, Sally,' said Gwen. 'She had to bring me into the loop so we could save your skin a few months ago, or had you forgotten how close to arrest you were? She put herself at risk to save you, then I signed it to keep her from going to prison.'

'Who made you sign?'

'The Brigadier.'

'Him,' he said, groaning in exasperation. 'Of course, it would be him. He's been trying to get her back in his clutches ever since she called him out on one of his most disastrous ideas. He's bound to want the two of you to do something grotesquely distasteful for him sooner or later.'

'Actually—'

'We're doing it now, aren't we?'

'More or less.'

'And you didn't tell me.'

'It wasn't meant for anyone to know,' she said. 'Our part was supposed to be brief and minor. But then came a Molotov cocktail to throw everyone's plans in disarray.'

'So you're interviewing the Caters because of what happened to Tony Danforth?'

'Tony Danforth was the target of the Brigadier's investigation, but he didn't order the attack. Now Iris and I are trying to find out why Tony was firebombed.'

'Why? To clear him?'

'Maybe. At least to protect him from further attack.'

'How do the Caters figure into this?'

'Because of what happened to Nancy Spurlock.'

'Which you wouldn't have known about if I hadn't brought it to your attention,' said Sally with a grimace. 'This is all my fault.'

'No, I'm glad you told me,' said Gwen.

'You said when you called last night that you specifically needed me on this trip. Why?'

'Because I am now a researcher for the BBC, and you are

my associate producer. And you have BBC identification, which I don't yet, as I've only just started my employment.'

'They'll raise hell at the office if they find out you're doing this.'

'No,' said Gwen. 'They won't.'

Parham was already at the restaurant when Sparks arrived. He stood to greet her when she came to his table.

'As this is official business, I am buying you lunch,' he said jovially. 'But don't break the department budget.'

'They don't serve champagne here, so you're safe,' said Sparks. 'Thanks for meeting me outside your office. I didn't want to risk bumping into my ex.'

'I didn't want to risk your bumping into any of my detectives,' said Parham. 'Let's order, then we'll talk shop.'

Tempted as she was to abuse Scotland Yard's hospitality (and deep down, she felt they owed her a few meals), she held herself to a portion of shepherd's pie and a pint of ale.

'How goes the Danforth investigation?' she asked.

'There's not much I can tell you,' he said. 'Not because I am withholding information, but because I really haven't made any progress. Any luck on that Cambridge connection?'

'We're still looking into it,' said Sparks. 'We've eliminated more possibilities than we've discovered, unfortunately. I had what I thought was a thought yesterday, but it may only be a fever dream. But those go well with fire, don't they?'

'You know that by now I take your ideas seriously, Miss Sparks,' said Parham.

'Thank you,' she said. 'Not everyone does. Now, I'm not prying into anything subject to any confidentiality requirements. My questions are about the actual mechanics of the petrol bomb. Would those fall within the parameters of our unofficial relationship?'

'Ask and I'll make the determination upon hearing them.'

'It seems to me there are two categories of how a petrol bomb can be used,' she said. 'Either it was already inside Mr Danforth's flat when he arrived, or it came in through the window after he opened it. Would you agree?'

'I would,' he said.

'If it was the first, then it would have been a booby trap and needed either a trigger of some kind to ignite it or a clockwork mechanism set to go off at a certain time,' she said. 'Given that Danforth's arrival could not have been predicted, we can rule out the clockwork. Did the fire brigade find anything that looked like a tripwire connected to some form of igniter?'

'There wasn't much to find by the time the fire burned down,' said Parham. 'They found fragments of a bottle, but nothing that looked like the remains of an igniter. We also considered the possibility of a fuse dangling from the window and lit from below, but there were no scorch marks on the outer wall or ashes on the pavement underneath.'

'How far from the window were the bottle fragments?'

'Scattered about, which one would expect from an explosion, but the pattern suggests that it happened five or six feet from the window.'

'That means it came in from the outside,' she said, nodding. 'He would have noticed it otherwise.'

'We're on the same page so far,' said Parham.

'The window was too high to reach from the street,' she said. 'Am I correct in concluding that you believe the bomb was thrown from the building across the way?'

'That seems to be the best theory,' he said.

'I don't like it,' she said. 'Have you ever thrown a full bottle of wine?'

'I have not,' he said. 'Have you?'

'It would be unlikely for undrunk wine to escape my grasp no matter how plastered I was,' she said. 'The roof of the building opposite Danforth's flat was set back from the base, which means that a heavy, ungainly, flaming object would have had to be thrown accurately some thirty feet through an open window. That would take an excellent arm. When you catch the fellow, send him to the Marylebone Cricket Club. They need a decent bowler right now.'

'We'll see if the fellow's arm is still good after he serves twenty years,' said Parham.

'Nevertheless, I don't think that's how anyone would fire-bomb a flat,' said Sparks.

'Nevertheless, the flat was firebombed,' said Parham. 'And that seems the most likely method.'

'Did you find any indications that someone had been on the opposite rooftop?'

'No. The only fingerprints on the door leading to the roof belonged to the caretaker, and he was listening to the radio with his family when it happened. So whoever was on the opposite rooftop wore gloves.'

'There's another possibility,' said Sparks. 'A rather insane idea, which is why I came up with it, yet I'm liking it better. But I need to know more before I bring it to you.'

'How soon will you know?' asked Parham.

'That I cannot tell you until I'm done investigating,' said Sparks.

'Why not tell me the idea and let me investigate it?'

'Because it involves areas that you shouldn't be stepping into officially,' said Sparks. 'Not to mention things I'm not allowed to mention.'

'I see,' said Parham. 'Someday, Miss Sparks, I am going to learn everything about you just to satisfy my curiosity.'

'When you do, please explain me to me,' said Sparks. 'My therapist is taking too long.'

THIRTEEN

'On to the Great North Road we go,' said Sally as they left London. 'I am renaming my Hornet Black Bess in honour of the occasion.'

'That was Dick Turpin's horse?' asked Gwen.

'Correct. According to legend, he rode all the way from London to York in fifteen hours. We could do it in five.'

'That poor horse,' said Gwen.

'Turpin was ultimately hanged for being a horse thief, so maybe there was some equine vengeance exacted.'

'I've grown quite weary of vengeance of late,' said Gwen. 'Let's talk about anything else for a while.'

'Gladly. How is Ronnie doing? Did you have a good visit this weekend while I was toiling away in the broadcast mines?'

'I didn't see him this weekend,' said Gwen guiltily. 'Iris and I were off tracking down a possible witness.'

'And we're already back to the vengeance,' he said. 'You'd better bring me up to speed.'

By the time she was done, he was shaking his head sadly.

'Poor Sauce,' he said. 'She died alone and in shame. I don't even know if bringing out the truth about what happened would serve to reclaim her reputation.'

'You know, I've never even thought about that as a goal,' said Gwen. 'The entire time I've been thinking about catching whoever did this to Tony. But he wasn't the first victim in this story, was he?'

'From what that Mrs Dorter told you, there may have been many victims whose stories never saw the light of day,' said Sally. 'Their predators may have been punished by other means, but one could hardly say those girls got any form of justice for what happened to them. And they never will.'

She was silent for a long while. He glanced over to see tears running down her cheek. He reached over and squeezed her hand for a moment.

'At least the world is safe from those two wolves now,' he said.

'That's not why—' she began. Then she shook her head. 'Sorry. A bad memory. Nothing to do with any of this. Could we stop for a quick lunch? I'm famished, and I need to fix my face.'

'Of course.'

He pulled off the road in Biggleswade and found a small tea shop where they had sandwiches. When they got back on the road he stopped the car at a junction for a moment, looking at the fingerposts pointing towards different towns. Cambridge was to the right.

'Do you want to pay your alma mater a quick visit on the way back?' she asked, noticing him looking at it. 'I've never been there. You could show me where you and Iris were moulded.'

'You've never seen Cambridge?'

'The Bainbridges were Oxonians,' she said. 'So were the Brewsters. I went to and from Oxford many times with my parents when they were either dropping off Thurmond or collecting him, and I now associate the place with my resentment for not being allowed to go. Plus, those rides were usually filled with Thurmond and me punching each other in the biceps in the back seat, despite his supposedly being too mature and me being too ladylike for that behaviour. But we had no close Cambridge connections back then, so I've never been. Have you been back?'

'Not since the war,' he said. 'I really haven't had the . . . not the desire to go. What would it be? The courage.'

'Why courage?'

'There is a reunion for my class coming up,' he said. 'I thought about attending for a split second, then rejected the idea.'

'Why?'

'Because I'm terrified of finding out how many of us, of my friends and colleagues, won't be there because they didn't make it through the war. I don't think I could take that right now. I'd spend the entire time mourning the ones I lost, despising the ones who avoided going and finishing with an aftertaste of guilt for having survived. And I wouldn't be able to talk about my own war because of the damn Act, so I'd stand around, holding my sherry, and lie about my career in Supplies.'

'You could talk to me now,' said Gwen quietly. 'I've been cleared for it, according to the Brigadier.'

He gripped the steering wheel tightly for a moment, then got his breathing back under control.

'Maybe someday,' he said. 'When I'm ready for you to hate me.'

'I could never do that, Sally.'

'You might, though,' he said. 'It may be better if we rip the plaster off quickly and find out what's underneath.'

'Please, not today,' said Gwen.

'No, of course not today,' he agreed. 'Let's save Tony first. His bandages are real.'

They drove on.

'Will Ronnie go to Oxford?' he asked.

'He's seven, Sally.'

'Decisions like that are made prenatally in some families.'

'All of his grandparents – well, the three living ones – expect him to attend Oxford,' she said. 'As if I had no say in the matter. What am I saying? As if Ronnie had no say. As far as I'm concerned it will be his choice. He can go to Oxford, or Cambridge, or the Sorbonne, or rodeo school in Wyoming if he wants. He's already wealthy and in line for a lordship someday. There's no need for him to make old school tie connections if he doesn't want them. As for the rest of my children—'

'Wait, what other children? I haven't noticed any crawling about since we've got involved.'

'Hypothetically speaking.'

'How many hypothetical children are you hypothetically going to have?'

'That would depend on when I hypothetically start having them,' said Gwen. 'One is no longer young.'

'You're not even thirty yet.'

'No, but it looms,' she said gloomily. 'From there, it is only a short leap into decrepitude.'

'You do own a mirror, don't you?' he said. 'Age cannot wither her, nor custom stale, et cetera, et cetera.'

'Cleopatra died young.'

'Older than you, self-inflicted, and she still looked good, by all reports. Don't keep any asps about and you'll be fine. Is Ronnie amenable to the idea of sharing his life with siblings?'

'He's in favour of it,' said Gwen. 'He wants a captive audience of smaller admirers who will do his bidding.'

'When does he come home from the country?'

'August. I'll be taking time off from work for two weeks.'

'Perhaps I could take him out to see a cricket match or something when you need a break,' said Sally. 'An all-male expedition.'

'He would love that, Sally,' said Gwen. 'So would I.'

They arrived in Kimbolton, passing the castle.

'Which of the six died there?' asked Sally.

'Catherine of Aragon,' said Gwen. 'I saw the room they kept her in when we stayed there.'

'You stayed in the castle?'

'I've stayed in many castles,' said Gwen. 'They're much more exciting when you're a child and don't care about the temperature of the room in which you're sleeping. There's the road east. Take that next right.'

Sally carefully followed her directions as they headed into the countryside. Eventually, they turned onto a long driveway that brought them to a sprawling brick mansion. The original building was two storeys tall and dated from the sixteenth century, but every fifty years or so some ancestor of the Caters must have decided he needed more space, so another building was appended to the first, some lengthwise, some crosswise, as if generations of architects had been playing a long game of dominoes.

'It's a bit of a jumble, isn't it?' commented Sally as he parked the Hornet near some other vehicles in front of a large entrance on the left side of the building.

'It's not bad,' said Gwen. 'It's certainly big.'

The door was answered by a maid.

'May I help you?' she asked.

'Mrs Gwendolyn Bainbridge and Mr Salvatore Danielli,' said Mrs Bainbridge. 'We have an appointment.'

'Certainly, Mrs Bainbridge,' said the maid. 'You are expected. Please come in.'

She led them to a room that took up one entire side of the house, with a twenty-foot ceiling and one entire wall taken up by glass panels overlooking the grounds. The room itself was filled with furniture that dated to different eras, each piece having in common only that in each of those eras the owners had overpaid. The maid showed them to a pair of nineteenth-century high-backed armchairs that had some vaguely Indian motif.

'I will inform Lady Cater of your arrival,' she said, and left, closing the double doors behind her.

'I think every place I've ever lived in could fit inside this room at once,' said Sally.

'Speak softly,' said Gwen. 'The ancestors are judging us.'

He glanced over his shoulder at a wall holding an array of paintings of the various Lord Caters, some in wigs and stockings, some in uniforms and plumed hats, the most recent in tailcoats, leaning against cannons or horses or grand pianos, depending upon which background matched the outfit.

'Bruce didn't make it to the portrait portion of his life,' observed Sally.

'It's only the men,' said Gwen. 'None of the ladies merited preservation or display. I don't even see a photograph of the current family anywhere.'

The doors opened and the maid stepped in.

'Lady Francesca Cater,' she announced.

The woman who entered was small, almost doll-like in her appearance. Her make-up gave her skin a porcelain smoothness – so brittle it looked as if it could shatter if she smiled broadly.

There did not appear to be much risk of that happening.

The two rose to meet her, and she reared back, startled as Sally reached his full height.

'Gracious!' she exclaimed. 'You're quite the specimen, aren't you?'

'How do you do, Lady Cater?' he said in his most genteel tone. 'Salvatore Danielli, BBC.'

'And I'm Mrs Gwendolyn Bainbridge,' said Mrs Bainbridge. 'We spoke on the telephone yesterday. So good of you to welcome us to your home. It is quite lovely.'

'Thank you,' said Lady Cater, gesturing for them to sit again. 'It was good of you to come all the way from London. We don't get as many visitors nowadays as we did before the war, especially with our children having grown up and gone out into the world.'

'I can imagine this must have been quite a lively place back then,' said Mrs Bainbridge.

'Oh, we had our occasions to shine,' said Lady Cater modestly. 'Of course, Kimbolton society, such as it was, was dominated by our cousins, the Montagues. Alas, they have fallen upon hard times.'

'So I've heard,' said Mrs Bainbridge. 'Such a pity. I attended a few soirées at Kimbolton Castle when I was younger.'

'I thought your face looked familiar,' said Lady Cater. 'What was your name back then?'

'Brewster. I hadn't been presented yet, so was relegated to the ranks of the other adolescents, but we had our fun.'

'I'm certain you did,' said Lady Cater. 'Perhaps you encountered my son, Bruce, when you were there.'

'I do remember him. He was kind enough to dance with me, even though I was such an awkward gangly thing back then.'

'I highly doubt that,' said Lady Cater. 'So you work now?'

There was a faint hint of distaste in her pronunciation of the verb.

'Yes, isn't it exciting?' burbled Mrs Bainbridge. 'They say television is the wave of the future, and I was quite lucky to get in on the ground floor. I've never had a full-time job before. My poor husband gave his life for King and country several years ago, and I've been very much at loose ends since our son went away to school. Mummy pulled some strings and I just started a few days ago. This is my first assignment, in fact!'

'I'm afraid that television hasn't reached us yet,' said Lady Cater, 'but I suppose the invasion is inevitable. I'm not sure I like the idea. I have made my peace with the radio, but it does dictate one's choices, doesn't it? But at least when it's on one isn't bound to a single location and may wander about the room doing other things. Television, on the other hand, confines you to a single seat for the duration of the experience. I don't relish being held slave to an armchair.'

'You still have the choice as to whether or not you'll watch it,' said Mrs Bainbridge. 'I've found that it has brought many aspects of the world to my attention that I might not have been aware of before. I'm hoping to do the same for others now.'

'You make your work sound positively altruistic,' said Lady Cater. 'What is this project that you've come to see me about?'

'We're putting together a programme about the civil war in Spain,' said Mrs Bainbridge, pulling out her notebook and pencil. 'We believe that enough time has passed to give us some perspective on it, especially now that we've had a chance to see General Franco in action for a decade, so we want to revisit and reassess the war as a precursor to the greater war that followed.'

'How does my late son factor into this?'

'We are interested in the different types of Englishmen who volunteered to fight in Spain on either side, as well as the circumstances and family backgrounds which led them to join. Was there anything in particular about Bruce's life here that you believe inspired him to go to Spain?'

'There was nothing about his upbringing that precipitated that,' said Lady Cater.

'Then you wouldn't say that he developed socialistic tendencies from living here?'

'Look around you,' said Lady Cater. 'Does anything you see, does anything about this place smack of socialism?'

'Not in the slightest,' said Mrs Bainbridge. 'But one needs to ask, then, if you believe that perhaps he joined the International Brigade as a reaction to his upbringing?'

'Not at all. The very idea is appalling. Bruce embraced every aspect of the Cater traditions, as well as the Cater wealth, wholeheartedly. We gave him every advantage, and he took advantage of everything we gave him.'

'Interesting,' said Mrs Bainbridge. 'Do you think the trans-
formation occurred because of his time at Cambridge?'

'I don't think that he ever turned away from who he was or
where he came from,' said Lady Cater. 'Despite falling among
some questionable companions while he was there.'

'Who, for example? Did he join the socialists? Or the
communists?'

'He did not,' she replied hotly. 'He never would have shamed
the family like that. He took his degree and eventually would
have taken his rightful place on that wall with his father and
his father's father.'

'Yet he joined the anti-fascist side,' persisted Mrs Bainbridge.
'What do you think prompted a decision like that?'

'Some reckless impulse of his, I suppose,' she said. 'We never
knew the reason, and never will.'

She's lying, thought Gwen.

'Our understanding is that he may have gone in part because
of an incident at Cambridge,' she said.

'Where did you hear that?' snapped Lady Cater.

'Mr Danielli, my associate, heard something about it from
his time there.'

'Oh? You were at Cambridge?' asked Lady Cater.

'I was,' said Danielli. 'A year behind Bruce.'

'I was unaware that they let people like you in there,' said
Lady Cater.

'Tall people?' replied Danielli. 'There is an unofficial quota.
They hand you a helpful guide to the shorter doorways so you
can avoid concussion.'

'So you knew my son.'

'I didn't know him well, but I knew him, as well as some
of his friends. I remember he was in a little satirical singing
group with Kevin Pickard and— oh, who was the third one?'

'Anthony Danforth,' she replied, hesitating slightly on the
name.

'Tony, of course,' he said.

'Anthony Danforth?' said Mrs Bainbridge. 'I saw his name
on a list of Cambridge men who went to Spain. Did he and
Bruce join together?'

'We think Danforth may have put the idea in Bruce's head,' said Lady Cater.

'Really? You wouldn't by any chance have any way of reaching him, would you?' asked Mrs Bainbridge. 'I'd love to get his account of what happened.'

'No, I do not,' said Lady Cater. 'I have no intention of ever speaking to that . . . that . . . I'm sorry, there are no polite words.'

'I'm so sorry, I didn't mean to upset you,' said Mrs Bainbridge. 'It does sound like you blame him for what happened.'

'What happened to our son can neither be changed or rectified,' said Lady Cater huffily.

'Of course,' said Mrs Bainbridge. 'So it wasn't the incident at Cambridge that propelled him into Spain.'

'There was no incident,' said Lady Cater in exasperation.

'What about your younger children? Did they go on to Cambridge as well? I understand it's a family tradition.'

'We thought after Bruce died that the school would hold painful associations for the other two children, and we were quite unhappy with how it was becoming overrun by leftists,' said Lady Cater. 'Nathaniel, my second, went to Oxford instead. As for Charlotte, well, she wanted to go to Cambridge in spite of everything. She idolised her brother and wanted to do everything he did, but we put our foot down.'

'Where did she end up going?'

'We sent her to Manchester to stay with some relatives and go to university. She loved it there, fortunately. You should hear her talk about it. She can do the funniest impressions of the locals. She did them at Christmas parties here, and her accent was spot on.'

'She sounds quite entertaining,' said Mrs Bainbridge. 'Would it be possible—'

From outside the doors, a man's voice was heard, speaking gruffly to someone. They heard the maid's voice in reply. A second later, a man burst through the door, the maid quivering behind him. He was in his sixties but robust and energetic, his grey hair slicked back with pomade, his moustache full and immaculately shaped. It wasn't hard to recognise him as the subject of the last portrait on the wall of Caters.

'Francesca, what the devil do you think you're doing?' he said to his wife, ignoring the others.

'Arnold, this is Mrs Gwendolyn Bainbridge and Mr Salvatore Danielli from the BBC,' she said, flinching slightly. 'They're interested in Bruce's story.'

'Are they?' he said, finally deigning to look at them. 'Are they indeed?'

He walked towards Danielli, who rose to meet him. Lord Cater looked up at him, examining his face, unintimidated by his height.

'Danielli,' he said. 'You're an Eyetie, aren't you?'

'English,' said Danielli. 'Born and raised here.'

'Not English in my book,' said Cater. 'We just fought a war against your people.'

'I know,' said Danielli. 'I was part of it.'

'For which side?' asked Cater.

'As I said, English,' replied Danielli calmly. 'Royal Army.'

'Doing what?'

'Supplies,' said Danielli.

'Oh, very brave, very brave,' sneered Cater.

'Necessary,' said Danielli. 'I did my part.'

'While better men than you died on the front lines.'

'No doubt,' said Danielli. 'I honour their valour and their loss.'

'Hmph,' said Cater. He turned to Mrs Bainbridge. 'I will be brief. There is to be no mention of my son in any broadcast or story. You may leave. Now.'

'But Lord Cater,' she began.

He turned and walked away. His wife looked after him mournfully.

'I'm afraid he took Bruce's death rather badly,' she said. 'The first son and heir, you see. They were quite close. I apologise for his behaviour, but I'm afraid I have no choice in the matter now.'

'No apology necessary,' said Mrs Bainbridge. 'We're sorry to have caused any upset. May I use the loo before we leave? It's a long drive back.'

'Certainly. I will have my maid show you.'

Mrs Bainbridge followed the maid down a hallway to a door. She went through, hiding her frustration.

She was close, she thought. Only she had no more time to learn anything. Lord Cater's anger, combined with his immediate lowering of the family portcullis, made him a prime candidate for further investigation. She wondered if she could manage to break into the Cater house later and search for something informative, the problem there being the massive size of the place.

She washed her hands, then opened the door.

'Mrs Bainbridge, a word with you. In private.'

She turned, startled, to see Lord Cater standing by a door down the hall. He turned without saying anything else and disappeared into a room.

Is this going to be an apology? she wondered.

Somehow, she doubted it.

The room turned out to be a small study. Lord Cater closed the door after she entered, then sat behind a walnut Italianate desk with a wine-red leather insert on top and legs covered with gilded carvings, ending in four brass lion's paws. There was a matching work cabinet behind him with a collection of photographs on top, mostly of earlier versions of Lord Cater standing proudly with a younger man at various stages of his life. Bruce, she thought. The scenes were largely of hunting expeditions or visits to various European capitals. The latter for the most part included Lady Cater and the two other children. The younger brother resembled Lady Cater. The sister, smallest of the three, was a combination of both parents. She clung to Bruce's hand in several of the pictures, looking up at him with adoration.

'That's Bruce in most of those hunting shots,' she said.

'Yes,' he replied. 'So you did know him.'

'I can't say I knew him,' she said. 'Only that I remembered meeting him at Kimbolton Castle.'

'Sit, Mrs Bainbridge,' he said, indicating a leather-covered chair in front of the desk.

She took her seat and waited.

'You are Lord Harold Bainbridge's daughter-in-law, if I'm not mistaken,' he said.

'I am.'

'I'm surprised that you would bother with such a mundane job, given your status.'

'It interests me,' she said.

'It may also interest you to know that Lucinda Kendall is my goddaughter,' he said. 'We speak frequently.'

'Do you?'

'Yes. In fact, she mentioned receiving a visit from you last week,' he continued. 'You and another woman were attempting to locate her brother, Kevin.'

'Yes,' she replied. 'Sadly, it turned out that he died in the war.'

'Which I would have expected you to know before making your visit,' he said. 'Being the keen reporter that you are.'

'What exactly are you getting at, Lord Cater?'

'I paid little mind to your visit to Lucinda until you showed up at my home this afternoon,' he said. 'You made no mention to her about your employment, which means that you were either there or here under false pretences, perhaps both.'

'If you care to verify my employment with the BBC—'

'I do not,' he said, standing abruptly. 'What I demand is that you immediately cease prying into my family's affairs or those of the Pickards. I've made some enquiries about you, Mrs Bainbridge. You have a reputation for sticking your nose in places where it doesn't belong. I won't have that.'

'Why did you let your son flee to Spain, Lord Cater?' she asked. 'What were you protecting him from here?'

He strode quickly around the desk towards her. She propelled herself from the chair before he could get to her.

'Stay away from me, or I will call for my colleague,' she warned him, backing away.

'He won't hear you from there,' said Cater. 'And if you won't listen to reason, I think stronger methods are called for.'

He reached for her. She waited for him to get close, then grabbed his right elbow from underneath with her left hand, his wrist with her right hand, and pivoted to her right, forcing his arm down. He wasn't expecting any resistance and was caught off guard, his body following his arm downwards.

'Are you the one who taught him?' she shouted. 'To treat women like toys, then discard them when they were broken? Is that another one of your family traditions?'

He tried to straighten, but she applied more pressure to his elbow, the pain forcing him to his knees.

'Are you insane?' he gasped.

'Used to be,' she hissed into his ear. 'Now, I'm only angry. Bruce went to Spain to avoid the scandal of what he and Kevin Pickard did to Nancy Spurlock, didn't he?'

He grunted in distress.

'Answer me!' she said.

'He could have gone anywhere!' he said. 'We didn't care where he went, as long as he stayed away until we hushed everything up here.'

'Are you still hushing everything up? Is that why Tony Danforth was attacked?'

'Danforth?' he asked in confusion. 'What does he have to do with anything? He's in China somewhere.'

'You didn't know he had returned?'

'No! I swear it! Dammit, woman, you're going to break my arm!'

She released him, retreating towards the door.

'If you want my silence about Bruce, you will stay here until I leave,' she said. 'Others know that we're here, so don't try anything. It will go badly for you and your precious family reputation if you do.'

With that she left him, still on his knees, clutching his arm in agony.

Sally was waiting for her in the front hall.

'Shall we go?' he asked.

'We should. Rather quickly, in fact.'

He asked no questions, nevertheless wondering at her expression and flushed appearance. She watched out the rear window as they drove away. It wasn't until they reached the end of the driveway that she turned forwards, taking a deep breath.

'Are you all right?' he asked.

'I am now,' she said. 'I had an unexpected conversation with Lord Cater.'

'Is he our firebomber?'

'No,' she said. 'He didn't even know Tony was back in England.'

'How can you be sure if he was telling the truth? Did you use your cold-reading skills on him?'

'No,' she replied. 'I used a different method. Much more satisfying, although I probably shouldn't make a habit of it.'

'It's too bad we came all this way for nothing,' said Sally.

'It's all right,' said Gwen grimly. 'I found what I needed to know. Let's go and see Iris.'

Sally pulled up by the *Cecilia* at six thirty. Iris opened the door as they crossed the gangplank.

'Oh, good, you're back,' she said, motioning them inside. 'Any luck?'

'A good working theory,' said Gwen as she came in. 'The Caters believe Tony talked Bruce into going to Spain, so they blame him for his death. It wasn't vengeance for Nancy that led to the attack. It was vengeance for Bruce. Only Lord and Lady Cater didn't know he had returned.'

'So it wasn't them?'

'No,' said Gwen. 'But Bruce had siblings. A younger brother and a little sister who worshipped him. They were only children when he died, which would explain why they didn't take action when Tony came back from Spain.'

'But they would be adults now,' mused Iris. 'So we need to find them next.'

'No, we don't,' said Gwen. 'One of them found us. His little sister, Charlotte. She's Evelyn Lowle.'

Iris stared at her for a moment. Then a smile spread slowly across her face.

'Perfect,' she said. 'That's the piece that explains everything.'

FOURTEEN

The three of them sat around the small dining table in the narrowboat's saloon.

'How do you know that Evelyn Lowle is Charlotte Cater?' asked Iris.

'Charlotte went to Manchester for university,' said Gwen. 'Her mother said she was expert at doing the Mancunian accent.'

'That isn't enough,' said Sally.

'I also saw a few family pictures in Lord Cater's study,' said Gwen. 'Charlotte had a younger version of Evelyn's face, although she was brunette then.'

'Hah!' cried Iris. 'I knew she wasn't a real blonde!'

'In any case, she couldn't have been more than twelve or thirteen when Bruce was killed in '37,' continued Gwen, 'which would explain why it would be unlikely for her to try to kill Tony when he came back from Spain in '38. But that was nine years ago, which means that Charlotte—'

'Is now old enough to be a killer,' said Iris.

'The problem is how do you prove they are the same person?' asked Sally.

'The Brigadier would know Lowle's true name,' said Gwen, looking at Iris.

Iris shook her head.

'We can't go to him with this,' she said. 'Not yet. We need something more tangible, or he'll just shut down the operation and she'll get away with it.'

'There's another problem,' said Gwen.

'Which is?'

'Parham said Lowle had an alibi for the time of the attack,' said Gwen. 'She was at her flat, and her landlady verified it. There may be other boarders there who could as well.'

'Or the landlady was lying,' said Sally.

'No, I agree that she was nowhere near Grenville House when it happened,' said Iris.

'You do?' exclaimed Gwen. 'You mean you think she wasn't behind the petrol bomb?'

'No, she was,' said Iris.

'Do you think her brother was involved?'

'No,' said Iris. 'But I have a theory that has been made considerably stronger by this.'

'What are we going to do to prove it?'

'Search Lowle's flat, for starters,' said Iris. 'Unfortunately we can't risk that tonight. She'll be going to her ministry job tomorrow. You and I will meet up at The Right Sort in the morning to get her address, then go from there.'

'What if she speaks to her father in the interim?' asked Gwen. 'She might know that we're looking into her family by now.'

'Protocol for maintaining a cover means no contact with one's real family,' said Iris. 'That was the best part of the job when I was doing it as far as I was concerned. You only just saw the Caters today, so if we move quickly, we should be able to break in before she's on to us. Right, if there is no further business, I hereby declare this meeting over and adjourned until further information is gathered.'

'Isn't what you're planning burglary?' objected Sally.

'No,' said Gwen. 'We're only committing burglary if we do this at night. I looked that up once for another situation.'

'But it's still illegal,' pointed out Sally.

'Oh, yes,' said Iris. 'Don't worry, Sally, it will just be the two of us. I have a plan.'

'Oh, goody – a plan,' said Sally. 'What can possibly go wrong? Well, then I guess you have no further need of me. Goodnight, Sparks.'

'Goodnight, Sally,' said Iris as she showed them to the door. 'Thank you for everything. Goodnight, Gwen.'

'Goodnight, Iris,' said Gwen.

The two walked back to Sally's car.

'I'll drop you off,' said Sally as he held the door for her.

'No,' said Gwen, getting in, then looking up at him. 'You'll come in with me. Iris may have no further need for you, but I do.'

Mrs Cowell had just finished hoovering her sitting room when she heard the doorbell ring. She glanced at the grandfather clock. It was ten o'clock in the morning, and she wasn't expecting any visitors or deliveries. She peeked through the curtains to see two young women standing at her front door. One was a tall, elegant blonde, while the other was a short, nervous brunette whose eyes kept darting about in all directions.

Wondering, she went to open the front door.

'Yes?' she said.

'Good morning,' said the tall woman. 'Are you Mrs Cowell?'

'I am.'

'How do you do? I am Mrs Aurora Chesworth. This is my secretary, Mary McTague. Am I correct in stating that you are the landlady for this building?'

'Why, yes,' said Mrs Cowell eagerly. 'Are you interested in renting a room?'

'It's not for myself,' said the tall woman. 'My cousin's daughter is coming to study in London and I have been asked by the family to find suitable quarters for a young woman where proper behaviour is strictly observed. Miss McTague, after some investigation, thought your establishment might be appropriate.'

'Oh, I keep a sharp eye on my girls,' said Mrs Cowell. 'They are home and in bed by ten thirty each night, or they can't stay here, and no visitors allowed, of course. It's all spelled out in the lease.'

'Excellent,' said Mrs Chesworth. 'Do you have any vacancies that we might inspect at the moment?'

'You're in luck,' said Mrs Cowell, stepping back. 'Do come in.'

She showed them into the sitting room, then hastily unplugged the vacuum cleaner and coiled the cord.

'You'll have to pardon me,' she said with a nervous laugh. 'I was just finishing up my cleaning. Cleanliness is next to godliness, as they say.'

'Amen,' said Mrs Chesworth piously.

'Amen,' echoed Miss McTague, suppressing a smirk which escaped Mrs Cowell's notice as she rolled the vacuum cleaner down the hall into a cupboard.

'Well, let's talk business,' said Mrs Cowell as she returned, wiping her hands on her apron. 'When will the young lady be arriving?'

'The autumn term starts the first week of September,' said Mrs Chesworth.

'Which school?'

'The London School of Economics, so you see how your location is so very convenient,' said Mrs Chesworth. 'We wouldn't want her returning through any unsavoury neighbourhoods at night.'

'This is a safe area, I can assure you,' said Mrs Cowell. 'There's usually a bobby walking the street every half hour, and there's no pubs close by. It's the alcohol what causes the most trouble after the sun sets. There's none allowed here in the house, neither. That's another rule of mine.'

'You run a tight ship,' commented Mrs Chesworth approvingly. 'May we see the available rooms?'

'Of course, of course,' said Mrs Cowell. 'Please follow me.'

She led them up a narrow staircase to the first storey which had a hallway with three rooms on either side and a bathroom at the end. Mrs Cowell produced a bunch of keys from her apron. Miss McTague watched her closely as she unlocked one of the doors.

'Do all the rooms have their own locks and keys?' asked Mrs Chesworth.

'They do, but I've got a master, as you can see,' replied Mrs Cowell. 'I don't want any secrets kept under my roof.'

The room was sparsely furnished with a single bed, a chest of drawers, a simple writing desk with a straight-backed chair and a built-in cupboard. The window faced another from a similar building across a narrow alley scarcely wider than the bins it accommodated.

'Not much of a view,' commented Mrs Chesworth.

'We wouldn't want to distract her from her studies, would

we?' said Mrs Cowell. 'But I've got another one on the next level that looks out onto the street.'

'Let's take a look at that one.'

The next level was very much the same as the first, including the furnishing of the room, but the street view was more cheerful, at least, despite some oncoming clouds. Mrs Chesworth gazed out of the window.

'I think she would prefer this one, don't you?' she asked Miss McTague.

'Depends,' said Miss McTague. 'You've forgot something quite essential, ma'am.'

'Ah, you mean the bathrooms,' said Mrs Cowell. 'Very important to us ladies, aren't they? Come take a look.'

She led them down the end of the hall to the bathroom and opened the door, revealing a free-standing bathtub on iron-clawed feet with a hand-held shower head running from a tall pipe at the end, alongside a toilet and sink that were old but clean and well-maintained.

'There's as many as six girls sharing it when we're full up,' said Mrs Cowell. 'So there can be a bit of a mad scramble in the mornings, but we haven't had any fights break out over it.'

'It seems adequate,' said Mrs Chesworth with a sniff.

'Mrs Cowell, I was wondering if I might put it to the test,' asked Miss McTague. 'I'm in rather desperate need at the moment.'

'Certainly,' said Mrs Cowell.

'Perhaps you and I could return downstairs and discuss potential terms,' suggested Mrs Chesworth. 'We do have two other places to look at today, but I am already leaning towards this one.'

'Of course, of course,' said Mrs Cowell. 'Let's go and talk business while your secretary does her business. Take your time, dearie.'

'Thank you, Mrs Cowell,' said Miss McTague gratefully. 'I'll be down in a few minutes.'

She slipped inside the bathroom and shut the door, then pressed her ear against it until she heard the footsteps and voices fade down the staircase. Then she stepped out into the hall, reaching for her lock picks.

Room 2C, thought Sparks. Hopefully Gwen will keep Lowle's landlady talking for a while.

The lock was a simple one. She had it open in seconds. She opened the chest of drawers first, feeling under the neatly folded clothes, then checking for anything taped underneath the drawers. She found nothing.

She moved to the desk, noting with reluctant approval the stack of books on one corner. She probably reads more than I do, she thought with chagrin. The desk itself revealed nothing. She quickly flipped through the pages of each book, looking for notes concealed within.

There was a copy of *The History of the Peloponnesian War* in the stack. She really did do her homework, thought Sparks, impressed. I wonder if she bought it with her own money, or if the Brigadier—

She picked it up and turned to the title page. Thucydides. The Jowett translation.

She copied down the publisher and the edition number, then replaced the book in its place in the stack.

She didn't have much time. There was a jewellery box on the bedside table. Sparks flipped it open to find the usual assortment of earrings, hairpins and a necklace. There were no secret compartments that she could discern. She was about to close the box when one pair of earrings caught her attention.

They weren't made from any precious metal, nor did they hold any gemstones. They had small, thin metal hooks at their ends and were bedecked with soft filaments – no, fragments of feathers that had been dyed yellow and pink, which flowed in the air as she picked them up like—

Like wings.

Rather pretty, she thought as she replaced them.

She closed the door behind her, hoping Lowle would blame its unlocked status on Mrs Cowell, then returned to the bathroom and flushed the toilet. She ran the water in the sink for a moment to complete the performance, then went down the stairs to rejoin the others.

'Sorry I took so long, Mrs Chesworth,' she said apologetically. 'Something I ate last night disagreed with my innards something fierce. Mrs Cowell, you were a lifesaver. Thanks awfully.'

'Not at all, dearie,' said Mrs Cowell sympathetically.

'I'll be sure to call you soon with my decision,' said Mrs Chesworth, rising to her feet. 'You have been a most gracious hostess, Mrs Cowell. My thanks for your hospitality.'

'It was nice to meet you, ladies,' said Mrs Cowell. 'I hope your cousin comes to join our little group soon.'

The two women exited into the street and walked away.

'Any luck?' asked Gwen.

'I think so,' said Iris. 'I need to get to a telephone right away.'

Mrs Cowell's place was on a side street off Theobalds Road. They found a telephone box on the corner. Iris looked up a number in her book, dropped a coin in the slot, then dialled. A moment later, a man answered.

'It's Sparks,' she said.

'Sparks?' barked the Brigadier. 'You're not supposed to have this number.'

'No time for that, sir. I need you to do something.'

'Do you? May I remind you how the chain of command works here?'

'I think I can crack the book code for the messages hidden in Danforth's flat,' she said. 'Would that be of interest to you?'

'Tell me how you got this number first.'

'I was with Edwards when he rang you from the hospital, remember?'

'He's not supposed to let you see him dial.'

'He didn't,' said Sparks. 'But I know how to identify the numbers by listening to how long the dial takes to return to position. Satisfied?'

'Useful trick,' he said. 'Fine. Tell me about the code.'

'It's Thucydides, but you had the wrong translation and edition,' she said, pulling out her notebook. 'You were using the Crawley. Try the Jowett translation instead.'

She read off the publisher and edition.

'Got it,' he said. 'I'll send a man out to get a copy and see if you're right. Where did you find this book?'

'I'm not telling you until you verify that it's the right one,' she said. 'I'll call back in a few hours to confirm.'

'Sparks, either you tell me right now, or—'

She hung up, then leaned her forehead against the telephone.

'Promise you'll visit me in prison,' she said.

'I expect they'll let us share a cell,' said Gwen. 'What's all that about a book code?'

'Both parties need to have the same book. Then you use two numbers to locate a word. The first is the page number, the second is how many words from the start of the page. The process is tedious but impossible to crack without knowing which book it is. They found coded messages in Tony's flat after the fire that appeared to be encrypted by that method.'

'That sounds rather incriminating,' said Gwen.

'Very,' said Iris. 'Miss Lowle suggested they try the edition of Thucydides that he bought at Maggs Bros, but it didn't work.'

'Why not?'

'If I'm right, it's because she faked those coded letters herself and planted them to be found,' said Iris. 'Only she used the wrong edition and translation. She must have assumed he bought the newer version. I found a copy on her desk.'

'You are a wonder, Iris Sparks,' said Gwen with a grin. 'Now, if it's a match, what then? Do you think the Brigadier will absolve Tony?'

'Maybe,' said Iris. 'Maybe he'll only give Lowle, or Charlotte, the sack.'

'What do we tell Parham, then? He still has a case to solve.'

'And solve it, he shall,' said Iris.

She dialled another number.

'Detective Superintendent Parham, please,' she said. 'Miss Iris Sparks calling.'

She was connected a moment letter.

'Miss Sparks, good morning,' said Parham. 'Do you have something for me?'

'I do,' she replied. 'Is PC Godfrey your fingerprint man on the Danforth case?'

'He is.'

'Send him to Grenville House. Tell him to fingerprint the door to the roof there.'

'The roof of Grenville House itself? How could anyone throw a bottle into a window from the roof of the same building?'

'Trust me, sir. Send Godfrey, then come meet me outside Danforth's room at St George's at two thirty.'

'Why there? Do you think he has more information to give us?'

'If I'm right, the guilty party will be coming there later,' she said. 'Bring your handcuffs.'

She hung up.

'Lowle is coming to the hospital?' asked Gwen.

'The Brigadier ordered me last week to get Tony to add her to his visitor list,' said Iris. 'Tony agreed, but wanted to wait until Tuesday so he could get through his initial treatment.'

'Which is today,' said Gwen. 'So she will be coming by after work.'

'And we will be waiting for her,' said Iris.

They had lunch, then took the Tube to Hyde Park Corner.

'We're early for Parham,' said Gwen as they walked in.

'That's fine,' said Iris. 'I need to call the Brigadier and find out if I was right about that book. And I need to ask my new boyfriend Carlton something.'

Edwards was lounging near the telephone boxes when they came in. Iris went straight up to him.

'Got a minute?' she asked.

'You could at least pretend to make this look casual,' he said irritably. 'Come on.'

The three of them moved further back into the room where they were somewhat concealed from view.

'You know she's part of this, right?' said Iris, nodding at Gwen.

'Yeah. So?'

'The night Danforth was attacked you were following him, weren't you?'

'You don't think I had anything to do with it, do you?' asked Edwards, bristling.

'I don't,' said Iris. 'But did you maintain surveillance on Grenville House after he came home from his date?'

'Yeah, I stayed across the street from the entrance,' said Edwards. 'I didn't see the Molotov go off. I heard it, ran to the corner and saw the flames, so I went to call 999 like a good citizen.'

'I assume you kept track of anyone going into the building after Danforth.'

'Where are you going with this, Sparks?'

'Did you see anyone carrying fishing gear?'

'I did, come to think of it,' he said. 'Male, thirties, five ten, black hair.'

'Would you recognise him if you saw him?'

'That is my job,' said Edwards huffily.

Iris smiled.

'First drink will be on me,' she said. 'I need to call your boss and let him know his new girl is a bad girl. And she's not going to have her second date with Danforth today.'

'Wait, you mean Lowle?' said Edwards. 'She's already having it.'

'What do you mean?' exclaimed Iris. 'She's supposed to come after work.'

'She got here about five minutes ago,' said Edwards. 'Gave me a wave. Amateur.'

'We've got to stop her,' Iris said, turning to move towards the lift.

'Hold on,' said Edwards, grabbing her arm. 'You can't go up there. You'll muck up the whole operation.'

'Let go of me!' said Iris, trying to pull away. 'I think she came here to kill him.'

'You're not going anywhere,' said Edwards as he grabbed her other arm. 'Not until I know what's—'

He stopped abruptly, sagging against her as his arms fell to his sides. Then he crumpled to the floor.

She turned to see Gwen standing over him, her umbrella still raised with the reinforced handle up high for a second blow. Iris stared at her in shock.

'Go!' Gwen commanded her. 'I'll take care of him.'

Iris turned and ran to the lift. Gwen watched until the doors closed, then called, 'Excuse me? I need some help here! This man needs medical assistance!'

She sat down on the floor by Edwards who was coming to, groaning and clutching his head.

'I'm so sorry,' she said, patting his shoulder sympathetically. 'I've never used this before on a live target, and it's so difficult to gauge how hard to swing it to disable temporarily without causing permanent damage. Can you hear me?'

He grunted something unintelligible.

'I do hope it's not a concussion,' she said. 'I had one of those last year. Long story. In any case, let me explain to you what's going on right now.'

The constable on duty outside the room checked her ID, then consulted his list.

'There you are,' he said. 'There's a nurse in there with him. You'll have to wait until she's done.'

'That's fine,' she said.

A minute later, the door opened and the nurse came out.

'Oh, are you here for our Mr Danforth?' she asked.

'I am.'

'I'm afraid he's asleep right now,' said the nurse sympathetically. 'He's had rather an exhausting set of procedures, and he's heavily sedated.'

'Oh, no!' she exclaimed, tearing up. 'It's my first chance to see him since, since it happened, and I begged the afternoon off from my job to come here.'

'Oh, gosh, are you Miss Lowle?' exclaimed the nurse.

'I am,' said Lowle. 'How ever did you know?'

'I was the one who read your note to him,' confided the nurse. 'Goodness, I was crying myself by the time I was done. Oh, dear, I wish he was awake for you. I know he was looking forward to your visit.'

'Do you think perhaps that I could just sit with him for a while?' asked Lowle. 'Maybe he'll sense my presence somehow. I'm sure it will do him some good.'

'Of course you may,' said the nurse. 'Come in. I'll put the chair by the bed.'

They went in together, and the nurse moved a chair up by the head of the bed. Lowle sat down and looked at him.

'He seems so peaceful right now,' she whispered. 'Could you close the door on your way out? I'd hate for anything to disturb him.'

'Certainly, dear,' said the nurse. 'Call out if you need anything.'

'I will. Thank you.'

She waited until the door closed, then leaned over, put her lips close to his ear, and whispered, 'Tony.'

There was no response.

'Tooooony,' she half-sang more loudly. Then she followed it with a sharp 'Tony!' accompanied by a shove.

He kept sleeping.

'Damn you,' she muttered, sitting back in her chair. 'I'm very disappointed by this, Tony. I really wanted to have one last conversation with you. I've had this moment planned for so long, and you are refusing to play your part in it.'

She looked up at the intravenous bottle hanging from a hook on the pole over him, then opened her bag and pulled out a hypodermic needle.

'It's a pity about the sedatives and the painkillers,' she continued, holding it up and depressing the plunger until a drop of clear liquid appeared at the end of the needle. 'I wanted you to feel this. I wanted there to be suffering involved right up to the end. I would have liked you to have known that it was me who brought it about, but I guess you can't have everything. Oh, by the way? The kiss wasn't all that great. In fact, I ran upstairs and threw up the second after I closed the door.'

She stood and reached for the IV bottle with the syringe. Then Sparks burst through the door and hurled herself at her, grabbing Lowle's wrist and twisting it. The syringe fell onto the pillow, close to Danforth's face.

'Let go of me!' shrieked Lowle as she spun and drove her left hand at Iris's eyes.

Sparks ducked the blow, causing her to relinquish her grip.

'It's over,' she said. 'Stop.'

'Here, what's this noise about?' said the constable as he came in.

'She attacked me!' cried Lowle.

'She's trying to— no!' yelled Sparks as Lowle made a grab for the syringe.

She leaped at the other woman and wrapped her arms around her in a bear hug.

'Look at her hand!' Iris yelled to the constable. 'Get that needle away.'

'I don't know what the hell this is about, but the two of you have to stop this,' said the constable.

He stepped forwards to separate them. The instant Lowle was free, she whirled and hit him in the throat with the heel of her palm, sending him to the floor, choking. Then she faced Iris.

'My brother died because of him,' she said.

'Your brother was a bastard and a rapist,' said Sparks. 'He deserved everything that happened to him and more.'

Lowle screamed in rage and charged at her. Sparks sidestepped her and tripped her up, shoving her down hard as she passed. Lowle's head slammed into the radiator as she fell. She dropped to her knees and Iris grabbed her left arm, twisted it behind her back, then pressed her down to the floor and sat on her.

'That's one thing I can still do better than you,' she said, panting.

'Miss Sparks, what's going on?' came a voice from the doorway.

She looked up to see Parham looking down at the two of them, a pair of constables behind him.

'Is this the person I'm supposed to be handcuffing?' he asked.

'One of them,' said Sparks. 'She just tried to kill Mr Danforth. Again. The syringe is lying over there somewhere. Oh, and she assaulted your constable just now. Sorry about the timing – I was expecting her later.'

Parham went over to the constable and helped him to his feet.

'Are you all right, lad?' he asked him.

The constable nodded, still coughing and rubbing his throat.

'Go find yourself a doctor,' ordered Parham. Then he turned back to Iris. 'That's Miss Lowle you're sitting on.'

'It is,' said Sparks. 'I'll hold her until you get the cuffs on.'

Parham squatted by Lowle and handcuffed her. Sparks got up, and Parham hauled Lowle to her feet.

'Take her to Serious Crimes,' he called, and one of the constables with him removed her.

He turned back to Sparks.

'One of them,' he said. 'There are more?'

'One other,' said Sparks. 'Hang on.'

She retrieved her bag from where she had dropped it before coming into the room, then pulled out a piece of paper and handed it to him.

'The man you want is Kenneth Lonsdale,' she said. 'One of our clients, the one Lowle dated before Danforth. That's his address. Send someone to pick him up and search his place. I'll explain everything on the way to your office. Oh, did you happen to see Mrs Bainbridge on your way in?'

'Yes, I was going to mention that,' said Parham. 'There was a commotion going on in the lobby. There was some talk about arresting her for knocking out a porter.'

'Talk them out of it, please,' said Sparks. 'I suspect the man won't be pressing charges.'

'I'll see what I can do,' said Parham. 'Ah, there's the syringe you mentioned. I'd better take that.'

He pulled a small manilla envelope from his coat and placed the syringe inside. Then he looked down at Danforth.

'This chap slept through everything that happened,' he said.

'Yes,' said Sparks. 'Whatever they gave him, I'd like to get some to take away.'

FIFTEEN

Inside the Curtis Green building at Scotland Yard, Parham led the two women to a small room in the basement level with a pair of speakers mounted on the wall and a small table with four chairs around it.

'You'll be able to hear everything in here,' said Parham. 'I don't want them to see you. I'll come back if I have any questions.'

He walked out, closing the door behind him, then walked down the hall to another room with a padded door. He entered it without knocking. There was a constable sitting at one end, a police stenographer sitting at a desk at the other, and in the middle, seated behind a desk and handcuffed by one wrist to a bar bolted into the wall was a man with a sour expression.

Parham sat across the desk from him, then glanced at his watch. He nodded to the stenographer.

'My name is Philip Parham,' he said to the man. 'I am Detective Superintendent at the Homicide and Serious Crimes Command. Is your name Kenneth Lonsdale?'

'Yes,' said the man.

'You are being charged with the attempted murder of Anthony Danforth of Grenville House, as well as with arson and related charges for the use of an incendiary device in the commission of that crime,' said Parham. 'We have matched your fingerprints to some found on the door to the roof of that building. An eyewitness who was across the street at the time has identified you as having followed Mr Danforth into the building carrying a fishing pole and a tackle box, and we have recovered from your flat a set of sketches of the building with handwritten estimates of the distance from the rooftop to the window of Mr Danforth's flat. We believe that you introduced a petrol bomb from the rooftop through his open window by means of the fishing pole. Do you wish to say anything in answer to the charge? You are not obliged to say anything unless you wish to do so, but whatever you say will be taken down in writing and may be given in evidence.'

Lonsdale slumped in his chair, pounding his free hand on his knee. Then he sighed.

'Have you ever done any fly fishing?' he asked.

'When I was young,' replied Parham. 'An uncle used to take me when we visited out in Shropshire.'

'Ah, out on the Severn, I suppose,' said Lonsdale, nodding. 'I've taken some good-sized trout out that way, twenty-five pounds and up.'

'Have you?'

'I have.'

'This sounds like quite the passion of yours.'

'There are times,' said Lonsdale wistfully, 'when I am standing up to my hips in a cold running stream with nothing but the sounds of the water rushing by, the leaves rustling in the breeze and the birds singing to each other in the distance, when I feel completely at one with the world. I feel a tranquillity then, a soothing of my soul like no other. The pole, the line flying out from it, the fly tied at the end, become extensions of my being, reaching out for connection to another living thing. And when the strike comes, I feel an exhilaration beyond measure.'

There were times to ask questions, and there were times to let people speak, Parham knew. He let Lonsdale continue.

'The war brought me to London, and I was cut off from all that. I couldn't breathe the air here, I couldn't hear my heart-beat amid all the noise. And I could not find anyone who understood me. I have been so lonely here, so intensely isolated in these vast, overwhelming, stinking crowds. I would sit in my flat and tie flies, remembering with each one my past moments of happiness as they drifted further and further away from me. I cast my lines here, and they landed on dead, stagnant waters and lay there undisturbed.

'Until I met her. That very first date, I felt that connection. It was a surge of almost a primal energy. And she felt it as well, I could tell. We talked, God how we talked, and then she asked if she could see my collection of flies, the real work of my life. I took her back to my flat and showed them to her, and she took my hand as I did, and the next thing I knew . . . well, all I knew of heaven before was nothing compared to her that evening.'

'This was Miss Lowle?' asked Parham.

'Evelyn,' said Lonsdale. 'Yes.'

'Then what happened?'

'Afterwards, she broke down and started crying. I was concerned, of course, and asked her to tell me why. She told me that she had come to London to search for the man she held responsible for her brother's death, and that she had signed up with The Right Sort because she had learned that he was a client of theirs. But then she had met me, and that changed everything. She didn't want to leave me, not even to continue her quest.'

In the listening room, Iris and Gwen looked at each other.

'So that's how she talked him into it,' said Gwen.

'She set the hook and he took it immediately,' said Iris.

'What did you say to this?' asked Parham.

'I told her that I would help her find justice for her brother,' said Lonsdale. 'She said that she couldn't possibly ask me to do anything that would put me at risk, but I was adamant. I would have done anything for her.'

'What was the plan?'

'I had to tell the ladies at The Right Sort that the date had gone poorly,' said Lonsdale. 'They were used to that with me. I also told them I was done with them, so that would free me to help Evelyn. She came over every evening after that, and for most of the weekend, and we made love and planned how it would happen.'

'Whose idea was the petrol bomb?'

'Hers. It was how her brother was killed, and she thought it the appropriate instrument of execution. She got the address by breaking into the office of The Right Sort after they closed for the day. I came up with the idea of swinging the bomb through his window with the line and rod. It wasn't difficult once I knew the length of line to use. I followed him into his building, then went to the roof and peered down until I saw his shutters swing open. Then I lit the end of the rag stuffed into the bottle, lowered it, and swung it inside as the flames reached the petrol. The explosion detached it from the line. I pulled the remainder back up, packed my gear and left the building with everyone else.'

'You could have burned down the entire place,' said Parham.

'I was going to call the fire brigade once I got out but someone beat me to it,' said Lonsdale.

'Good of you,' said Parham.

He took a small envelope and poured out the odd feathery earrings that Iris had seen in Lowle's jewellery box.

'Do you recognise these?' he asked.

'Yes,' said Lonsdale. 'Two of my prized creations. A matched pair of yellow and pink badgers. I was going to try them out for salmon in Devon, but Evelyn thought they would make lovely earrings to remember me by, so I gave them to her as a keepsake.'

'I think she will remember you quite well, Mr Lonsdale,' said Parham. 'We will type up your statement and have you sign it. Take him away, Constable.'

The officer uncuffed him from the bar and guided him out of the room.

'Need a break, Miss Martin?' Parham asked the stenographer.

'He was a talker, wasn't he?' she said, cracking her knuckles. 'I'm ready for the next one when you are.'

'Back in five,' he said as he collected the fishing flies.

He walked back to the room where the two women had been listening.

'You were right,' he said to Sparks. 'Both about the fishing pole and the man using it. What tipped you off?'

'I tried to think as a detective would,' she said. 'As I told you at lunch, I thought of another way to get that bottle through the window, and once I thought of swinging it in by a line I thought about fishing poles and that took me to Miss Lowle's prior match. That was information we had that you did not. And once I saw the fishing flies in her jewellery box – the badgers, he called them? – I was certain.'

'May I see them?' asked Mrs Bainbridge.

Parham pulled out the envelope and shook them onto the desk.

'They are lovely,' she said, peering at them. 'Little works of art in their own way. I was thinking as we listened that if only he had bared his soul like that to us when he first came to The Right

Sort, we could have done a better job of finding a woman who could have appreciated a man like him. We could have saved him.'

'Maybe you've saved your other female clients from a man who is willing to kill,' suggested Parham. 'He and this Lowle woman seem to be a match made in hell.'

'So you're saying we did our job too well,' said Sparks.

'She should be down by now,' he said, glancing at his watch. 'I'm going back in.'

He collected the earrings and went back to the interview room.

This time, a WPC was sitting at the side and Miss Lowle was the one in the chair with her hand shackled. There was a large ugly bruise running across her forehead, but her gaze was alert, focussed on Parham when he entered. He sat across from her.

'Is your name Evelyn Lowle?' he asked.

'It is.'

'How's the head doing?'

'Down to a dull throb,' she replied. 'Thanks for asking.'

He told her the charges and read her the warnings. When he had finished, she sighed.

'This is all quite ridiculous,' she said.

'Why?'

'I had nothing to do with the fire, or the attack on poor Tony.'

'We've heard otherwise.'

'From whom?'

'From Kenneth Lonsdale, for one.'

'Oh. Him,' she said, her expression perturbed. 'I was afraid it was going to be something like that.'

'Something like what, Miss Lowle? He gave a detailed account of a conspiracy between the two of you.'

'But that's the ridiculous part, don't you see?' she said earnestly. 'Yes, he and I dated, and honestly, I was looking for some fun, you know? It had been a while since I had any. And the lovemaking turned out to be rather extraordinary, I must say, so I came back for more the next couple of nights. But as good as it was, I realised this wasn't going to last, so I tried to explain that to him. He refused to accept it, and that's when I began to see he was a bit off his rocker.'

'How so?'

'He told me over and over that we were meant to be together for all time, and he got more and more agitated. He was starting to frighten me, so I told him it had been lovely, but I was done and moving on. He asked if I was going back to The Right Sort and I said, yeah, that was why I signed up, and he said he'd make sure the next man wouldn't end up with me. I'm afraid I didn't take him seriously enough.'

'When was this?'

'Our last day together. The Sunday before he attacked Tony.'

'You had already received an invitation from Mr Danforth for a date by this point.'

'Yes.'

'But you continued to see Lonsdale.'

'Like I said, the lovemaking was good,' she said, shrugging. 'Spectacularly good. And a girl can date more than one man at a time, you know.'

'Why didn't you tell me this when I interviewed you after the incident?'

'I was scared,' she said, looking down. 'I hadn't taken Kenny seriously, so when poor Tony was attacked, I thought you'd somehow think I had something to do with it. I'm sorry. I should have told you.'

'You should have,' agreed Parham. 'You should also have told me your true name.'

'My what?' she exclaimed, startled.

'Your true name,' he repeated. 'Miss Charlotte Cater, is it not?'

'I've never heard that name before in my life!'

'You are the younger sister of Bruce Cater, who died fighting in Spain in 1937,' he said. 'He was a classmate of Mr Danforth, who your family blamed for persuading your brother to join that fight. Your entire family, including you.'

'I have no idea what you're talking about,' said Lowle.

'What about this afternoon, Miss Cater?'

'My name is Evelyn Lowle,' she insisted.

'You tried to kill Mr Danforth by means of a hypodermic syringe filled with enough morphine to cause a fatal overdose.'

'I don't know anything about that,' she said.

'Miss Sparks saw it happen.'

'She's mistaken. It was probably left in the room by one of the nurses.'

'And you made statements to her at the time—'

'Then she's lying,' said Lowle, her expression contemptuous. 'She came in and attacked me out of the blue. She had to come up with some story to justify that.'

'You also struck a police constable.'

'I was defending myself from Miss Sparks,' she said. 'Everything was in the heat of the moment. I didn't realise I had hit him.'

'She's good,' commented Gwen as they listened.

'She's been trained,' said Iris glumly.

The interrogation went on for over an hour. Lowle never broke or deviated from her story.

'He still doesn't know about her Intelligence role,' said Gwen. 'The operation. That could help him connect the dots.'

'We can't tell him about it,' said Iris. 'Not without permission. We've skated perilously close to the edge as it is.'

The door opened, and Parham came in.

'I don't know if I can charge her for the first attack,' he said wearily. 'She paints a plausible picture of Mr Lonsdale as a jealous lover. Not that I believe it for a second, but a jury could. It would be her word against Sparks for the second attack.'

'What about the constable who came into the room?' asked Sparks. 'Surely he saw or heard something to support the charges.'

'He was too involved in breaking up the fight between the two of you to notice whether or not she had the syringe. And once he had been hit in the throat he was down, choking and trying to breathe again. He didn't hear what was being said in the room during that.'

'There's still my word,' said Sparks.

'Yes,' he said. 'But what occurs to me is that she rendered a constable hors de combat with a single blow. That's not something a woman can normally do—'

'I can,' said Sparks.

'So can I,' said Mrs Bainbridge.

'Normally,' he repeated. 'You've both had training. I suspect she's had some as well. And if that's the case, then I think there may be more to this mess than is apparent. Given what I know about your background, Miss Sparks, as well as your early involvement in this matter, I am asking you directly: is there something crucial that you're not telling me? Something that you can't tell me because of security reasons? If there is, then you may not be allowed to testify against her.'

Mrs Bainbridge looked at her partner imploringly, but Sparks shook her head.

'You're a very good detective,' Sparks said to him. 'How long can you hold her without charging her?'

'Realistically, until the morning,' he said.

'Let me see what I can do,' she said.

The cab pulled up in front of the entrance to the courtyard. They climbed in and Iris gave the driver the address. Then she heaved a sigh as they pulled away.

'Come on, it might work,' said Gwen.

'No, it wasn't that,' said Iris. 'I'm just thinking about every poor decision I've made in my life to bring us to this moment.'

London, 1938

Sparks was engrossed in a report on increases in German steel output by Reichswerke Hermann Göring since the Anschluss, jotting down notes and statistics, translating on the fly the sections she'd incorporate into her own report. She didn't see Mr Pelton, her supervisor, approaching until he was nearly on top of her, leaning over her desk and cutting off the light from the overhead dome lamps.

'His Nibs wants you,' he said. 'He needs that report.'

'Now?' exclaimed Sparks. 'But it's due tomorrow. I'm not done updating the conclusions.'

'Bring what you have, give him the gist orally on the end bits,' said Pelton. 'You can type those up later. Move, girlie. He doesn't like to wait.'

'Blast,' she muttered, gathering the stacked completed sections along with her handwritten notes.

Her desk was one of dozens down in a large room in the

bowels of the Foreign and Commonwealth Office building on King Charles Street. The undersecretary was three storeys up. She clutched her papers to her chest and slid sideways through the array of similar desks until she reached the hallway, then she half-walked, half-ran, dodging clumps of conversations clogging her route until she reached the staircase.

She was mentally rehearsing her conclusions as she walked into the undersecretary's anteroom. His secretary glanced at her, then more pointedly at the mantel clock which sat under a portrait of Edward Wood, the current Secretary of State.

'He's been waiting,' she said ominously.

'I was only told eight minutes ago,' said Sparks.

'Then you should have been here four minutes ago,' replied the secretary, picking up her telephone and dialling. 'She's here. Yes, sir, I'll send her right in.'

She hung up and pointed over her shoulder to the oaken door to the inner office. Sparks walked up to it, knocked and went inside.

Rab Butler, the undersecretary, was seated behind a massive desk, with a pair of green banker's lamps flanking the blotter. There were all manner of maps mounted on easels on one side of the room, while a large, burgundy leather-covered sofa took up the other side, a low table in front of it. A man she had never seen before was sitting there, observing her while smoking a Dunhill, his cigarette case on the table.

'Good morning, Mr Undersecretary,' she began. 'I understand you wanted my report now instead of tomorrow. I was going to finish typing it this morning so as to incorporate the newest production statistics, but I'd be happy to summarise my conclusions orally.'

He waved off the proffered stack of paper.

'All a ruse to fetch you here, my dear,' Butler said with a genial smile. 'I wanted you to meet someone. Brigadier Thomas Meredith, may I present Miss Iris Sparks, one of our best and brightest.'

'How do you do, Brigadier?' she said, turning to him as he rose from the sofa.

'Miss Sparks,' he said.

'I'll leave you to it,' said Butler.

Sparks stared in surprise as he walked out of the office and closed the door. Then she turned back to the Brigadier.

'What is this?' she asked.

'Direct question, right to the point,' said the Brigadier. 'What do you think it is?'

'You have a military title but you're not in uniform,' she observed. 'You look too young to be retired—'

'Thank you,' he said drily.

'So some branch of Intelligence?'

'Soundly reasoned, Miss Sparks,' he said. 'Anything else?'

'Your name isn't Thomas Meredith,' she said. 'The initials on the cigarette case on that table are S.P. Unless you stole it.'

'Or unless I meant for you to see it and assume that,' he said. 'You came to the Foreign Office a few months ago.'

'Yes, after graduating—'

'From Newnham College,' he said. 'With top marks and a reputation for both a brilliant mind and a somewhat reckless approach to university life.'

'You're only young once,' she said.

'Multilingual,' he continued, walking towards her. 'And you spent a term in Berlin.'

'Yes, at the—'

The slap came from his right. She blocked it with her left hand, the report tumbling to the carpet by her feet. He nodded approvingly.

'Good,' he said. 'I also was given to understand—'

This time, it came from the left, but she was anticipating something of the kind and merely stepped back as his hand passed safely in front of her face.

'—that you've had some self-defence training,' he continued calmly as if nothing had happened.

'Yes, sir. Care for a spar?'

'Not at the moment,' he said. 'I'm recruiting, as you no doubt have guessed by now. Depending on how your training goes, I could keep you here analysing what information comes in or I might send you out into the field.'

'The field. Meaning Germany?'

'Quite possibly,' he said. 'The current appeasement policy is only forestalling the inevitable, despite what our leadership believes. Work for me, and maybe we'll gain an edge on events.

It will be vital work, Miss Sparks. It may also be dangerous.'

'I like a little danger in my life,' she said. 'I haven't found any in the basement here.'

'There's something else you should know up front before you commit,' he said.

'Which is what?'

'You're a very pretty girl,' he said, looking her over. 'That can be an asset for certain types of operations. If you come aboard I may ask you do certain things that conventional society would consider a moral compromise.'

An image flashed across her mind. Her hand holding a Buck's Fizz in salute as Kevin Pickard smirked from across the breakfast table.

'That won't be a problem, sir,' she said. 'I'm well acquainted with those.'

London, 1947

Carruthers slowed the car down to a halt short of the gate. The Brigadier looked up from his newspaper.

'Damn,' he said.

'Still want me to shoot her?' asked Carruthers.

'No,' said the Brigadier. 'Besides, she has Bainbridge with her.'

The two women were standing in front of the gate, their arms folded. Carruthers killed the engine, then got out.

'How is it going to be, Sparks?' he said.

'We've come to negotiate, so we'll behave,' said Sparks.

'There is nothing to negotiate, Sparks,' said the Brigadier as he got out. 'It's done. Go home.'

'Parham needs to know more to charge her,' said Sparks.

'She's going to be released tonight,' said the Brigadier. 'The orders have already gone through. She's too valuable an asset to waste.'

'After what she did? You really want a psychopath like her working for you?'

'She's perfect, Sparks,' said the Brigadier. 'In the span of a few short days she improvised a plan to seduce a man she'd just met into committing a murder for her, and there is nothing about it that can be traced back to my department.'

'You said you weren't trying to kill Danforth,' said Sparks.

'We weren't,' said the Brigadier. 'But we were not unhappy with the result. Danforth in the Foreign Office poses a genuine and immediate threat to our operations. Now at the very least he'll be out of commission for some time. If he's still keen on continuing his career, we'll be watching him even more closely.'

'You weren't trying to kill him,' said Mrs Bainbridge. 'But you knew she was Bruce Cater's younger sister, didn't you? You knew about the connection between Cater and Danforth.'

'I did,' said the Brigadier.

'So you recruited her specifically to put her in a position where she could exact vengeance upon him,' said Mrs Bainbridge. 'And then waited to see what would happen. Like a stupid little boy playing with a chemistry set seeing if he might set off an explosion.'

'What are you going to do with her now?' asked Sparks.

'Train her further, find another mission for her particular set of talents,' said the Brigadier. 'She's going to be the operative you never could have been, Sparks. Do you know why?'

'Tell me,' she said.

'Because she lacks the flaws that held you back,' he said. 'You had a conscience and a sense of remorse. She doesn't.'

'She's still young,' said Sparks. 'She may still develop them. If she does, they will break her. They broke me.'

'I know, Sparks,' he said. 'Otherwise I would have made more of an effort to keep you. Go home. Parham has a criminal to charge, Lowle vanishes into a new identity, everybody gets what they need.'

'Not everybody,' she said.

'Everybody who matters,' he replied.

'We won't be doing you any more favours,' she said. 'Be clear about that.'

'And if you attempt to punish us for that, we have left letters detailing this shambles of an operation with someone we trust,' added Mrs Bainbridge. 'Not Mr Danielli.'

'No, he would be too obvious a choice,' said the Brigadier. 'I'll be sending a man to collect Lowle's records from The Right Sort tomorrow. We're through, ladies. Goodnight.'

He stepped between them, opened his gate, then went inside.

'I could give you a lift home,' offered Carruthers.

'We already beat up two of your colleagues today,' said Sparks. 'Would you like to be the third?'

'Some other time,' he said.

He got back in the Bentley and drove off.

They returned to work the next morning, trying to match people who they hoped wouldn't end up in any criminal conspiracies. Around two thirty, they heard footsteps ascending the staircase. Then Carlton Edwards appeared in the doorway.

'How are you feeling?' asked Mrs Bainbridge with concern.

'Still woozy, no thanks to you,' he said.

'You're off hospital duty, at least,' said Sparks.

'Yeah, the boss wasn't exactly thrilled with my performance yesterday,' he said. 'I let two women get the drop on me.'

'It was a good thing you did,' said Sparks.

'He sent me to collect her files,' said Edwards. 'Wouldn't even give me a day to rest up.'

'I have her file here,' said Sparks. 'Oh, and you'll need the index cards.'

The two women each rifled through their boxes of eligible women and pulled out Lowle's cards. Sparks clipped everything together and handed them to him.

'Are you up for that drink?' she asked.

'That was a serious offer?'

'I'm always serious when it comes to drinking,' she said.

'Not today, Sparks,' he said. 'Have to wait for the noggin to ease up.'

'Some other time, then,' she said.

'See you around, Sparks.'

He left.

'Are you all right?' asked Gwen.

'You know me,' said Iris. 'I am sustained as always by my innate cheerfulness.'

'That was the last part, wasn't it? I guess we're done.'

'Not quite,' said Iris.

CODA

She sat at the head of the bed, her back against the headboard, her legs drawn to her chest, her arms wrapped around them. 'Is something wrong?' she asked softly.

'I'm sorry,' he said disconsolately. 'I don't seem to be able to manage it.'

'Is there something I could—'

'It's not you, Sparks,' he said. 'You are perfection.'

'Hardly.'

'Remember the night when we escaped the anti-fascist rally?'

'Vividly. Our first kiss. And our second.'

'Do you remember me telling you that I was in an experimental phase?'

'I do.'

'Well, this is the experiment,' he said, looking away from her. 'Hypothesis: Tony Danforth is not homosexual. Experiment: Tony will make love to the most desirable woman he has ever known. Result: abject failure. Conclusion: Tony Danforth is homosexual. I'm sorry to be such a disappointment.'

She crawled across the bed to hold him.

'You are not a disappointment,' she whispered. 'You will never be one. You are my dear friend, and always will be. I'm so glad you've finally told me.'

'You suspected?'

'It's taken this long to get you into bed with me,' she said, leaning her head on his shoulder. 'I wondered if that was the case. It's good that you didn't force yourself to go through with it. It would have only made things worse later. Do Kevin and Bruce know?'

'They've been making snide comments,' he said. 'Dropping nasty little hints about my failures with women. Those eased

off when you came into my life. There were quite a few specu-
lations as to what would take place between us this weekend.'

'But they don't know.'

'They would cut me off completely if they did,' he said. 'It
would get out around the entire university and dash to pieces
all of my hopes to join the Foreign Office. Hell, to have a career
in anything worthwhile in this country. My desires are
prosecutable.'

'Listen to me, Tony,' she said, turning him to face her. 'You are
worthwhile, much more so than this wretched, backwards country
we are forced to live in. So I promise you this: your secret will
always be safe with me, no matter what. And you are going to
spend the rest of the night in my bed, and we will emerge for
breakfast looking exhausted but triumphant. If the others ask, I
will blush becomingly and you will be reticent but quietly proud.'

'You would do that for me?' he asked. 'Risk your reputation
for me?'

'Do you know my reputation?' she said, laughing. 'One more
conquest for Iris Sparks will raise very few eyebrows. Now, put
those pyjamas back on and let's get some sleep. Oh, one more
thing.'

'What's that?' he asked.

She reached up and ruffled his hair vigorously for a few
seconds, then sat back and admired her handiwork.

'Now, you do mine,' she said.

He reached forwards and gently tousled her hair, then held
her head gently with both hands and kissed her.

'I am forever yours,' he said.

'Likewise,' she said. 'Come, we can still cuddle under the
covers without sabotaging the experiment.'

He put his pyjamas back on, slid under the bedclothes, and
embraced her. They fell asleep and stayed in that position.

Until the screaming began.

East Grinstead, 1947

When they had stabilised him enough they transported him by
ambulance to the specialised burn facility. His regular nurse

rode in the back with him, maintaining the morphine drip when each jolt caused him to gasp in pain. Once there, she kissed him on the cheek and whispered, 'God save you,' then took the train back to London, crying all the way.

There came a series of debridings and skin grafts, each requiring its own recovery period. The days became a blur, and he spent much of his time asleep. Then one morning, he woke to see a familiar pair of eyes inches from his.

'Sparks?' he said. 'Am I dreaming?'

'You dreaming of me would be extremely flattering, given everything,' she said.

She was sitting next to his bed, leaning with her forearms folded on the edge, her chin resting on top so she would be face to face with him.

'How extraordinary of you to come all this way,' he said.

'It's not that long a trip,' she said. 'And I have three questions for you.'

'All this way for three questions,' he said. 'I feel like an oracle. Ask and be enlightened.'

'Why did you kiss me outside the Barley Mow that night?' she asked.

'I'm sorry about that,' he said.

'I asked you why, not to apologise.'

'I spotted a man following me,' he said reluctantly. 'I've been fearful ever since I came back that the Foreign Office would discover my preferences, and I thought they had sent someone to catch me in pursuit of them. I thought maybe a brazen display of blatant heterosexuality would appease them. I'm sorry my paranoia led to your discomfort.'

She looked at him for a long time. He couldn't read her expression. Then she nodded.

'You weren't being paranoid,' she said. 'But you were wrong about the reason you were being followed. Did Parham tell you why you were attacked?'

'Not in detail,' said Tony. 'Just that it was a man who had dated Evelyn before me. I assumed that it was out of some insane level of jealousy.'

'That was part of it,' said Sparks. 'There's more.'

'How is it that you know this?'

'Forster wrote something pretentious before the war that nevertheless has stuck with me,' she said. 'That if he had to choose between betraying a friend and betraying his country, he hoped he would be strong enough to save his friend.'

'I don't want you to commit treason on my behalf, Sparks,' he said softly.

'That isn't the problem,' she said. 'The problem is what to do when you also believe said friend is also a betrayer. Which leads to my second question: what did Sauce tell you when you drove her from the Pickard mansion to the train station?'

He was silent.

'Did she tell you that Bruce had raped her?' she continued. 'That he did it repeatedly while Kevin held her down, and that your two close friends then traded places? That this was all happening while you and I slept unawares in Kevin's sister's bed?'

'Iris, please,' he whispered.

'I think she told you,' said Sparks. 'Because I asked you when you got back what she had said, and you refused to answer. Which means that instead of helping her, instead of helping a woman who had been brutally victimised by your two dear friends, you took their side instead.'

'So did you,' he said.

'No, I took no position,' she said. 'I didn't have the knowledge of what she said happened. I asked her after the weekend, but she shut herself down. I'm not saying I came out of this clean. I should have trusted my suspicions. But you made your choice based on much more information than I had. Why?'

'Because they were my friends, and she wasn't,' he said. 'I couldn't let them go to jail. I had no idea Sauce would kill herself. Then when Bruce spiralled down afterwards I offered him a grand soul-cleansing adventure, which ended up killing him. I've lived with that guilt ever since. Guilt over them both.'

'She was my friend, Tony,' said Sparks. 'So were you. You should have told me.'

'Were?' he said, his voice breaking. 'Is this your judgement upon me?'

'You've already been punished,' she said. 'And here is where I betray my country. I was an inadvertent instrumentality of that punishment.'

'How so?'

'You were being followed because you were suspected of being a communist double-agent,' she said. 'Whether for Uncle Joe or Chairman Mao, I don't know. I was asked to set you up with a British agent who would find out if it was true.'

'Evelyn Lowle?' he said. 'She works for the government?'

'Yes,' said Sparks. 'Only it turned out there was much more to her than that. How well did you know Bruce's family?'

'I met him and Kevin when I started at Cambridge,' he said. 'I only met his parents when they came to visit, which was infrequent. Why?'

'He had a little sister, Charlotte,' said Sparks. 'She's Evelyn Lowle. She was the one who got Lonsdale to attack you. No one knew she was planning this.'

'My God,' he said. 'But she wasn't charged with any of it.'

'Nor will she be,' said Sparks. 'Everything has been hushed up. Lonsdale will plead guilty and serve his sentence. She will continue on in another place under another name.'

'What about me?' he asked.

'They still suspect you,' she said. 'I imagine they always will. It may be true, for all I know. All I can say is if you are working for the other side, give it up now, Tony.'

'I suppose you're done with me, then,' he said bitterly.

'Almost,' she said.

'That's right. There's a third question to be asked. I dread hearing it.'

'This one is less painful,' she said. 'Our first date at the Whim. You were planning to take me to a film, but we got caught up in talking for the entire day. Do you remember?'

'I remember. What's the question?'

'Which film were you going to take me to?'

'*The Night Is Young.*'

'Why that one?'

He smiled, closing his eyes and remembering.

'Because Ramon Novarro was gorgeous,' he said.

'He was, wasn't he?' she agreed. 'Fine. No more questions. There's one last thing.'

'Which is what?'

'You're still a client of The Right Sort,' she said.

'I will withdraw my application—'

'We have a match for you.'

'What?'

'Her name is Virginia Barton.'

'Sparks, you can't possibly—'

'Like you, she doesn't want children,' continued Sparks. 'Like you, she wants someone to talk to at the end of the day. And, like you, she loves books. In fact, she's a librarian.'

'I don't know if this is a good idea, Sparks,' he said.

'That's too bad, because she's waiting in the hall outside,' said Sparks, rising to her feet.

'But—' he protested.

She left. Then another woman entered.

'Good morning, Mr Danforth,' she said. 'I'm Virginia Barton. I believe Miss Sparks has told you about me.'

'Um, yes,' he said. 'Has she told you much about me?'

'A little,' she said. 'I am so sorry about your recent tragedy.'

'Ah, that,' he said. 'Forgive my appearance. It must come as a shock.'

'Oh, no, I'm not referring to that,' she said. 'I'm given to understand that you lost all of your books in the fire. It must have been terribly upsetting.'

'There have been many upsetting events in my life,' he said. 'Not being able to read is certainly one of them.'

'Then, with your permission, I would like to read to you,' she said, sitting by the bed and pulling a book from her bag. 'I was also told that you are a devotee of Thucydides. I took the liberty of bringing my copy with me. Would you like me to read it?'

'That—' he began. Then he started to cry. 'That would be lovely. Which translation?'

'The Crawley, of course,' she said, opening it. 'I think it's the better one. Don't you?'

'I do,' he said.

Sparks, listening outside, heard Barton begin: 'Thucydides, an Athenian, wrote the history of the war between the Peloponnesians and the Athenians, beginning at the moment that it broke out, and believing that it would be a great war and more worthy of relation than any that had preceded it . . .'

She left them there, and walked out of the hospital to the railway station.

London, 1947

They entered Brompton Cemetery through the north gate, then looked down the long main road.

'Emmeline Pankhurst is buried over there somewhere,' commented Iris as they headed south. 'My mother took me to the funeral. I was maybe ten years old. She kept telling me about the Suffragists and all that they endured. Yet here I am in 1947, and I still don't have an official degree from Cambridge.'

They walked along, yew trees towering over them on both sides. In the distance, the dome of the chapel poked up.

'This section on the left,' said Iris. 'There should be several rows of Spurlocks there.'

They walked among the graves as the stones became newer and newer.

'There she is,' said Gwen, pointing to one.

It was a simple stone, with the inscription reading NANCY SPURLOCK, 1917–1936. Underneath were the words, NEITHER CAN THEY DIE ANY MORE: FOR THEY ARE EQUAL UNTO THE ANGELS.

'What is that from?' asked Iris.

'Luke, chapter 20,' said Gwen.

They looked down at the grave for a moment.

'Do you mind if I pray for her?' asked Gwen.

'By all means,' said Iris.

Gwen put her hands together and closed her eyes, her lips moving. Iris waited, idly watching an iridescent golden-green beetle land on some wilting flowers on an adjacent plot. A rose chafer, she thought.

Gwen opened her eyes and said, 'I'm done.'

Iris knelt by the grave and placed a bunch of white lilies on it, then placed her palm on the grass over it for a moment. Then she stood back up.

'Let's go,' she said.

They walked back towards the gate.

'A point of clarification,' said Gwen. 'As an atheist, you don't believe in an afterlife, correct?'

'Correct,' said Iris.

'Then why put flowers on Nancy's grave if you don't think there's any chance of her knowing?'

'In case I'm wrong,' said Iris.

An hour later, they were back at the *Cecilia*.

'I've disconnected the shoreline, but I need your help with the gangplank and the ropes,' said Iris.

'Of course,' said Gwen. 'But first, in honour of your maiden voyage . . .'

She pulled a bottle of burgundy from her bag and presented it to her.

'Save it for when you've moored,' she advised.

'I will,' promised Iris.

She ran across the gangplank and inside the saloon to store it, then came back out and grabbed the ends of the gangplank's rails. Gwen reached down and grabbed the bottom of the other end.

'Heave ho!' cried Iris.

Gwen lifted the end up as Iris pulled the handles until it was vertical. Then Iris slid it inside the taffrail and connected the safety chain across the gap. Gwen untied the stern rope, coiled it, then tossed it across the narrow gap to Iris.

'I'd come with you, but I've got Ronnie,' said Gwen. 'Are you going to be all right on your own?'

'I'll be fine,' said Iris. 'I need to be alone for a while. Hopefully, it will clear my head.'

'Where exactly are you going?'

'I don't know,' said Iris. 'That's the beauty of it. When I've been gone for a week, I'll find a place to turn around and come back. Don't worry, I'll send you and Ronnie some postcards.'

'Ring me if the boat breaks down, or if you break down, or if you need bail or anything,' said Gwen.

'Will do,' promised Iris. 'Let me start up the engine, then you can untie the bowline.'

'Aye, aye, Captain,' said Gwen.

Iris disappeared into the boat while Gwen moved to the other rope and stood at the ready. A minute later she heard the engine rumble into life. Iris came out on the fore well, and Gwen untied the line, coiled it and tossed it to her.

They looked across at each other for a moment.

'Do you know,' said Iris, 'when I raced the Bumps at Cambridge, it took eleven of us brilliant women to get us on our way. You and I have just done it by ourselves. Do you realise what that means?'

'What, darling?' replied Gwen.

'That you are worth ten Cambridge women,' said Iris. 'Love to Ronnie, and mind the shop, won't you?'

'I will,' said Gwen. 'Bon voyage!'

Iris walked to the stern and grabbed the tiller. Slowly, carefully, she eased the *Cecilia* into the centre of the canal. She looked back at Gwen, blew her a kiss then throttled up the engine.

Casper, her neighbour and instructor, was watching with approval from his accustomed chair on the roof of his boat. As she passed him he lifted his pipe in salute and she waved, grinning proudly.

Gwen watched as the *Cecilia* slowly made its way down the canal and disappeared around a bend.

'Fair winds and following seas, Iris,' she said softly.

Then she turned and walked home to spend the rest of the day with Ronnie.

Acknowledgements

In addition to sources previously cited, the author gratefully acknowledges the following:

John Willis Clark, *A Concise Guide to the Town and University of Cambridge*, 11th Edition, 1938 (Bowes & Bowes, 1936)

Richard Davenport-Hines, *Enemies Within: Communists, the Cambridge Spies and the Making of Modern Britain* (William Collins, 2018)

Alice Gardner, *A Short History of Newnham College, Cambridge* (Bowes & Bowes, 1921)

Mary Agnes Hamilton, *Newnham: An Informal Biography* (Faber and Faber, 1936)

T.E.B. Howarth, *Cambridge Between Two Wars* (Collins, 1978)

Andrew Sinclair, *The Red and the Blue: Intelligence, Treason and the Universities* (Weidenfeld and Nicolson, 1986)

Rita McWilliams Tullberg, *Women At Cambridge* (Cambridge University Press, 1998)

New Pictorial and Descriptive Guide to Cambridge and District (Ward, Lock and Co., Limited, 1934)

The account of the protest against Oswald Mosley was found in part in 'Cambridge UNIVERSITY STUDENTS RAGS Chronicle', accessible through https://archive.org/stream/CambridgeUNIVERSITYSTUDENTSRAGSChronicle